Ask, Tell

E. J. NOYES

2017

Bella Books, Inc.
P.O. Box 10543
Tallahassee, FL 32302

This is a work of fiction. Names, characters, businesses, places, events and incidents are either the products of the author's imagination or used in a fictitious manner. Any resemblance to actual persons, living or dead, or actual events is purely coincidental. The publisher does not have any control over and does not assume any responsibility for author or third-party websites or their content.

Printed in the United States of America on acid-free paper.

First Bella Books Edition 2017

Editor: Cath Walker
Cover Designer: Judith Fellows

ISBN: 978-1-59493-530-5

PUBLISHER'S NOTE

About the Author

E. J. Noyes lives in Australia with her partner, a needy cat, aloof chickens and too many horses. When not indulging in her love of reading and writing, E. J. argues with her hair and pretends to be good at clay target shooting.

Acknowledgments

Writing a book is a strange experience and one I may not have survived without the help of some very important people. Thanks must go first and foremost to Ash. I've no words to express my gratitude for your guidance and encouragement through every step of this process. I couldn't have done it without your unwavering faith in me. Go Bears!

Thank you, Kate, for your staunch friendship and (sometimes painfully) honest opinions—you were right, I'm sorry, you're pretty. Paula, I wouldn't have kept my sanity without your laughter...and your wine. Thanks to Dina, Steve and the Scribbers for your time, enthusiasm, knowledge and support.

Thanks to my (favorite, but don't tell the others) cousin, Adam, for answering my endless questions about your job—last question, I promise. I'm so grateful to Mary Buchanan who shared her knowledge with me, and to Dr. Michelle Warman who went on a trawling mission among her colleagues to supply me with more information. Thank you, Liaison Extraordinaire Trish and CPT Melissa Kalis for the fascinating insights into your day-to-day life.

A world of thanks to my editor, Cath Walker and the team at Bella Books for making my first publishing experience so exciting and wonderful. It's been everything I'd ever hoped for. And a bag of chips.

Finally, my eternal gratitude to my partner Phoebe who never laughed when I told her I was writing a book. Pheebs, thank you for talking me out of my panic every other day and making me feel like this was the most important thing in the world. I love you. You've always felt like home to me.

Author's Note

The United States military policy *Don't Ask, Don't Tell* (DADT) is an important part of LGBT history. Prior to its implementation in 1993, homosexuals were banned from enlisting, and if discovered once serving were dishonorably discharged—their careers finished.

In addition to the stigma, personnel lost their military pension, insurance, healthcare (including treatment for physical and mental injury acquired during their service) and financial aid for social welfare assistance or education. They lost their entitlement to a military funeral, were barred from wearing their uniform or medals in public and in some cases even prevented from voting or owning firearms. They were often denied bank loans and found their past viewed unfavorably in job applications.

All because of their sexuality.

It was considered by some that openly gay and lesbian service members could potentially undermine the integral structure of discipline in the armed forces. DADT was developed as a strategy to prevent discrimination without compromising the military's culture of regulation and hierarchy. The policy was simple: *Don't Ask* anyone about their sexual orientation. *Don't Tell* anyone about your sexual orientation. Pretend the "problem" didn't exist. It meant that one could not be discharged for simply *being* gay or lesbian, only for engaging in homosexual conduct. A person could still be dismissed but discharge was no longer automatically dishonorable. Clearly DADT was inherently flawed.

Openly homosexual personnel were still subject to discrimination, so service members were forced to conceal their sexuality. They couldn't share important aspects of their lives with the men and women with whom they lived and died. They couldn't discuss the birth of a child, be supported when a partner died or comforted during a breakup. In short, DADT still denied gays, lesbians and bisexuals the same human rights and respect as other members of the armed forces.

In 2010, as a necessary step toward allowing gay and lesbian service members to live and serve freely, a study by the Department of Defense was undertaken to gauge the effects of repealing DADT. The risk to military unit effectiveness, order and morale was considered low and the process of repeal continued. DADT officially ended on 20th September, 2011.

A bill has since been passed to give service members who had received less-than-honorable discharges due to their sexual orientation the opportunity to have their discharge records corrected to reflect their honorable service.

* * *

The Army base that sets the scene for this book is fictional but based on the workings of a military base in Afghanistan. As a person who has never served in the armed forces, I received assistance from a number of veterans and serving members, but any inconsistencies that remain may be laid squarely at my feet.

CHAPTER ONE

FOB Invicta Military Hospital, Khost Province, Afghanistan
August, 2009

I've wanted Rebecca Keane from the moment I first saw her perform surgery. I'd only been deployed for three days on my first tour and instead of concentrating on our patient, I found my eyes drawn to the strands of wavy blond hair that had escaped her scrub cap. Wide, dark blue eyes creased when she smiled over her mask at me and I forgot how to verbalize, mumbling something stupid about a liver.

My shallow thoughts about her beauty took a backseat when I saw how effortlessly she negotiated what seemed to be a lost cause. Confident, yet never demanding. Skilled and calm. She tilted her head as she asked my opinion, then her eyes held mine as she agreed with it.

My want of her isn't anything deep or well thought out, but more the way you see a coat in a store window and think right away *I want that*. Then you remember you already have a coat. A coat named Victoria that's been yours for almost nine years.

* * *

I run with sluggish footsteps and a wandering mind, trying to take my thoughts away from here. Away from war, bullet wounds and dismembered limbs. Away from the dust and dry heat of Afghanistan and a man I couldn't keep alive. Away from the expression on Keane's face when I told her I'd lost him. Away from her look of disappointment and away from my own failure.

It's not working. I can't stop thinking about it. I need a better distraction or I'm going to cry. I shove my thoughts to the opposite end of the scale. Instead of disappointment, I imagine Keane giving me a look that is lustful. Perhaps as I push her against the wall of a shower cubicle and kneel to slip my—

"Sabine." Mitch interrupts thoughts that are fast becoming inappropriate.

"Mmm?"

He isn't even panting. "You're fuckin' slow. My mama runs quicker'n you."

The fantasy is gone. I slide my tongue over dry lips as I turn my head toward him. Even in sunglasses, I'm squinting and the dust in my mouth coats my tongue like a gritty blanket. I can't think of a witty comeback. I'm going to have to let this one go. Slow, my ass. I clamp my lips together and increase my pace.

Mitch moves ahead. I try to keep up. He laughs and increases his speed again, taunting me. I drop my shoulders and burst into a sprint. We race each other around the track, jostling and giggling, and I manage to keep up with him for twenty feet or so before the length of his strides allows him to break away. Mitch Boyd, my best friend and a fellow surgeon, is well over six feet tall and athletic. I can't compete when he decides to outpace me.

With his beefy arms raised to make a V above his head Mitch crosses an imaginary finish line. He tosses his cap high in the air before bursting into a warped victory dance. The smug bastard looks ridiculous as he shakes his ass and I'd tell him so if I wasn't so breathless. I reach him as he leans down to pick up his hat.

"Really thought you could outrun me? Maybe you should borrow some stilts," Mitch teases in his molasses drawl. His voice always reminds me of barbeque on a Sunday afternoon.

Texan and stupidly good-looking, he would probably be my type if my type had balls. I suppose it's possible I'd be Mitch's type, if his type had tits.

I manage one word between gulping air. "Asshole." My friendly punch goes wide, hitting Mitch's shoulder as he straightens. He recoils in mock horror, as though my fist actually registered instead of just glancing off his bulk. I swat him again as we begin a cool-down lap around the track. Somehow a dead bug has made its way into my mouth.

Mitch tugs his cap on. "I got an interestin' email yesterday."

"Yeah?"

"There's a rumor Congress is gonna repeal Don't Ask, Don't Tell."

I scoff. "I doubt anything will come of it. It'll take years to reverse policy. If the bill even gets through." And I don't hold much hope it will. The army policy on gay and lesbian service members is clear. Keep it to yourself and do your job.

"You never know, darlin'. It could happen. Then you can invite Keane to come stay the night in your bed. I know you've got a little crush going." Mitch caught me eyeballing Keane when we first arrived on base and he refuses to let it go. He's not wrong, I do have something, but it's not just a schoolgirl crush.

Rebecca Keane. My boss. Dimpled. Accomplished and inventive surgeon. Owner of a number of very pleasing physical attributes. Wearer of my favorite perfume. Flag football devotee. Most certainly an excellent lay. Shorter than me, I could probably pick her up and carry her to a bed. Don't start that shit again, Sabine.

Mitch is waiting, watching me with an eyebrow raised. I'm so busy fantasizing that I haven't responded to his teasing. I fling my arm out to hit him. "Don't even start. As if you haven't got your eye on someone too."

Mitch stretches his arms up luxuriously. "The list is longer'n my arm."

I raise my eyes to the sky. Of course it is. We continue walking without speaking—our friendship is long past needing to fill silences with inane conversation. We're halfway around the track when the siren starts with a persistent screech that reverberates through my bones. Speakers across the base blare an "Attention on the FOB!" message to tell us casualties are on the way.

Our FOB, Forward Operating Base Invicta, is a secured area in a massive, miles-wide valley between stunningly stark mountain ranges. We're one of the smaller units and the hospital is our most important feature, but you wouldn't know to look at it. It's deliberately unremarkable—nestled among the obligatory military structures of quarters, mess halls and equipment sheds.

Everything at Invicta is laid out with pleasing symmetry in uniform colors of cream, khaki and brown. Some buildings are permanent, or as permanent as things get around here. Others, like the mailroom, are plywood shacks that amazingly never fall down when a hot windstorm blows through.

All day and night the base hums with people at work inside the fence, locals outside it, and transports coming and going. In high wind, the razor wire and chain-link fence encircling Invicta rattles and clinks. I live with constant noise and dirt. I live with the omnipresent smell of diesel, dust and aircraft fuel. I live with other people's blood on my uniform.

The incoming alert keeps blaring. It reminds me of a smoke alarm. I feel it like fingers gripping the back of my neck, forcing me to respond. I can't ignore or sleep through the sound. No matter how tired I am after thirty-seven hours running on adrenaline, bad food and coffee, I will wake up and I will respond. Some of the more experienced team members tell me they can feel the helicopters approaching before they hear them. Maybe on my next deployment I'll somehow gain this extra sense but for now I have to rely on regular old hearing. I stop, hold my breath and strain to listen for the heavy thrum of the helicopter rotors.

Mitch shields his eyes, pointing out toward the horizon. "I hear the birds over yonder." This means we have maybe seven minutes. He breaks into a sprint just before I do and our feet leave heavy prints on the dusty ground as we race one another again, only this time it's not for fun. Fucking assholes.

Goddamned fucking assholes. I've already been in surgery for over eight hours today. I'm hot, sweaty and tired. I should be getting ready to enjoy some personal tension relief in a shower cubicle.

The air-conditioning shocks me when I burst into the building and a deep shiver builds at the base of my neck. I tug at my shirt as we jog through the hallways among other Medical Corps personnel. Most of them are also pulling pieces of uniform off as they move. My sweaty shirt sticks to my skin as I try to yank it over my head. I grunt as I wrestle with it, my hip hitting the wall. Frustration burns in my throat but I push it back down. I need to be calm, focused and professional. Not some idiot ranting about a T-shirt.

Bobby Rodriguez, one of our anesthesiologists, and John Auger, a general surgeon like Mitch and me, reach the pre-op prep room as we do. I pause to let them pass and Rodriguez looks at me, wearing his best shit-eating grin. Outside the theater I am fair game, but once inside he wouldn't dare. I greet them breathlessly. "Bobby. John."

"Hey runners." Rodriguez drags his words out. "Timely interruption. Wouldn't want you two getting even hotter out there." The joke is old and tired.

There are rumors on base about Mitch and I being involved. We do not confirm, or deny because it's easier to maintain a charade than to risk exposure. Sex is everywhere here, and yet it is nowhere. It's something we talk about constantly, but at the same time it's not allowed.

Bobby and John grin at us. Mitch rewards them both with a hard back slap. This ritual is some unspoken bro code that I can never be part of. Every night, men all over the world sit in bars, get physical with each other and discuss their latest conquests.

"Did you fuck her?"

"You fucking bet I did. She could suck a melon out the tailpipe of a sixty-five 'Stang."

Cue masculine laughter, more back slapping and another round of beers.

If women had a ritual, it would probably be the age-old question asked over a glass of wine: "Did he make you come?" A wry smile would be the response. No. Of course he didn't.

The grin I give the boys is forced. See? I'm part of the game too. Mitch holds the door so I can slip through. He turns to me, his blue eyes wide and I suppress a laugh. Yes, Mitch, I know it's an act for you. I leave him and cross the room without looking at anyone else.

I'm an automaton. My equipment locker is orderly, everything organized within easy reach. I quickly unfasten my thigh holster and leave my weapon on the shelf. Hop around to pull boots off, wet wipes to get rid of dust and sweat, back into scrubs. Chug some water, wristwatch off and drag my hair into an even tighter bun. The ends feel ragged, like it's dangerously close to being out of regulations. Tomorrow I will go to the base salon to have a few inches lopped off.

I catch sight of myself in the mirror stuck to the back wall of my locker. My dark eyes appear almost black from the reflection of shadows nestled under them. I look tired. Is that a line near my nose? I lean closer, rubbing at my face. No. Good. Thirty-five is too young to have wrinkles.

The room has filled in the three minutes I've been in here. Conversation hums around me. Doctors. Nurses. Men. Women. All in various stages of dress and undress. All pay grades. All ranks. No wandering eyes. In here, we're sexless. Anticipation and adrenaline, and perhaps profound fatigue cause a slight tremor in my knees, but not my hands. My hands are surgeon's hands. They do not waver. I pull on my scrub cap and tie a tight double knot.

The door connecting the prep room to the scrub area and theaters swings open. "We have three incoming, ETA five minutes. IED. Four lower amps, one upper. Blast trauma. We'll know more when they arrive." Her voice. Cultured. Mellow. Sexy.

Stop it Sabine.

Lieutenant Colonel Rebecca Keane stands in the doorway holding her cap. She now has everyone's undivided attention, which isn't difficult. Perhaps ten years older than me, she has an empathetic yet commanding air. Her manner is straightforward and confident, but never belittling. I classify all of these as important qualities for a boss and team leader. I also classify her as extremely attractive.

I look away and force myself to focus. IED. Improvised Explosive Device. When I first heard the term, I imagined someone hastily cobbling a bomb together with whatever they had lying around. I mused to myself about how bad it would really be if they put some effort into it.

Now on my second deployment, I know better. Improvised doesn't mean a fucking thing. Four lower and one upper from three casualties. I do the math. Today, a soldier might have lost both legs and possibly an arm. War. What is it good for? Not much it would seem.

"Captain Fleischer!"

I straighten, turning toward Keane with my chin lifted. "Ma'am?"

Keane keeps her eyes on me. "You, Auger and Rodriguez take casualty A with Thorne for ortho." She assigns all the other surgeons into teams as I'm pulling shoes back on. I finish my laces then look up in time for the last of her briefing. "…you all know the drill. Nice and steady, no mistakes." Keane's eyes sweep the room, lingering on me for a moment before she exits.

Wait. I have a brief moment of panic as I mentally run through my past three days in surgery. Does she think I made a mistake this morning? That was unavoidable. Nobody could have saved him. I can't think of anything else. All my reports are completed and I've only lost one patient this week. Less than everyone else. Shit.

I pause, tuck a wisp of hair into my cap and rush after her, intending to ask if there's anything amiss. Mitch grabs my arm before I reach the doors. "Good luck," he says, eyes bright.

My gaze moves to the swinging doors. Keane is gone. "Luck is for suckers." It's our standard response. I pull my arm free and leave him to assemble with the members of his team.

CHAPTER TWO

Hot wind sweeps in from outside as three casualties are rushed through in a flurry of bloodied uniforms and rank body odor. I finish pulling on disposable gloves and quickly tie my gown in the back. This crew is one I've never met before. I throw a hurried introduction at them. "I'm Doctor Fleischer. Bring A into this bay here please."

One of the Combat Pararescuemen—PJs we call them—turns to me. "ALOC since the blast, been given packed blood. Below knee and partial arm amp."

Altered Level of Consciousness could mean anything. Seems this guy is very new and needs his hand held a little. "Has he been conscious at all?" I ask.

"Briefly ma'am, at first contact."

"Okay, let's roll him on." We transfer the casualty onto the gurney, careful not to dislodge the lines attached to his body. He is extremely pale, his torso heaving with ragged breaths. Hello shock, hello massive hemorrhage.

I run my hands over the man on the stretcher and make mental assessments while more stats and details of drugs administered are thrown at us. The fetid tang of blood and voided bowels from the patient's hastily-removed uniform hangs in the air. Facial trauma, one arm, one leg and two messy stumps. What shitty fucking luck. I almost let out an audible sigh, but catch myself and cover it by clearing my throat. We rush through the rest of our checks and he is taken from the assessment bay to the theater.

Bobby is already in there when I bump up against the scrubbing sink and reach for a mask. I fit it carefully, tying it with more double knots. The disposable nail pick digs into the sensitive skin of my nail bed. My nails are short and scraped many times a day. Nothing ever accumulates under them.

My gaze moves between my hands and the window in front of me where I can see nurses unpacking sterile kits and placing instruments onto trays. My favorite nurse Sarah pauses to respond to a question from Bobby then rushes away to keep prepping.

After many months of operating with me, they all understand how I like my trays laid out. When I walk into the theater I know my forceps will be set at the perfect angle against my clamps and I'll have exactly the right scalpels and needle holders. Mitch calls it OCD. I call it organization.

The iodine impregnated scrub sponge has an odor that sticks to the inside of my nose. The scent will stay there for at least ten minutes, assuming nothing more noxious invades my nostrils. Nate Thorne and John Auger step in beside me, reaching to pull a mask each from the box on the shelves above us.

"I fucking hate IEDs." John's Boston accent is more pronounced than usual. He's upset. "Give me a bullet any day. Something we can fix. Not this chop and drop bullshit and a 'Sorry we couldn't fix your limbs because some prick blew them off and they are God knows fucking where' speech at the end." The muscles of his cheeks bulge as he vents and he finishes with his molars clamped tightly together.

John loathes injustice and hates to be ineffectual. Lately it feels as though these two things are in steady supply around here. His ranting is nothing new and I've heard it almost every day for the nine months we've been deployed together. Ninety-two days left on this, my second deployment, until I am rotated out. Ninety-two more days of listening to him going on and on about things which are out of our control. You can do it, Sabine.

Nate says nothing. He's shy, one of those people who blends into the background, and he rarely talks unless it's to ask for something during surgery. I stay silent too, but nod to show I'm not ignoring John. His words fade out into background noise and my mind wanders. My hands and forearms are now stained yellow-orange. I think of Oompa Loompas. I think of watching movies with my younger sister.

When I was fifteen, I decided I wanted to be a surgeon. My sister Jana was the first person I told. I expected encouragement but instead, she laughed at me. When she was done, she asked me how someone so prone to random thinking could manage to focus long enough to perform surgery. Some days I'm not even sure how I do it myself. On days like today, days when someone dies, I almost feel like I'm just playing at being a doctor.

"Doctors?" Sarah stands at the window in front of us, her voice soft behind the glass.

Nate glances up, and John and I answer together. "Yes?"

"Are you ready to get going?"

She's telling you to hurry up, Sabine. I splay my fingers and scrub harder. John resumes talking. I think I catch the word *occlusion*. He must think about surgery constantly. I'm not really listening, so I don't know what to say in response. I make a musing sound. Good enough. When I'm not in the operating room, I want to think about anything but surgery. I want to think about my pets, the beach, skiing, dancing and drinking. Maybe my girlfriend. My family.

I became a surgeon because it was what I wanted. I joined the army because my family boasts three generations of military service before me. My great-grandfather fought and died in *World War I*, leaving a young son for the second. After he'd done his duty in *World War II*, my grandfather grabbed his pregnant wife and they left Germany for America. Oma and Opa produced three sons who the New Homeland gobbled up eagerly for the Vietnam War. Only one was regurgitated. My father.

I once gave a brief summary of my family background to Mitch and watched with amusement as he made the connection. During both World Wars, my family fought for the *other* side. I told him I'm proud of my heritage. I didn't tell him how as a surgeon, the literal translation of my German last name to The Butcher delights my dark sense of humor.

Anguished wails from the operating room beside mine startle me out of introspection. It's something I've never quite got used to, listening to them before they are anesthetized. No doubt, I'd be making similar noises if our situations were reversed. Be honest, Sabine, you would be louder.

I glance at the clock on the wall, bump the faucet handle with my elbow and bend to get my arms under the flow. "See you in there." Before either of them answer, I push backward through the door to the theater.

When I spin around I come face-to-face with Sarah, holding a ready towel. While I dry my hands and arms, my gaze drifts to the table where the patient has been settled prior to being knocked out. Everyone bustles around me. Another nurse wrestles with the x-ray and CT machines, trying to get images up for us to work with while Bobby runs another vitals assessment. I'm tempted to speak up to tell Bobby my expert medical guess is that the patient's vitals are present, but unimpressed with current body conditions. He probably wouldn't find it funny.

Sarah already has my gown ready and I slide forward into it with arms outstretched. I turn for her to tie the straps and when I rotate back around she offers a right glove ready for me to dive into. I give my fingers a quick wiggle to seat them before she hands me my left glove. We dance this dance many times a week and she knows my routine so well it's like she lives inside my head. Poor woman. My fingers interlace, ensuring the thick latex is snug against my skin. I lean forward so Sarah can fit protective glasses over my eyes. She smiles when I wink at her.

Each moment we wait increases the risk, but I can't begin until the patient is intubated. Time is written on his stumps in black marker, telling me when tourniquets were applied. They have been on those limbs for almost an hour and a half. I fidget. "How's it going, Bobby?"

"Can't get him yet, Sabs. His larynx is ground beef, not much left of his mandible," Bobby responds. "Glidescope please, I'm going to video-assisted." Sweat is beading along his sideburns. Bobby rarely sweats. There is no point demanding he hurry up. I know from experience that being pushy gets us nowhere.

One of the nurses turns to me. "Images are up."

"Thank you." I glance at Bobby one more time, then stride across the linoleum to the monitors. I'm impatient, which makes everything feel like it doesn't fit right. I roll my shoulders to shift the gown, wrinkle my nose against the material of the mask and make a conscious effort not to check the progress of the intubation. He won't go faster if you're leaning over his shoulder, Sabine.

I focus on the images in front of me, tracing organs and structures quickly with my eyes. His intestines are a mess, but repairable. I don't think you'll need a colostomy, sir. Moderate internal blunt force blast trauma. Lucky man. Relatively speaking.

John sidles up beside me, his eyes sweeping the images. "Messy, but not the worst." His pale blue eyes move from the monitor to my face. "You good?"

I nod and take another moment to ensure I've got all the information I need. Behind me, I hear Nate's small sound of agreement.

"We're golden, guys. He's on." Bobby sounds relieved. He hooks up the anesthetic machine and tosses his laryngoscope onto a tray.

The team gets right to work. I've performed so many surgeries like this that it's all muscle memory and I barely even have to think. We converse, but it's all mundane and focused on the casualty, except for ten minutes where Bobby chatters about an upcoming preseason Bears game. John and I exchange exaggerated eye rolls. The nurses snigger. We've all heard Bobby's Bears predictions before. They'll probably lose the game. Nate murmurs something about the Broncos.

"Can I move up?" John asks. He wants the space.

"Give me a moment, I've got a little bleeder." I glance up.

"You got it?" he asks calmly.

It only takes a few moments to control. "Yep, done." We all shuffle around, except for Bobby who is sitting down with his legs outstretched. Lazy prick.

* * *

When John and I are both satisfied we've done all we can, my personal complaints can finally be acknowledged. After almost four hours of surgery, a deep ache has taken up residence in my left shoulder and gnawing emptiness turns my stomach. I haven't showered in over thirteen hours, three surgeries and one twenty-minute run. I feel disgusting and I really need to pee. We finish up and leave Bobby to recover the patient.

I drop my dirty gown and gloves into the hazardous waste receptacle and before I can reach for the chart, Sarah is holding it out to me. I'm wriggling my toes inside my boots, trying to ignore insistent messages from my bladder. The patient's name is Corporal Gleason. "Call me as soon as he's awake please." Sarah nods, giving me an accommodating smile while I sign my name at the bottom of the last page. "Thank you." I snap the chart closed and pass it to John.

Scrubbing out takes a few minutes and I use the time to run through the surgery. I relive each step for the report, which I'll begin as soon as I shower and change. The sound of water has woken my bladder up. I begin to jiggle. The paper towel sticks as always and I have to tug it hard to get the dispenser to relinquish a square for me to dry my hands. Piece of shit equipment. Someone clears their throat, startling me. I hadn't noticed Colonel Keane at the sink to my right. I sneak a look at her.

Keane shakes her hands out, not bothering to dry them before she pulls her cap off. The lighting in this room highlights the deep gold tinge in her blond hair. I toss the paper towel and try not to stare as I wait for her to approach me. Outside the operating rooms there is no need to salute but I lift my chin and straighten up. "Ma'am."

"Initial surgical report, Captain?" Her tone is crisp, but her dark blue eyes are not.

John and Nate are still in the theater, so it's on me to report. I run my tongue over my lower lip before speaking. "Casualty is on his way to recovery, Colonel. Nate attended to the amputations and we've left the sites open. We'll watch for infection, then tidy up more when we're more certain about viability. John and I repaired damage to liver and large intestine. There was a small amount of bleeding but we were able to contain it. I expect no issues." I feel like a younger version of myself, the nerdy teen with braces having to explain a complex math equation to the class.

"Very good. I expect the written by tomorrow."

I'll have it completed sooner than that. "Of course, ma'am." I pause and take a shallow breath. "Have there been any issues with my other surgeries or reports from this week, Colonel?" Worry sits uncomfortably in my chest, the sensation of thinking something I've done may not be good enough.

Keane stares at me, the crease between her eyebrows deepening. "No Sabine. Why would there be?"

"No reason, ma'am, I just thought..." What am I going to say? I was watching you and I saw you watching me when you mentioned mistakes? Of course not. I clear my throat. "I just wanted to make sure everything was in order, ma'am. You seemed disappointed in me, in my outcome from this morning." I'm acutely aware of how pathetic I sound.

Keane gives me a patient smile. "Disappointed? I was, yes. For you, not in you, Sabine. Everything is fine." Her left cheek is creased with a dimple. I try not to look at it.

I exhale, releasing a fraction of my anxiety. "Thank you, ma'am."

Keane folds her scrub cap in half. "Enjoy the rest of your day." She nods her dismissal of me and walks off.

My eyes stray to her ass as she leaves the room. "You too, Colonel." I count off thirty seconds to be sure she is gone, then race to the bathroom.

CHAPTER THREE

There's a skinny local boy of about eight trying to catch my attention from the other side of the fence, calling out and pointing at the vehicle shed that's two hundred feet to my left. They call him Motor Head because he comes by at least once a week from the village a mile or so further into the valley, hoping to see the helos and massive trucks up close. He mills around, usually only for a few minutes until our guys give him an aggressive order to leave. Then the boy runs off with his arms outstretched like a plane. Every single time.

I want to wander over, hook my fingers in the chain-link, and talk with him about the awesomeness of the Pave Hawk helos the PJs use. To describe the roaring power of takeoff in a C-17 plane, and how uncomfortable it is being jammed in a Humvee. But I can't, ever. Two guards are already moving closer with weapons ready, calling for the boy to move on.

My teeth close around the soft skin inside my cheek. I can't even chat to a kid about a shared love of aircraft without worrying if he's spying on the base, has a grenade in his pocket or is wearing a suicide vest. I keep my distance but offer him a cheery wave and am rewarded with a huge, gap-toothed grin before he sprints away.

I continue to the office and give the status board a cursory glance, trying to judge the likelihood of casualties arriving in the next few hours. Then I spend a few moments doing a calculation I devised on my first deployment. It's complex, taking into account a number of things. I work out current missions in progress, then factor in Murphy's Law of how much I've slept in the past forty-eight hours and if I've eaten or peed in the past four. Thirty-two percent chance of having to operate. Good enough. I jog back to my room to grab my shower bag and a fresh uniform.

The whirring fans in the shower block make it very hard to have a conversation, yet it doesn't stop some of the other women. I sneak in and claim a stall away from their noisy chattering. The last thing I feel like doing with my tits out is to converse over the top of shower stalls. Especially about things like last night's chow or if I think the patient from yesterday will need more of his stump removed before we send him to Germany for recovery.

I pull out my tweezers and compact mirror, tidying my eyebrows while I wait for the water to heat. War is no excuse for neglecting these shapely babies, or so Mitch likes to remind me. By the time I'm done, the water is still only lukewarm. My shower is short and with the barest of pressure, and I hate every moment of it. I want to soak in a tub or take a long, hot shower. Preferably with Vic.

My stomach flips when I think of the way my girlfriend likes to push me against the shower wall. Cold tiles against my skin. Her hot tongue on me. In me. The flutter in my stomach slides south but before I can do anything about it, giggles float over the top of the stalls. The interruption stops my arousal like a pin to a balloon. Fuck this place. I finish up and rush from the bathroom before I can be dragged into any semi-naked conversations.

Offices are reserved for the higher ranks, but the surgical staff share a space where we can complete paperwork away from the cacophony of the common areas. I grab a coffee and something to eat, settling at one of the stations. While the reporting system loads I pick listlessly at a dry muffin. I write out my usual concise thorough report, do a quick double check of my spelling and send it through to Keane. Mine will be the first one she receives. You suck-up, Sabine.

As I leave the building, Sarah finds me to tell me Gleason is in recovery and conscious. Post-op checks don't take long and it's too early for chow, so I make my way to the main ward hoping to find Mitch. Maybe I'll do some unofficial rounds. Wandering through the wards is oddly calming, despite the loss and pain hanging in the air. I rationalize it as a non-asshole version of Schadenfreude. A reminder to be grateful for the things I still have.

I choke down a protein bar while I walk, the fake chocolate grit sticking to my teeth. There should have been a subject in med school about eating, dressing and writing while you walk. My life feels as though it's always in motion and when I'm stationary, I begin to feel off-kilter. I turn a corner and almost bump into Mitch. He grunts when I elbow him in the ribs.

"Watch it, oaf. How'd it go?" I stuff the last bite into my mouth.

My best friend leans against the wall. "Double leg and more. We lost him." His shoulders are slumped in disappointment.

"Shit. I'm sorry, Mitch." I grab his forearm and squeeze it.

"Happens. I'm gonna shower." Mitch shrugs, feigning nonchalance. I know him well enough to realize how upset he really is. I give him what I hope is a sympathetic look as he pats my arm, then walks off. His steps have the slow, clumping sound of defeat I know so well.

The rubber soles of my boots are barely audible on the floor as I continue into the wards. I see my roommate, surgeon Amy Peterson, doing rounds in the post-op rooms. She hasn't changed after surgery, her scrubs are crumpled and have what looks like a melted chocolate stain on the thigh. Maybe it's dried blood. Either way, it's gross. You're all class, Peterson. Tall, willowy and stunning, Amy looks like she should be a model or the CEO of a billion dollar corporation, rather than calling for *some more fucking suction* with blood up to her elbows.

Amy gives me a cheery wave and a rude gesture. Before I can return either, she goes back to her chart. I've had a few roommates rotate in and out during my deployments and she is unquestionably my favorite. Polite, fun and carefree, she's as respectful of my space as I am of hers. Amy has a wicked sense of humor, a filthy mouth and is exactly the sort of person I would normally be attracted to. Thankfully, I'm not.

She's prone to pawing through my uniforms while I'm asleep, or out of the room, to leave candy in my pants pockets. Amy is also the only other person on base, aside from Mitch, who knows about my longtime girlfriend, Victoria. I've never explicitly told her or even alluded to it, but she is intuitive and sharing a room with someone makes certain things hard to hide. It's never been an issue with us, it is just one of those things. Don't ask me, and I won't tell you.

Most of the casualties are sleeping, but some who are awake acknowledge me politely as I walk past. Others turn their heads as if pretending I'm not there means I will go away and not bother them. Denial and anger are everywhere here, because we never have casualties long enough to witness them cycling through stages of grief to acceptance. We keep soldiers until they are stable enough to be moved on for their next level of care. Some are grateful when they leave. Others are angry.

It's a classic post-traumatic pattern and I suppose they are entitled to be cold toward me. Sometimes it stings, but I sympathize with them and try not to take it personally. They are dealing with massive loss, confronting their mortality while coping with physical pain. I'm sure I'd be pretty fucking unfriendly if I'd just had my legs removed.

There is a patient of mine halfway along the row of beds. He will lose the sight in his right eye, and his right forearm is gone. He was scooping out a cathole to take a dump but dug up a small explosive device instead. The soldier turns his head in my general direction as I approach. Both eyes are still bandaged and he has shrapnel wounds all over his face and upper chest.

I grab his chart from the end of the bed. "Private Holman, Doctor Fleischer. How are you doing today?" I thumb through the pages and write my name and the time on his chart while I wait for an answer. He is silent. I try again. "How is your pain?"

Holman says something unintelligible, but I imagine *fuck off* features in his dialogue. I'd probably tell me to get fucked too. Still, I push on. "Your vital signs look good. We'll do some more tests on your eyesight in a few days and then take it from there. Any pain in your residual limb?"

Nothing. Come on, soldier. I sigh quietly, lifting my eyes to the ceiling as if I might find some inspiration there. Nope. As a rule I try to stay away from clichés, promises and uses of the word luck. Just once, I would like to tell them how sorry I am and agree that this is really shitful but of course I can't.

"If your pain levels are unmanageable, remember you have the button or you can call a nurse," I remind him as I lean over to check the settings on his PCA machine. I move the button so it's touching his hand and he can press it to administer pain meds if he's uncomfortable. He snatches his hand away as the plastic touches him. Don't mind me, soldier, I'm just trying to help.

As I step from the room, I catch a waft of Keane's perfume. She comes into my peripheral vision a few seconds later, waving a chart at me. "Fleischer, a word?"

"Of course, Colonel." She smells so good. Stop it, Sabine.

She walks away, leaving me to follow. I keep a respectful distance between us as we move to stand beside the nurses' area. There are no nurses there. We're alone and I'm very aware of it. Keane smiles as she flips the chart open and steps closer to me. "I wanted your opinion on something, Sabine."

I've noticed whenever she says my name, she puts a slight French inflection on it. She makes it sound so sensual that I'm not bothered she's chosen the wrong accent. I tuck Holman's folder under my arm and glance at the name on Keane's chart.

Her patient from this morning. I raise my eyebrows. She could have asked Peterson, who was operating with her or she could have figured it out herself. "Yes ma'am." I lean over to get a better look, careful not to touch her.

Keane glances sideways at me. "He's in recovery but still unconscious and showing vastly decreased brain activity."

I frown. Her patient was a leg amputation, no visible head trauma. "He didn't present as neurologically impaired?" I ask, running my finger over the text as I read. She has beautiful, elegant handwriting. I lift my gaze to her face.

Keane is watching my hand. "No, completely responsive on arrival." She raises her eyes to mine. They are the same blue as the ocean, the color of the water just as you get past the breakers.

I take a shallow breath. "Head CT?" The patient is now almost six hours out of surgery and should be awake. Weird.

Keane gives me an encouraging smile. "I'm waiting for it but I thought you might have an idea."

She's so close to me that I feel her body heat as I chew the inside of my lip, thinking. Why is she asking me? "All I can think of is PCS, ma'am." Post-concussive syndrome. Brains do not like shock waves from IEDs. "We had that case last month…but he wasn't symptomatic until a day or so post-op." I check the chart one more time. "I'm sorry, that's all I can think of."

Keane is watching my hands again and I realize I've been gesturing as I talk. Mitch often tells me talking with me is like having a conversation with an orchestral conductor. I drop my hands to my sides.

"Thank you, Captain. That was my thought too. I'm pleased to know we're on the same page," Keane says softly. She is flushed. This is new.

My eyes widen at her tone. "Yes ma'am. I'm sorry I don't have more for you." I move slightly to the side. Something is making the pit of my stomach tight, as though this is edging into borderline flirting. I'm interested in flirting but I'm not interested in being disciplined. Or worse.

Colonel Keane straightens up abruptly, leaning away from me. "As you were." She snaps the chart closed then strides away without waiting for me to respond.

I stare after her, confused. What an odd reaction. She seemed almost…guilty. Was *she* trying to flirt? It certainly seemed so to me. Don't be ridiculous. You're imagining things, Sabine. I'm still holding Private Holman's medical chart. Shit. I power walk back to his bed and drop it into the holder. I pause a moment and stare at him, trying to decide if there's anything more I can say. There isn't.

CHAPTER FOUR

Victoria is a disembodied voice. "I can barely see you. Why don't you just call tomorrow?"

"Vic, we're here now. I don't know what'll happen tomorrow. I may not get time." It's hard to keep my tone even. I'm tired and want to sleep but this is our scheduled weekly video call, so here I am. It's close to midnight here, which is convenient for Vic. Not so much for me. Now she wants me to hang up and call her some other time. I want to tell her that I specifically stayed awake for this, but it will only cause an argument and I cannot be fucked dealing with it.

The lounge area is occupied by four of us, including Mitch. We are dotted around the room, seated at tables or sprawled, as I am, on one of the worn couches. I sit facing the room so nobody can see my laptop screen. If anyone queried, I would just tell them she is my sister and the lie would stand because we share dark hair and high cheekbones. Mine comes from my mother's Mediterranean heritage meshing with my father's Germanic bone structure. Vic's is the result of a skilled hair colorist and genetics she isn't sure about.

I would prefer not to lie, but I also don't want to be called in to address a complaint of homosexual conduct. The inevitable shitstorm of formal investigation and discharge are not worth it. I've never had to explain her away like that because nobody has ever seen our calls, or even a photograph of her. Vic loathes the secrecy. Her opinion lies somewhere around *fuck the institution*.

That attitude is part of what attracted me in the beginning, her carefree nature offset my love of order perfectly. Now I feel her digs at the army serve no purpose other than deliberate antagonism. She wasn't always like this but the longer I stay in the military, the more bitter she becomes.

I'm in the lounge because the connection in my room was awful, but here it's no better. There must be a storm coming and it's messing with the Wi-Fi, one of the relatively small, yet annoying issues that creep into my daily life. Mitch is curled up on an easy chair hiding from his roommate's snoring. He is reading yet another zombie horror novel, but I'm sure he's also listening in on my call.

I adjust my headset, plucking the speakers away from my ears then letting them fall back into position. I keep my voice low and the headset means her words stay private. "What time's the show?" I tuck my legs underneath me and shift the laptop. The heat on my legs is becoming uncomfortable.

"Starts in two hours. I'll have to leave in twenty minutes." At least the sound is fine.

Something moves against my thigh and I lift my butt off the couch to dip a hand into my pocket. A half-melted chocolate bar. Amy. How did I not notice that in there? I toss it onto the couch and lean closer to the screen, as though it would somehow fix the connection. "How many artists?"

When I first deployed, I struggled with accidentally calling her baby or honey whenever we spoke. Now those words don't even seem to enter my lexicon, or hers it would seem. We are perfunctory. Almost bored with one another. Early in the deployment, she would spend our calls listing all the things she missed about me, and missed doing to me. Her graphic descriptions left me blushing and unable to respond for fear of someone overhearing, and when we hung up, I would rush to my room or the showers to relieve the throbbing between my legs.

Eventually, her lists faded away and turned into meaningless conversation. Now we rarely mention anything soft or endearing. Instead, we speak of the mundane, avoid the important and argue about the tedious. Before I left on my first deployment, a year apart with only the vague possibility of two weeks leave back home seemed unbearable. Now, nine months through my second, I wonder why I thought I couldn't do it.

Vic's image focuses, then distorts again. "Just three. Paul thinks I'll make a few sales. We'll just have to see."

Sales are important for her, more for her ego than our bank balance. Her first exhibition and sale was celebrated with a bottle of champagne as expensive as one week's rent. We did the same at my graduation from medical school, but not when I graduated from Commissioned Officer Training. We've hardly celebrated anything about my army career.

"Send me some photos of the work?" I squint, trying to make out her features. Her wide eyes and thick wavy hair. The quality of this call is woeful and I can't help but feel disappointed. Regardless of the issues in our relationship, in the nine years we've been together I have never stopped being awed by her physical beauty. It's a pity other things fade away. Things that once excited now aggravate and annoy.

When I speak to her, I have to remind myself why we're together. Why we love one another. Things that help me when she's detached, or I'm tired and upset. I make myself remember how we fell in love when I was in my final year of med school at Ohio State. We used to spend our time hiking through state parks, camping, laughing and enjoying one another.

For our first date we got lost and drove for hours trying to find a drive-in movie theater. We settled at the edge of the field to watch the second half of *Gone with the Wind* and drink margaritas poured from a thermos. I licked salt from the edge of the glass and Vic said my lips were the fullest, most sensuous lips she'd ever seen. Then she kissed me.

I skipped study sessions when she told me the huskiness of my voice drove her mad with desire, after which she threw me down onto the bed where we stayed for almost two days. Now I can't imagine spending slow time in bed with her. What would we even talk about once we were done fucking? Movement in the doorway catches my attention and I look up in time to see Colonel Keane pause, her laptop tucked under an arm. Her eyes have a wide deer-in-the-headlights look as we make eye contact. My boss opens her mouth, closes it abruptly and walks away without coming into the room. I'm still looking at the doorway when a peeved voice bursts through my headset. "Sabine!"

"Mmm, sorry. What was that?"

"I asked if you got my last email. About the back door?"

"Shit. Yeah, sorry I haven't replied. Just hire someone to repair it, or I'll sort it out when I get home."

"I'll leave it for when you get back, then you'll be happy it's the correct one. I mean, what's another three months with a sticking door handle, right?" She's pissed off. I'm sure it's because I never replied to her email, and because I didn't respond right away just now. I'm pissed off because there's no reason she can't do it and now it's one more thing for me to deal with when I get back.

Mitch materializes beside me, his eyes on my chocolate bar as he dog-ears a page of his book.

Victoria must have caught sight of him. "Hi Mitchy." The video pixelates before I catch sight of her twisting her hair up and shoving a hair stick through it.

I tug the headset away from my ear. "Vic says hi."

Mitch leans down, waving in the general direction of the camera. "Hello darlin'. Ugh, what a God-awful connection." He must assume his voice carries through my microphone to Vic. Mitch snatches the candy bar from the couch and waggles it at me, eyebrows raised in silent question.

I give him a vague wave. Whatever. Eat it, you uncontrollable chocolate addict. There's a blur of movement on the screen before a furry shape is presented to me. The video stabilizes for me to see Vic smile as she holds up our cat, Brutus. He is limp when Vic gently moves him close to the webcam. I have no idea if he can see me but I know he hears me when I raise my voice slightly. "Hello, my precious baby!" Brutus leans forward, straining toward the sound of my voice.

Mitch stops unwrapping the chocolate long enough to snort. I lift my middle finger and wave him off. He departs the room with the remains of my candy bar clutched in his fist. Thief. Vic sounds bored as she strokes Brutus's black fur. "He's gained weight again. The vet says he needs less kibble, even though he's on the special protein one." She likes the cat well enough, but she doesn't love him like I do. Whenever she emails me, there is always a picture of Brutus to satisfy my feline cravings but I suspect she has taken them all at once to dish out at intervals.

"Maybe feed him less again or swap it for all wet food?" I regret saying it immediately. She'll take it as criticism. Vic doesn't respond. Instead, she bends her head to watch Brutus, who has begun a vigorous grooming ritual on her lap. I watch the cat lick a front leg and rub it over his ears a few times, and feel an urge to cover the awkward silence. "How's Caesar?"

For a moment an expression I don't recognize crosses her face. "He's good." Before I can comment, Vic whistles and our Doberman shoots into view, his whole butt moving as he wags his tail. From his position on Vic's lap, Brutus swats the dog half-heartedly with a white paw. How rude. Et tu, Brute? Vic pushes the laptop back, tapping the table and pointing to the screen. "Look!"

Caesar jumps up, paws on the table and sniffs, his nose wet against the webcam. I lean closer. "Hey buddy!" The dog tilts his head, seeming confused before he jumps down and runs off. Vic and I laugh together for what seems like the first time in ages.

"He was never very smart," she concedes. I make a noise to show my agreement, but not too strongly because the dog is her favorite.

I lean back on the couch with a dull sort of sadness in my chest. All my people are living their lives back home without me. Some nights, the thought keeps me awake and I have to get up and wander the hallways to rid myself of the heaviness, bumping into other insomniacs or people coming and going from a shift. These are the times I think of all the things I miss about my girlfriend.

I miss the feel of her hair, soft curls loose against my bare skin when I wake up. She knows how I take my coffee, right down to the exact amount of milk I like. Sometimes I think she makes it better than I do. I miss her laugh, always just a little too loud. I miss her hands, long fingered and callused from holding paintbrushes. Pianist's hands, though she's never played aside from clinking out the first notes to "Heart and Soul". I miss the way she used to make me feel.

When I remember these things, it makes me feel worse because it always segues into things I do *not* miss about her. Her snide comments about my job and how I only joined the army to please my family—she's right, of course, but that's beside the point. The way we fight about it never changes. We've always fought and I used to think I would worry when we stopped fighting, because that would mean the spark had gone. Now I know that's not true. The spark can go out just fine all on its own. It happens gradually, but it happens nonetheless.

A short burst of electronic static startles me. "How's work?" Vic asks because she feels she has to. The reality is she doesn't like to hear about the awful, gory aspects of my job.

I shrug. "The usual." I don't like to get into specifics. The evasion works well for us and stops arguments. Once fiery and passionate, they used to end with us tumbling into bed. Fight and fuck. Now that I'm deployed, they end with no contact until something triggers her desire to speak to me again.

Our first major fight, we yelled at one another for hours because we had to move for my residency. Then, the trailer we were towing rocked with the movement of the car while we made up in the backseat, our lovemaking frenzied and passionate. We fought again when we had to move to D.C. for my army posting, then when I left for my first active duty. I think we're still fighting about that one, but I'm not sure we've made up this time.

There are a few boxes stacked behind her. "What's with the boxes?" I ask, tilting my head to try to see them better.

"Art supplies," she answers quickly. Vic stretches an arm to the side and when her hand comes back into view she's holding a glass half-filled with ice and amber liquid. Glenmorangie with a splash of soda. It wouldn't even be dark in D.C. yet. How nice to be her, at home drinking in the twilight. There's a sudden rush of saliva in my mouth as I imagine how she would taste if I were to kiss her at this moment. A deep ache starts between my legs. I look around, feigning casualness. "I can try the connection in my room again. Amy is doing rounds." Vic will understand what I mean.

"I have to get going for the gallery show, Sab. There's hardly any time," she says carefully. "Is it even worth it?"

Of course it's worth it. My teeth find the inside of my cheek. I want to snap at her but instead, I force a nonchalant shrug. "Well. I suppose not then." My tone is neutral, though rejection twists my gut. "I miss you."

"You too. Hey, I've got to go. Talk soon." Vic waves and the video call shuts off abruptly, leaving me stunned. I close the laptop, tuck it under my arm and trudge back to my room to take care of the ache myself.

CHAPTER FIVE

This morning I'm alone for breakfast, sitting in a corner of the chow hall with my back to the room. I take a too-large bite of toast and turn the page of my tattered book, leaving a smear of peanut butter on the paper. I contemplate licking it off.

"Captain Fleischer."

I drop my things and spin around. Keane is directly behind me, which means I can't push my chair back. I twist and squirm, and manage to stand with my ass wedged against the table. I throw an unnecessary salute, trying to buy some time to frantically chew. When I manage to swallow, it feels like it's stuck against my sternum. Should have chewed a little more, Sabine. I scrunch my eyes against the pain in my chest and finally manage to acknowledge her. "Colonel Keane. Good morning."

She studies me, cheek lifted in a half smile. "Do you need some liquid to wash that down, Sabine?"

I swallow hard, still trying to push the lump of food down. "I would appreciate a moment for that, ma'am. Please excuse me." I grab one of my mugs and turn away from her to take a deep gulp of lukewarm coffee.

"Take your time, Captain."

I swallow another mouthful then set the mug back down and run a thumb over my lips. "I apologize, Colonel. I wasn't expecting company. How may I help you?"

Keane smiles, wide enough to show her dimples. "I need you, Sabine."

She needs me. I stare. What? I distinctly recall waking up this morning. My voice is pitched a little deeper than usual as my heart rate picks up. "Ma'am?"

"We've just had a sergeant come in who needs his gallbladder removed." Her thumb and forefinger are a quarter of an inch apart. "This close to rupture. I want you to assist me with the laparoscopic chole."

Of course. Surgery. Not *needs* me. You idiot, Sabine. "That sounds very interesting, Colonel. I appreciate the opportunity."

"We're just waiting on a room to be prepped, so you have time to finish your breakfast." Her eyes flick to the book I had flung onto the table. Kafka. In German. Embarrassing. Keane looks back to me. "Fifteen minutes?"

"Yes ma'am." I snatch up the book and the rest of my breakfast. Ugh. Why not just ask her for an autograph, Sabine? She's the only superior officer that makes me so flustered. I know it's because I'm aware of my lust and how I should *not* be thinking of her that way. Cerebral logic dictates that I can't help acting like a wide-eyed kid around the object of my crush.

But this thing with Keane is more than a crush, or lust or an infatuation. It's all those, sure, but it's also a feeling of…wanting to be seen by her. Of wanting to *know* her, beyond all of this. Wishful thinking and nothing more. You're an adult, Sabine. Now act like one.

Keane is finishing up at the sink when I step up to scrub. I haven't removed a gallbladder or done a laparoscopic surgery since residency and I'm a little worried. Our main function is trauma, stabilizing casualties so they can be moved on for further treatment. We treat contractors, detainees and occasionally some Afghan nationals and also deal with any emergency medical issue a member of the coalition forces might have. Like a gallbladder that could rupture en route to Germany.

Colonel Keane rinses her hands. "Are you ready, Sabine?"

"Just running over the procedure again, ma'am."

"I'll be right there helping you. I know the scopes can be awkward if you're not used to them but it really does help get them back out there faster." She bumps the faucet and shakes water from her hands.

"I know, and I'm excited to have the chance to brush up on my skills, Colonel."

"You're lucky, once upon a time we had to do it the old-fashioned way. Then the year before your first tour we had an unusually high number of incarcerated hernias, angry gallbladders and appendixes." Keane smiles, looking like a kid at Christmas. "That's when I wrote a thorough report on the benefits of laparoscopy and our requisition was approved."

Her smile is contagious and I find myself returning with a grin of my own. "Sounds like you were very persuasive, ma'am." She could certainly persuade me to do a few things. Sabine…

Keane backs through the door, still smiling at me. "See you in there."

I turn back to my scrub and finish running the steps in my head. When I'm sure I've got them down, I push into the operating room. As I'm getting gowned and gloved, Keane is preparing the ports for the laparoscopes, making swift incisions and inserting the scopes. I cast my eyes over the equipment, trying to recall the controls. Keane looks up at me, her eyes crinkled over the top of her mask. "You're up, Sabine."

She is patient with me as I manipulate the instruments while watching what I'm doing on a screen. Operating via a monitor allows no sense of depth perception and I feel like a student. A dumb student. To add another element of difficulty, the floor has been vibrating every five minutes or so since before we began. It's an operation outside the wire, not troops practicing.

Keane shuffles closer to me, her hip brushing the top of my thigh. "Change your angle slightly, Sabine." She laughs as I move the scope in the wrong direction. "No, no. Here, go in like…this." Her hand closes over mine and she helps me make a minor adjustment to the pitch of the scope. "Excellent. There. Now clip, cut and dissect."

My tongue shoots out the side of my mouth as I quickly place clips, cut the artery and duct then dissect the gallbladder away. Bingo.

"Perfect. Now bag and remove." The approval in her voice is clear.

I allow myself a victorious smile as the deflated organ is placed in a bag like a piece of trash and dragged out of a tiny incision. I'm alternating between watching the monitor intently, and watching Keane's hands as she moves her instruments around. Keane nods. "Looks good. Let's close up." She peers at me for a long moment, as though she's waiting for me to say something.

I catch her eye. "Yes ma'am. I agree." We finish and leave the sergeant to be taken to recovery. I watch Keane checking the chart. Her eyebrows are furrowed, the way they do when she's concentrating. Keane smiles at one of the nurses before signing the chart and handing it to me, her smile still in place. I scrawl my name on the page and rush ahead to hold the door open for her.

She waves her hand under the automatic soap dispenser. "Would have taken courage to hide the pain from that gallbladder as long as he did."

"Yes, indeed it would have." I point at the dispenser to indicate I need to use it. "Excuse me." She shifts her position fractionally but I still have to reach across her. "Apologies ma'am."

Keane seems unconcerned about my invasion of her personal space. "Excellent surgery, Captain." She snatches at the paper towel, offering me a few squares before she pulls another bunch down for herself.

"Thank you." I pause as the floor vibrates again. "…Colonel." The back of my neck feels strange, like someone is grabbing and squeezing with cold fingers. After so long I should be blasé about fighting nearby but it still makes me nervous.

"Are you okay, Sabine?"

I realize I've been staring at the floor. I look up at her. "Yes ma'am. Perfectly all right." That didn't sound convincing.

Keane gives me a sympathetic smile. "Just think, if you can do a lap chole with the floor vibrating under your feet, you can do one anywhere." My boss leans against the sink. "Make sure you put it on your résumé." She's teasing me. The laugh lines around her eyes crease as she waits to see how I'll respond.

I decide to play along. "May I use you as a reference for this particular skill listing, ma'am?"

Keane chuckles, seeming pleased. "Of course, Sabine. I'll make sure I'm effusive, should anyone ever ask." She tosses her paper towel in the trash, still smiling. "I'll see you later."

I return her smile. "Thank you, Colonel. Have a pleasant afternoon."

"And you."

As I walk outside, I can hear distant gunfire from outside the base. Maybe we're going to be busy soon. My hand strays to brush against the pistol holstered on my thigh and I quicken my pace toward the barracks to collect my gear. Mitch is in his room, reading, and barely looks up when I knock on the open door. I rest against the doorway. "Gun time! And I'm not talking about your biceps."

He sets the book down. "Heard you had a lap chole. How was it?"

I shrug. "It was interesting. A little confusing." Perhaps it was equal parts interesting and confusing. Keane grabbing my hand was certainly interesting.

Mitch sighs. "Come on, let's get this over with." His apathy permeates everything as he collects his gear.

We run to the armory and collect three boxes of ammo each. As always, the clerk glances at my tits. I give him a tight-lipped smile. Nope, sorry pal. We are the only ones on the outdoor range, so we choose two stations next to one another and set up. After we affix new targets to the metal backings Mitch is unusually quiet on our way back to the stations. Presumably, he's sulking because it's shooting day.

He'll sulk even more if he fails his yearly weapons qualifications. At least twice a week I make sure to drag him to the range to keep our pistol and rifle skills up to scratch. Plus I really like it and it's one of the few things that I'm better at than Mitch. If I didn't push him he'd probably never practice, and he only just passes quals as it is. I kick up dirt with my boots and try to ignore the vibrating ground. It's more pronounced out here. I look around, checking beyond the fence but don't see anything.

I check the Beretta to ensure everything is in order. I load an extra magazine, fit my hearing protection and pull on my safety glasses. When I'm ready, I raise a hand to signal the range officer. He gives a short blast on the siren and puts up a large red flag to let people know there is live fire inside the wire.

It takes me just over fifty seconds to empty my first magazine of fifteen rounds, while Mitch is still thumbing rounds into his spare. He's procrastinating. I make sure my pistol is empty and configured safely before picking up my binocs to check my grouping. I can see without the optics, but I want an exact view of where my shots have landed. They look good. Except one. Fuck.

Mitch has fired eight shots. I wait for him to finish his set before leaning over to see how he is doing. Not great. The muscles in his cheeks bulge with tension. Oh dear. I work through the second magazine and again, wait for him. Mitch finishes his minutes after me and stares blankly down the range. I yank my earmuffs off, leave them looped around my neck and peer through the binocs at his target. "Better, but you're still snatching at it."

Mitch nods silently. We're competitive about everything, but he begrudgingly admits I'm a better shot and has always accepted my instruction. It's a small win, but I'll take it. The range officer is watching us. "You're clear to go down range." He sounds bored as he changes flags again. I wonder what he did to get stuck on range duty today.

Mitch and I jog down to change targets. He lets me win. Shit, he's really sulking. I grin at the tight groupings on my target. Twenty-five holes all within a grapefruit-sized space just to the left of where a sternum would be. Sorry, paper target heart but you're probably pretty fucked. There are five embarrassing strays which would do nothing more than nick a right lung.

Mitch stares at my paper then yanks his down with his mouth set in a thin, petulant line. Looking at his, I can tell which grouping is from his first magazine and which is from his second. The second set is compact and centered over the left pectoral, but his first fifteen look like he was sneezing every time he pulled the trigger.

I clamp my lips together to stop myself from smiling as he tucks the paper under his arm. He'll sulk even more if I mock him too hard. I decide I'll mock him lightly. "Well, I suppose you've hit pretty much every vital organ. It'd take a lot of patching up." It's always been a source of amusement to me, practicing doing one of the things we spend so much time fixing. I suspect my superior marksmanship is because I like shooting whereas Mitch does not.

I write the date and time on my target then set up another. If I ever wanted to chart my best time of the day or week, I would have the data I needed. Hypothetically.

Mitch pins up his second target. "I always want to aim for the head," he admits. He looks like a teenager admitting a secret porn stash to his mother.

"You read too many zombie books." I turn to walk back up range.

"I do," he agrees. "At least someone 'round here will know what to do in the zombie apocalypse." His eyes are bright as he looks at me. He is serious. So many years of listening to his talk have drained me of all responses.

We spend another hour working through the rest of the ammo while the range officer repeats his monotonous flag up, flag down, siren routine. Mitch holds the armory door open for me and I duck under his arm. He dumps his targets in a trash can just inside the door. I shake my head, but bite my tongue. Maybe if he charted his progress he might improve more. He leaves me to claim a table in the room adjoining the armory while he fetches water. I sit in front of the rattling air-con unit, tilting my head up to catch some cool air.

Mitch sets two bottles on the table. "Plain, not sparklin'. I hate this place."

"You're a snob." I begin to break down the pistol.

He shrugs. "I like nice things, darlin'. Still don't explain why I spend so much time with you." My best friend's smile is saccharine sweet.

I ignore his fake barb and begin to methodically clean and oil my pistol. We don't speak as we check mechanisms and apply tiny dabs of grease. I give each part another once-over and begin to reassemble the Beretta.

"I'm thinkin' of applyin' to FST." Mitch's declaration comes from nowhere.

My hands pause. "What?"

"FST." He is watching me, gauging my response as he runs a cleaning rod through the barrel again.

Forward Surgical Team. Small units which are packed up and moved closer to combat. My brain sticks on the word *combat*. It's far more dangerous than what we are doing now, stationed in a combat support hospital a safe distance away from most of the major hostile areas. My mouth hangs open for a few moments before I manage to blurt out a squeaky, "Why?"

"It'll look good on my résumé, Sabs," he says earnestly.

I can't argue. He's right. We are both Commissioned Officers with the rank of captain, but the glaring difference between us is that I have no real aspiration to move beyond my automatic promotion to Major Fleischer in a few years. Mitch thinks Lieutenant General Mitchell Adam Boyd sounds amazing. My cheeks puff and I force the air out. "It would be a great opportunity." My tone is even, I'm trying to keep my own needs out of it.

"Just a thought. I ain't made a decision either way," Mitch says. He knows me well enough to have read my response.

I lean back in the chair, quickly finish putting my pistol back together and insert a full magazine. I check and re-check it is on safe before I secure the weapon in its holster. I'm upset about his unexpected news but not altogether surprised. Perhaps it's selfish, but I'd always pictured us staying together, being deployed in the same place until I was done with my military service. I've always known he would stay on even once I'd left.

Vic and I made an agreement where I would only fulfill the minimum obligations that came with me using the Army Health Professions Scholarship Program for med school. The HPSP contract I signed means seven years of active duty, then I can move on to a private job back home and spend four more on the Individual Ready Reserve roster.

Lately I've been thinking about staying on past my minimum. Part of me wants to please my father. The other part of me, the one that's cowardly, wants to be away from the unpleasant atmosphere that's been slowly filling my house for the past few years. I didn't even get to tell her my carefully prepared story about wanting certain deployments versus uncertain reserve call-backs. The moment I said *thinking about extending my contract*, we started to fight. I'm breaking the terms of our agreement.

I'm trying to keep a neutral facial expression when Keane pushes through the door. Mitch and I slide our chairs back and jump to attention. I speak first. "Colonel Keane, good afternoon." My posture is perfect. If only my father could see me now. Slap me on a recruitment poster, boys.

She stops next to me. "Boyd, Fleischer. As you were."

I relax my posture slightly. Her eye protection sits atop her head and it seems so casual, like she's just come inside from being at the beach. Keane sets her earmuffs and cleaning gear on the table. "How was your session?" The question is directed at both of us, but she's looking only at Mitch. My stomach twists. Have I done something?

Mitch side-eyes me. "Very productive, ma'am."

"I'm pleased to hear it." Keane glances down at my targets still folded on the table. She reaches for them, unfolds and shuffles through each one. Keane finally looks at me. "These are yours, Fleischer?"

"Yes ma'am." I'm mortified about the fact that they are marked so fastidiously with both date and time.

"Very good, Sabine. You should think about a Marksmanship Badge or even competition." She offers the targets back to me.

I hold the paper in front of myself, as though I could use it as a shield to stop my embarrassment escaping. “I’d never thought of either, Colonel, but I’ll give it some thought. Thank you.” The tips of my ears feel warm. Damn it. Mitch is silent beside me and I know from his posture that he is holding back laughter.

Keane picks up her things and inclines her head, giving me an amused smile. “Enjoy your afternoon.” She walks away with her cleaning case swinging in her hand, leaving me to sit down and refold my targets. I am still very aware of the heat of my ears.

Mitch lets out a deep chuckle. “I think she likes you. She never mentioned my shootin’. Maybe I should keep all them targets after all.” Mitch mock-pouts at me and puts his cleaning things away. He closes the case with a loud click. “Oh yeah, by the way, you got dirty gun grease on your forehead, darlin’. Real smooth.”

CHAPTER SIX

The mailroom should open at six, but this morning the clerk is late. I'm taking a standing nap against the outside wall, waiting with Mitch for mail handout. Last night was nonstop surgery and I haven't slept yet. The door swings open and hits the wall beside me, startling me fully awake. I stifle a yawn and step inside. "Fleischer, S."

"Number?"

Automatically, I recite my ID number. The clerk rummages for a minute then holds out a package, which will be from my sister, and a small stack of letters banded together. He glances down at the stack. "Flee-shur."

Mitch sniggers. My eyebrows flick upward for a moment as I stare at the clerk. Are you kidding me? I literally just pronounced my name for you, you asshole. I give him a tight smile and take my mail, resisting the urge to snatch it up and shout *Fleischer* his face.

Mitch moves forward, his forearms resting on the counter. His posture reminds me of someone trying to charm free drinks from a bartender. "Boyd, M." Mitch offers his number without being asked. He turns to face me, giving me a slow and exaggerated wink.

"Boyd!" The clerk hands Mitch a parcel. It is the same every time we collect mail. No letters and just a monthly parcel from either my sister or my mother. I rub my hand across my stomach, as though I could dispel the awful feeling building there. Mitch is exuberant. "Thank you, adopted family!"

I glance at the package in his hand and force a grin. "Bigger than mine, you family-stealing asshole."

Mitch and I became friends in pre-med and both made career choices with family in mind. Mine were to continue tradition. His were an attempt to regain favor with his parents, who disowned him at sixteen when he told them he was gay. In the almost seventeen years I've known him, he has had no contact with a blood relative.

We are long past dissecting his family's motivations, yet I never stop feeling a pang of sympathy when the only mail he receives is from *my* family. It fills me with indignant outrage that his cannot move past his sexuality to focus on what a good, talented and kindhearted man he is. My family latched onto Mitch quickly, and he them. It didn't take long until he was invited to our events, slotting in as though he was born a Fleischer. Holidays are always spent with my family and they never fail to gift him with something for his birthday and Christmas.

Oma and Opa taught him German expletives. My sister still tries to set him up with workmates who invariably turn out to be straight. He watches ball games with my father while my mother frets over him being single. When I think of him being adopted by my loved ones, I feel humbled and grateful for my family. They have been supportive of my entire life and also embrace others who are gay.

Mitch is drumming his fingers on Jana's package as we walk back to our quarters, no doubt eager to open it and see what goodies she has included. I tuck my package under an arm so I can sort through my stack of letters. Mom, Mom, Oma…Vic.

Vic. Weird. She loathes writing letters, preferring the instant gratification of an email to the humble handwritten page. Both of my mother's envelopes feel thick, as usual. There will be news articles from the local paper with her humorous annotations on them. She will have included recipe clippings, as though I could somehow make an apple cinnamon Bundt cake here.

Mom's letters read more like a journal of randomness, her daily activities and gossip about the neighbors. I look forward to them because they are so normal and full of boring day-to-day things. We pause outside my room where I shuffle the letters into a neat pile. Mitch stares at my hands. "Is that—?"

"It's nothing," I interrupt, shoving Vic's letter to the back. I knock softly on the closed door to give my roommate a chance to respond before bursting in on her.

"All good!" Amy calls from behind the closed door. Good start, I'm not interrupting her napping or masturbating. She is sitting cross-legged on her bed with a headset on, in the middle of a call with her husband and young son. Amy lifts a hand in silent greeting. Shit, I forgot it was her call time. Mail will have to wait.

"Workout?" Mitch asks from the doorway. It's not against the rules for men and women to be in the same room if the door is open or there is someone else present, but Mitch has never stepped over the imaginary line across the doorway of my room.

"Mhmm." I leave my mail on the bed, give Amy an apologetic smile and pull the door closed.

The gym is empty, which means we can talk without filtering. I warm up while listening to Mitch prattle about his upcoming rest and recreation leave, or R and R as we call it. The running joke is that it's actually I and I. Intoxication and intercourse. The latter is particularly true for him.

He has a four-day pass to go to Qatar for where he will meet up with a few guys from other units who share his preferences. The location makes me uneasy because the culture means they have to be careful. He seems unconcerned, which makes me even more worried.

I feel strangely weak today and my only excuse is that I'm tired. When I almost drop a warm-up set Mitch chastises me, like some personal trainer who is intent on remodeling a client. "Come on, Betty Spaghetti." He settles the bar back in the cups.

"How about you do some backflips for me, Mitch?" I grumble at him, sitting up and wiping my face with the bottom of my T-shirt.

He pouts. Mitch is far too burly to do any sort of gymnastic activity. When I'm feeling particularly puckish, I do a few casual roundoff back handsprings in front of him, digging out my gymnastic training from when I was eleven and interested in such things. In third year med, I offered to teach him after we'd been drinking. The memory of his one attempt at a flip always cheers me up. The stitches I put in his eyebrow as he lay on the kitchen table in our tiny, shared apartment didn't even leave a scar. I should have gone into plastic surgery.

"You're cruel, Sabine, you know?" He adds another five pounds on each side. Prick.

"I do." I lie back down.

Mitch watches from above, ready to spot me if I wobble again. "I say, Sabs, you and the Colonel looked mighty friendly when I wandered past the wards the other day," he says slyly.

I falter midlift and have to work to push the bar all the way up, my cheeks puffing with the effort. Thanks for the distraction, buddy. "I didn't see you." I grunt the words out.

He gives me a knowing smile. "Of course you didn't. You were too busy. Checkin' charts was it?"

"It's not like that. She wanted an opinion."

"About what? Whether her tits look good in her uniform?"

"Fuck off." I push out another repetition, trying to ignore the fluttering in my stomach. Colonel Keane is very attractive and there's nothing wrong with enjoying it, so long as I don't give myself away. I can't deny she makes me feel strange, like the time I thought about shoplifting a denim jacket in high school. It was wrong, but I still thought about it.

Mitch won't let it go. "I think it is like that. Don't even try telling me you ain't ever thought about her. I know you've had that little crush for a while now."

It pleases him to hear me admit weakness. I frown up at him. "You know I have. It's not some stupid schoolgirl crush, Mitch."

I'm worried. If Mitch saw something, then perhaps I wasn't wrong about her behavior earlier. Maybe I wasn't imagining it? I give myself a mental headshake. Mitch sees what he wants to and so do you, Sabine. I finish my set with quivering arms and stand beside the bench while Mitch adds weights for himself.

It's just that I respect and admire Keane's capabilities as a surgeon. I'm intrigued by the humor I've seen peeking out from under her calm exterior. She is warm and caring and sympathetic and you're getting carried away with your thoughts, Sabine. Everything is irrelevant anyway, because I am not a cheater. Plus there's the issue of her unknown sexual preferences and the fact she wears a wedding ring. Oh, and of course, that pesky thing called The Army and the even peskier thing called Don't Ask, Don't Tell.

Apparently my face gives my thoughts away. Mitch gives me a self-satisfied grin as he settles himself. "I see you got a letter from Vic."

I look around quickly, reassuring myself that we are still alone. "Yes."

"How's it goin'?"

I'm not in the mood for a relationship dissection but there's no point lying or being evasive. He will drag it from me eventually. "Not great. The usual, but something else is off. Something different. I can't figure out what it is." I chew my lip.

Mitch and I speak regularly about my relationship with Vic. He knows how I feel that the distance between Vic and me is expanding, as though we're tugging on opposite ends of a rubber band. We're both just waiting for it to snap. The band stretched slowly, almost imperceptibly, at first but now I think the pressure is greater, the tension more obvious.

It's taken us years to get to this point and my gut tells me the longer we go on, the more inevitable our split is. It's just a feeling I have. One which refuses to go away. One I've had for a while now. I lean on the cold metal of the press bar. "I don't know what to do about it."

"Sometimes there's nothing you can do. You work with what you got, or put it away and start over." He smiles, seeming pleased with his analogy. "Now, get those arms off my weights unless you want me to bench you too."

After another forty-five minutes in the gym, Mitch decrees it's time for breakfast. Because we work around the clock, the chow hall is always open. It is half full of people scattered around the room. Mitch and I split. I walk straight to the coffeepots to pour myself two small cups. If there was a suggestion box, I would write *bigger coffee mugs* on a slip of paper every single day. I add powdered whole milk and stir listlessly. I would sacrifice a non-vital organ for fresh milk. My colleagues tease me about putting milk instead of creamer in my coffee, but it's what I've always done.

The breakfast offerings are as uninspiring as ever. Bread here is only edible if toasted but I refuse to eat the cold, soggy toast that the mess staff leaves in piles for us. The rotating track of the mass toaster accepts my two pieces of whole wheat and I eat squishy grapes while I wait for my fresh batch to be done.

Being still lets my mind wander and it inevitably returns to the conversation I had with Vic the night before last. That niggling feeling returns. The toast burns my fingers and I grab a jar without checking what it is, smearing it haphazardly. Chocolate spread. Ugh. I nearly toss it and start over, but I'm anxious to get back to my room to read my letters and open Jana's package before I shower and wait for incomings.

Amy is gone by the time I make it back to my room. Vic's is the obvious choice to read first. It's almost a novelty. I open the envelope and fish inside for the single piece of paper, barely half a page of Vic's awful penmanship. Her written words always make me feel as though she is writing in the dark after drinking a bottle of wine during an earthquake. It's something I tease her about and without fail she responds with a quip about her handwriting reflecting her artistic flair. I read the first line and my stomach muscles tighten. I know what it is, but I didn't expect it like this.

Oh God.

CHAPTER SEVEN

Dear Sabine,

There's no easy way to say this and I don't think there's any point in wasting time with platitudes or metaphors. I'm seeing someone and I'm leaving you. I'm lonely and unhappy and have been for a long while. I know you are too. We can't fix this. Not while you're over there and I'm here. I know you want to stay in the army and I can't spend the rest of my life by myself.

I'm sorry to hurt you, I do love you, but I need someone with me. Call or email me if you want to talk things over. I'll leave your house and car keys in your sister's mailbox along with some other things for when you get back.

I'm taking Caesar and Brutus.
Come home safely,
Victoria xx

She may as well have addressed it *Dear Jane*. My heart is drumming and I feel the churn of nausea. I bite down hard on my lower lip as I read it again. Maybe I'm misunderstanding her awful writing? No. It's blunt and to the point which is typical-Victoria style. Fuck. Why not call, or email me?

The only reason I can think of for her sending a letter is because she needed to create something to express herself. Something concrete. If it's on paper then it's official. Fucking hell, couldn't she have waited a few months until I was home and done it in person? I lean back against the wall, trying to think while my stomach heaves. Every time I almost manage to hold on to a thought, it dances around my head as though it were a skittish horse shying away from having its bridle put on.

Seeing someone.

Taking the boys.

If this were a movie, sad music would swell right now. Close-up on my stunned face. Let the letter drop and show a slow-motion pan to fluttering paper. But this isn't a movie. I can't grab a fistful of popcorn and shake my head thinking *poor bitch, but hey she should have known it was coming.* This is real life and there's nothing here except for this mess in my hand as the only remnant of our relationship. There you go, Vic, there's your fucking metaphor.

I close my eyes, trying to conjure up some memories of us. Happy ones. Ones which will make it easier for me to be angry about what she's done. I can't think of anything right now. The only thing I can think is that she's cheating on me and she's taking the boys. My pets.

A nerve twitches in my cheek. I make a decision. I'm going to call her. I need to hear her say it and I don't care what time it is at home. Who the fuck ends a nine-year relationship with less than half a page of words? I fold the letter and shove it deep into the back pocket of my pants. My legs tremble as I walk to the phone room.

It's empty, so I choose the booth in the corner and drop heavily onto the chair. It takes a moment while the credit left on my phone card is calculated. I know her cell number by heart, even with international dialing requirements but when

I go to push the numbers my brain freezes. It's like the dream where I need to dial 911 but every time I try, I fumble it or can't remember the correct sequence.

I press the earpiece of the phone to my forehead. "Shit. Shit." Think. No, don't think. That's your problem, Sabine. You're overthinking it. I stare blindly out the window until it comes to me. I press each number hard, lifting the handset to my ear. It seems to ring forever. There's always a delay with these calls as if our words must bounce off all the satellites in space.

Finally, she picks up. "Hello?"

"Vic? It's me." I have to assume she still knows who *me* is. The sounds of laughter and live music reverberate in my ear. I glance at my watch. Nearly midnight in D.C.

"Sabine?" Vic sounds wary. She's probably unsure if her letter arrived. "Uh...hi babe. Give me a moment and I'll go outside." The irony of her calling me babe is not lost on me. I hear muffled sounds and I fidget for a minute before she's back. "Couldn't hear a damned thing in there."

I see no point in wasting either my time or phone credit. "I got your letter."

The sound of a lighter sparking clicks in my ear. "Oh. I was wondering about it." She says no more, leaving it for me to pick up the conversation. I hear her inhale on a cigarette. She's smoking again. She knows I've always hated her smoking.

"I'm not going to lie, Vic. I'm pretty fucking upset. Can we talk about it?" I am met with silence. I grind my teeth. "Hello?"

"I'm here. These damned calls. Look, Sabine, there's no point. Nothing's going to change. The distance and uncertainty. I can't handle it and now you're thinking of staying in the military..."

The implication hangs between us. It's my fault. As she speaks, I realize she isn't cold but very matter-of-fact. It hits me. She's been sitting on this for some time. She picked up and moved on from our relationship a long time ago. Far earlier than I had. I hear noise in my ear, but I barely hear her words. It's only when there is no sound that I realize it's my turn to say something.

The sound escaping my mouth is a cross between a snort and a choked grunt. "So we're just going to call it quits after all this time? Just like that? After nine fucking years? I'll be home in three months, Vic. You couldn't have fucking waited to tell me in person?" I'm staring out the window, watching a group of men running PT drills in the morning sun. I wonder why I'm fighting it instead of just lying down tamely. It's not like we haven't been moving toward this.

Vic inhales again. "Three months, then they'll send you back. I thought this was the best way, Sa—" I hear a muffled thud and a muted, "No, it's fine. I'll be back in a minute." She comes back on the line. "Look, I'm sorry, Sabs. I really am but I can't help how I feel. You know we haven't worked for a long time."

I suppose at least she made some apology. As a rule she never apologizes. Her standard is *I'm sorry if this upsets you* not *I'm sorry I upset you*. I clench my molars. "What's her name?"

The answer is immediate. "Kate."

"How long?"

There's a long pause before she answers me. "Almost two years."

It started during my first deployment. She was with this woman when I last came home. Oh God. The trembling in my knees increases. "Jesus Christ. Why didn't you tell me sooner? Why waste both of our time?" An even more terrifying thought comes to me. "Vic, do I need to get tested for anything?"

"No! Jesus, no and I don't know why I waited." Her voice is quiet. "I wasn't sure. I thought maybe you and I, maybe we could fix it."

Fix it after she's been fucking another woman for all this time. I snort at her audacity. "Where are you now? Where are you taking the boys?"

"I'm moving to Colorado, Sabine."

"Vic. Why the fuck are you moving to Colorado?" My left hand is a fist. I force myself to release it.

"Kate got a job there. We leave the day after tomorrow." Vic clears her throat and the sound of her taking another drag filters through to me.

A hot flush builds at the bottom of my neck as I realize what she is saying. "Why can't you leave the boys with Jana?" My voice cracks up an octave and the pounding of my heart makes me feel like I am choking. I can't deal with this. My stomach twists and I have to swallow bile to stop myself from puking on the floor.

Vic's voice is full of indignation. "Why? Because they are mine too, Sabine. You'll probably be sent overseas again and your sister works full time."

I sit slumped in the chair with my head hanging almost between my knees. She could have said something when we spoke the other day and then I could have at least known. Vic's not cruel. It makes no sense. I'm crying and I swipe my palm over my face. There is silence between us and I need to fill it.

"What about the house bills? How am I supposed to pay them while I'm away?"

"Well…it's your house so technically your problem. Maybe your sister could find time to collect your mail and pay your bills for you."

"Sure," I say weakly. "I just don't…I don't get why *now*."

Vic's inner cynic, the one I always tease her about, isn't so amusing when she says, "Because I realized that being a military wife won't work for me, Sabine, and I want to move on. Let's be honest, you're so afraid of disappointing your family that you're probably going to stay in the army for the rest of your life."

I say the first thing that comes into my head, spitting words through gritted teeth. "Fuck you, Victoria. FUCK. YOU. You fucking adulterous, animal stealing cunt!" I slam the receiver down as hard as I can and leap out of the chair. It wobbles and I help it on its way with a hard kick. The chair clatters to the floor, rocking back and forth. I contemplate picking it up and throwing it against something.

With my back pressed against the wall and hands cupped over my mouth, my chest heaves as I try to control my anger. I cannot even begin to process what has just transpired. Logically, I know she has cheated on me and we have now broken up but when my mind slides around to really thinking about how I feel about it, something slams down in my brain like a portcullis.

I need to tell someone. I pick up the phone again and dial my sister. Jana answers halfway through the incoherent message I'm leaving on her machine.

She listens wordlessly as I try to explain through hiccupping sobs and words tumbling over one another. She makes no judgment and offers no advice, simply asking me in a voice hoarse with interrupted sleep, "What can I do?"

I have settled down to where I can speak coherently and I give her my instructions. First, I want the bed gone along with all the linens, blankets and duvets. I want it gone. I can deal with the rest later, but for now the thought of Victoria in our bed with someone else sickens me. I want my locks changed so she can no longer get in to our house. *My* house. Vic said it herself—my house, my problem. My parents gave me money for a deposit as my graduation present, wanting me to have somewhere to settle once I'm done with the army. I'm the only one making payments and my name is the only one on the deed.

"Jana, can you just sell the stuff or give it away or fucking burn it? I just want it gone when I get home. Can you do that for me please? And pay the bills in the mail, and change the garage door opener too. And can you tell Mom and Daddy?" I choke on the last few words.

Jana's voice is soft, soothing. "Of course, Sabbie. Do you want me to get Caesar and Brutus?"

"I d-d-don't even know wh-where she is," I stammer. I haven't stammered since I was seven. Get a grip, Fleischer.

"Okay, okay, don't cry, honey. I'll sort it out for you."

"Thank you." I hang up the phone without a goodbye, because there are no more words left. I leave the chair lying on the floor. People are faceless when I stumble past them. I go past the chow hall, snatch up a water bottle and push my way outside, breathing in the hot dusty air. I continue on past the barracks, breaking into a jog. I need to move before I explode.

It is just before ten hundred hours and already the heat is oppressive, though there is barely any humidity. I pick up my pace, heading to the worn dirt running track and I don't slow down once I get there. Usually I would take a moment to admire the line of mountain range meeting deep blue sky but today I just don't care. I run around and around as the sun continues to rise and sweat begins to pour from my body. I want to run until all I can think about is how exhausted, hot and sweaty I am. I want to run until all thoughts of my life with my now ex-girlfriend have been detoxed in gallons of sweat.

I run for fifteen minutes. Twenty-three. Thirty-one. It's not working. Her words stay in my brain, repeating constantly in the rhythm of my running.

Taking them.

Seeing someone.

Nearly two years.

Colorado.

I imagine my pets having to go on a plane. Brutus will be shitty about being caged, howling and sticking his paws through the bars. Caesar will be excited to be in the car going for an outing, hanging out of the window with his ears flapping in the wind. He'll go into a crate without issues. I try to imagine what Kate looks like. Does she look like me, or is she my total physical opposite? I think of Vic fucking this faceless woman and have to stop abruptly to lean over the edge of the running track and vomit.

I stand bent over with my hands on my knees. I wipe my mouth and wait to see if anything else is going to come up. No. I swish water into my mouth to eliminate the bad taste. She's seeing someone. I know Vic. She would have fucked her in our bed. Does this Kate wear my clothes, or drink out of our cups and use our cutlery? Of course she does. I turn back to the track and start moving again. I don't know what to do. What can I do? I'm not there, I'm here. She has left me and taken them and gone to someone else, somewhere else. I'm fucking helpless.

Mitch jogs out of the barracks to join me. Someone must have told him I'm out running around in the sun like a crazy person. I wave him off and run away. I don't want to talk. I want to be silent. I want to forget. But I don't forget. If anything, it feels as though the horror of this experience is growing. It's a deep ache that sits right in the core of my body.

After fifty-eight minutes, my legs are jelly and my gait has turned from a run into a shuffle. Another person approaches. I ignore them too. When I come around near the building on the long side of the track, I see it's Colonel Keane. Fuck you, Mitch. He's sent one of the few people I can't ignore.

My lungs burn. I slow to a walk fifty yards away, moving toward her with my hands on the small of my back, trying to catch my breath. Keane stands relaxed as she waits for me to approach. I come to attention in front of her, aware my shirt is drenched and sticking to me. I'm sure my face is bright red from exertion. My feet hurt from running for so long in boots and now that I've stopped, I'm rather queasy. I keep my distance and try to gulp in air. "Good morning, Colonel." My breath probably smells like puke. I slide my tongue over my teeth.

She looks me over and offers me another bottle of water. "Captain Fleischer, may I inquire what you're doing out here running around in this heat?"

I tuck the empty bottle under my arm and take the full one from her. "Thank you, ma'am. I…I'm trying to acclimate for my New York Marathon training." Ha-ha. Good one, Sabine.

Her lips twitch. "They run that in fall, not summer." She steps closer to me. "I don't think it's comparable to current conditions." Keane pulls her shades off and stares me in the eyes. I am squinting without my own sunglasses. "Sabine, I cannot think of anything or anyone who is worth a dose of heat exhaustion. Go inside, get to the showers and cool down. That's an order."

"Yes ma'am."

I detect something in her eyes that looks like pity before she pivots and strides purposefully away.

CHAPTER EIGHT

People are staring as I trudge back to my room and their gaze makes my skin crawl. I can only assume they are gossiping about me. Whatever. It wouldn't be the first time and it won't be the last. Personnel on base talk and we talk about everyone. I sneak in to my empty room, collect shower things, a fresh uniform and mostly-full laundry bags ready for my sweaty clothes.

A few shower stalls are occupied. Why can't I ever just fucking shower by myself? The sound of two women conversing, loud and obnoxious, fills the space so I find a stall as far away from them as I can. I try to concentrate on the comforting familiarity of my preshower routine while I wait for the shower to heat up.

After a few minutes the water is still cold, but it will have to do. It's only when I'm halfway through my shower that I realize I never turned the hot water on. Well done, Sabine. I take my time washing my hair and wonder idly if masturbation would help me feel any better.

Before I make a decision either way, I'm surprised to hear my name float over from the other side of the room. I step out from under the spray so I can hear them better. Yes, they are talking about me. It seems the grapevine has flowered quickly today. I'm not surprised, very little escapes the eyes and ears of this place.

The conversation carries easily, though I can't quite tell who the two voices are. Ladies, don't you know the first rule of gossiping? Make sure the subject of your gossip is not in earshot. Amateurs. The thought of someone being so stupid would be amusing, if it weren't for my current mood. I rinse my hair, turn the water off and begin to dry myself.

Presumably, they haven't noticed someone else is here and they continue to dissect my behavior.

"It must have been pretty serious. I heard she tossed a chair."

No. I just kicked it.

"I get it. I mean I'd do a lot worse if David left me for some skank ho while I was deployed."

I don't know if Kate is a skank ho, but thank you for the assumption. Nice to know sisterhood is still alive and well.

"Isn't she with Boyd?"

No, multiplied by infinity.

"I wouldn't mind giving him a go." Laughter carries over to me.

Best of luck with that dream, ladies.

Both showers shut off in quick succession which makes the voices easier to hear. "What a prick. Poor girl, I feel sorry for her."

She actually does sound sympathetic, how nice. I lean my forehead against the cool tile of the shower wall. How did everything get so fucked up?

"What an asshole. Wonder how long he's been fucking around."

He. An interesting but not unwelcome twist to the tale. I exhale. Your secret identity is safe, Sabine. A chill skitters over my neck. I said Vic's name and anyone could have overheard it during what was obviously a breakup argument. You got lucky, idiot. I dress and pack my things into my shower bag as their conversation moves on to something else. The stall doors bang open and footsteps head in my direction.

I could stay hidden, but I am feeling uncharacteristically nasty. Why shouldn't I take some of my current mood out on someone else? Their indiscretion and stupidity practically demands it. I open the door and step out of the stall into the path of two of my colleagues. They both rank underneath me. I could have some fun. Silently, I stare at both of them, waiting for acknowledgment.

Their gazes are everywhere but on my face and when they speak together, it's strained. "Captain Fleischer."

I lace my words with fake sincerity. "Lieutenant Neal, Lieutenant Trotter. Thank you so much for your support. It means a great deal to me." Their mouths fall open as I stand before them, casually toweling my hair dry. Neal blushes. Before they can say anything else, I grab my bags and leave the block.

I pull my hair up while I walk across the base and just as I step into the barracks, Mitch appears ahead of me. He changes course to intercept and steer me around a corner. "What's goin' on? This place is all worked up 'bout you." His voice is calm, even.

I glance around to make sure we are alone, then fish listlessly in my laundry bag and pull the letter out of my uniform pants. "Vic's done. She's been fucking around. Almost two years apparently." I hear the lack of emotion in my statement. It's strange. My insides twist in turmoil.

Mitch's eyebrows shoot up as he takes the letter. "That cheatin' bitch. Christ! Of all the fuckin' things."

I slump against the wall, too disturbed to respond. I feel like I should take some of the blame, but right now, no matter how hard I try I can't. Maybe I should have just grabbed Keane, acted out all my ridiculous fantasies, and risked everything. Apparently, fidelity means nothing after all. Don't be stupid, Sabine. It isn't as simple as that.

Of course I've not been physically present in Vic's life, but it's not as though I'd left her. I'm working. Yes, I've eyeballed other women while away and feeling lonely, but not once have I acted on it in any way. I'm angry and hurt, but most of all I just feel really fucking sad. Despite how I feel, it's not really a surprise. We've been on this course since I left on my first deployment and I've been steering the bus as much as Victoria has. But I've never cheated.

Mitch takes a minute to read the letter properly, with his forehead furrowed and his mouth twisted into a sneer. He folds it in half and I take the paper, fold it over again and tuck it back into a pocket of my dirty uniform pants. Mitch grasps my forearm. "Where is she?"

My voice is the flattest of flat monotones. "Somewhere with my pets, getting ready to go to Colorado with her girlfriend. The one that isn't me."

The edges of his mouth are jammed downward. "I'm so sorry, angel. How fuckin' horrible." He steps close and pulls me into a hug.

My nose stings as though I'm about to cry but my eyes don't produce any tears. I feel numb. People say this all the time, like the drama isn't happening and it always makes me scoff. Now I know what they mean. It feels surreal. This is not my life. My arms steal around Mitch's waist as he holds me and gently strokes my hair. With my ear pressed against his muscular chest I can hear his heart beating. The regularity of its rhythm is comforting. "You don't have a heart murmur," I blurt.

"Huh?"

I step back, wiggling my forefinger at his chest. "Your heart. You are cardiovascularly sound." I give him a serious doctor expression.

Mitch shakes his head at me. I just want to feel normal again, to shake off this feeling pressing down on me. He sighs. "Well, it's a good thing y'all didn't race off to the East Coast and get married, otherwise you'd have to give her half that nice ol' house of yours."

He's right, but it doesn't solve my current issue of who will run the house when I'm away. I make a mental note to ask Jana if she knows anyone who might like to housesit when I am deployed next. My sister graduated law school, moved to D.C. almost immediately for a job and lives ten miles or so from me. I've often wondered if she only applies for jobs near me. We've always been close.

The sound of footsteps pulls Mitch and me apart. Regardless of the nonstatus of our relationship, neither of us wants to give cause for disciplinary action. I smell Keane before I hear her.

"Captains."

Mitch and I come to attention before Colonel Keane, offering a simultaneous, "Ma'am."

She returns our greeting with a nod. "Fleischer, I'd like to see you in my office please. Oh-nine-hundred tomorrow."

Why not see me now? Clearly, we're both free. Her expectant stare makes me stand even straighter. "Of course, Colonel." Surely it can't be anything wrong with my reports. They have been as thorough as always, listing everything I did in a concise manner. No fatalities in the past two days. What could she want?

"As you were." Keane continues up the hallway with my eyes following her ass.

Mitch waits until she is out of sight before grabbing my elbow and propelling me outside. "Girl. I know that look. You fixin' to be discharged?"

I give him a haughty look. "I'm single now, remember? There's nothing wrong with looking."

"I've heard it before and you're only *just* single."

I ignore him and hold my bags of dirty clothing up. "I need to drop these off."

The small laundry room is packed with personnel. Staring, staring. At me. Scrubs go into the communal laundry hamper—someone else's problem. I rummage through my dirty clothes, search through my pockets and pull out a piece of Amy's candy, which I toss to Mitch. He unwraps and shoves it in his mouth as I pat the rest of the fabric down. Paper rustles in one of the back pockets. I reach in and pull out Victoria's letter.

I stare at it for a moment then shove it into the pocket and seal the Velcro fastening. I once lost a letter from Oma this way, forgetting it was in there, and when I took my uniform out of the dryer it was nothing more than a pile of paper pulp. I shove my clothes into a machine before I can change my mind.

Mitch has been watching me. "Destruction by laundry. Interestin' technique." The candy bulges in his cheek as he speaks.

My response is flat. "Seems appropriate."

He shifts his treat to the other side of his mouth. "What're you gonna do?"

"I don't know," I tell him as the incoming casualty alert sounds.

Mitch laughs and slings an arm around my shoulder, pulling me against him. "Doctor Fleischer, I think I have just what you need."

I groan. "I'm off shift, Mitch. There was no all personnel call. They don't need me." My protests do no good and he manhandles me toward the operating theaters. I just feel like sleeping. I want to pretend that I am seven and if I hide under the covers then the bad thing will be over.

"Darlin', you gotta trust me. You're needed and this is what you need."

"I hate you," I deadpan. He shoves me through the doors and leaves me in the prep room, begging off with the excuse that he has to pack ready for his transport. Oh right, he's going on leave later today. Shit, what crappy timing. People are still staring at me. I still ignore them.

My head is full of expletives, every one directed at Mitch for dumping me here. I procrastinate at my locker, certain there is no need for me. Amy is sitting on a bench a few feet away, fiddling with her laces and hasn't noticed that I'm here. Space cadet Peterson. Colonel Keane walks in, breaking stride when she sees me. "Fleischer, you're not supposed to be on shift."

No shit. I shake my head. "No ma'am but Boyd thought…I thought perhaps you might need some extra hands." I try to sound convincing. I'm fairly sure I fail.

Keane looks at me with an unreadable expression. "I'd like you to assist me." She turns to Amy. "Peterson!" Amy jumps up and goes to Keane immediately.

"How long is it since you slept?" Keane asks before Amy can acknowledge her.

"Uh, twenty...seven hours? Ma'am."

"You're off. Get some rest."

"Yes Colonel. Thank you." As she turns away, my roommate catches my eye and gives me a shrug. I don't know either, Ames.

I snatch scrubs from my locker, change quickly, and by the time I step up to the sink Colonel Keane is at the end of her scrub. Annoyance flows through my veins like a toxin. The assessments have been done and I've no idea who I'm operating on. I make appropriate sounds in response as Keane briefs me on the casualty being prepped in the theater. Triple GSW, should be easy. I glance up at the wall clock. Two minutes twenty-six seconds, not long enough. I rub the sponge harder against my skin, as though it might make the time pass faster.

Colonel Keane turns the water on and rinses her hands once more. "I'm very sorry to hear of your relationship breakup." She's almost whispering. Before I can respond she turns away from me and shakes her hands in the sink. I watch her, dumbfounded as she pushes backward through the door into the operating room.

Did I hear her correctly? What an odd thing for her to say. I look up in time to see Keane glance back at me, our eyes meeting through the glass window before she turns away.

* * *

Three hours and forty-one minutes later, I tear my gown and gloves off and stare blankly at the chart in my hand. I don't remember doing half the things described on it. Good to see you're paying attention to all the important stuff, Sabine. I scribble my name and shoulder my way out of the theater. I am exhausted and still a little pissed about being dumped here and made to operate, though there's the buzz of adrenaline that always stays with me after surgery.

The annoyance makes no sense. I'm not usually one to hold on to displeasure. Keane signs the chart before she joins me at the sink. "Excellent work, Sabine."

"Thank you, ma'am," I reply with enthusiasm I do not feel.

She is standing at the opposite end of the sink, turned sideways away from me. It's a glaring contrast to how close we have been for the afternoon, our shoulders brushing as we clamped and sutured. There's no way to avoid being in someone's personal space during surgery. We have spent most of the day with our hands touching while we scrabbled for—

Stop it. I wash my hands harder. Maybe I should ask not to operate with her until I get my head together. Then I won't be watching her washing her hands and imagining her running them over my breasts. Christ Sabine. Stop thinking about it—this is not the time.

Keane's voice breaks me out of my inappropriate sensual thoughts. "Enjoy the rest of your day, Captain. I'll see you in my office tomorrow." Keane tosses her damp paper towel away as she leaves.

I speak to her departing back. "Yes ma'am." As if I could forget. I leave the building and stop by the men's barracks, and flounce toward Mitch's room. His door is open and bags are sitting on his neatly made bed, but the room is empty. He can't be far away. I back up to the wall and slide down it to sit in the hallway while I wait for him. My thoughts drift back to Keane's words. *Sorry to hear of my relationship breakup.* What does she know? How could she know?

Mitch comes back after a few minutes, carrying his electric razor. "Come to see me off?" He stares down at me, offering a hand to help me stand. "How was it?"

"Fine. Person. Bullets. Lived."

Mitch seems surprised by my unusual bluntness, but he leaves it be. "Carry this for me would you?" Before I can say no, he hands me his laptop bag and I sling it over my shoulder like a good little pack mule. The helo is idling when we get close and a few people have already settled inside. Their collective excitement about off-base leave is electric and rubbing off on Mitch, who is grinning like a fool.

"Be careful, yeah?" I say, a little more gruffly than I mean to.

Mitch winks at me. "Don't you worry, Sabs. This bag is ninety percent condoms."

"It's not just that and you know it." I'm more worried about the men he's *not* going to sleep with. The ones who could hurt him.

Mitch nods, his tongue sweeping over his lower lip. "I hate to be leavin' you like this. Sure you're gonna be okay? Don't wanna see you get all eat up while I'm gone."

What can I say? Give up your much-needed break to sit with me while I mope? These four days are like a lifeline for him. Mitch won't apply for R and R in the States, brushing it off with his usual shit about having no family back home. I know it's because he thinks it'll be easier for our colleagues to have stateside leave approved if one less person in the unit is asking. We get two weeks in every twelve months, but only if we've been deployed for two hundred and seventy days. Even then R and R is only approved if our boss thinks that team members being absent won't compromise the unit.

I brush his question off with a wave. "Don't even worry, you go and have a good time. I'll see you in a bit. Be safe, Mitch. I need you around." I hand him his computer satchel.

Mitch tips an imaginary cowboy hat at me, then I get a tight one-armed hug before he saunters away. He stops after a few steps and turns back. "Go to the office right quick, change your forms, send 'em to Human Resources. You don't want pay benefits goin' to the wrong person." Mitch spins and jogs to the transport with his bags bouncing on his shoulder.

He's right. I have to remove *my friend* Victoria from my notification of death and gratuity payment file. I sigh and shove my hands deep into my pockets, standing by myself with the rotor wash whipping dust up around me. I watch, motionless, until I cannot see the helo any more.

CHAPTER NINE

My sleep is fitful and broken with dreams that are more like nightmares. After jerking awake for the fourth time, I give up. Thankfully Amy hasn't been here to witness my crappy attempts at REM cycling. I'd feel awful for having interrupted her rest with my constant tossing, turning and gasping back to wakefulness. I need to relax. I slip a hand beneath my blanket, but the moment I close my eyes, all I see is Vic with her mouth on another woman. Ugh. Every shred of arousal I may have been able to conjure dries up like the Sahara.

The luminous dial of my watch shows three forty-seven and my body burns with nervous energy, refusing to lie still. I don't know if I should head to the gym to lift weights, or run, or read, or fire off sleep-deprived emails to my family. I walk the hallways of the barracks for an hour then steal over to the hospital where I wander like a shade through the rooms, looking at charts. When I realize it's close to seven thirty, I set down the chart I'm reading. I need breakfast and a shower before my meeting with Colonel Keane.

The chow hall is packed but there's a free space next to Neal, one of my opinionated bathroom gossips from yesterday. Excellent, a little light sport to cheer me up. No, don't be a horrid bitch, let the woman eat her breakfast in peace and go sit elsewhere. I settle at a table with a group of colleagues who are practically inhaling food. My roommate is among them and she is indignant. "Bitch, where'd you get the orange?"

"They're always hidden on the bottom of the pile, Ames. You never know where to look." I give her a patient smile, peeling the orange. I'm not sure why she's so excited. This orange looks as though it's a few days away from growing mold. I cut the fruit and give her half. "How was your night?"

"Thanks. It was fucking awful. Be glad you were sleeping and not on." Amy pulls a segment out and sucks the juice from it.

Be glad I was sleeping. Not quite. Obviously she didn't catch me sneaking through the wards. I begin to pull the orange apart. It's sour, musty-tasting and my stomach flips when I swallow. I force all of it and a piece of toast down quickly. Experience tells me if I don't eat I will crash in a few hours. I gather the remnants of my breakfast and push my chair back. "I have to go. Meeting with Keane," I explain to the group.

Amy grins and a few of the others try to hide smiles. Evidently the consensus appears to be that I am in trouble. Perhaps I am. "Good luck," Amy singsongs. "Is that peanut butter?" She snags the leftover piece of toast from my plate and waves me off with it, grinning.

Thanks, Ames. You could at least pretend to be concerned about my potential ass chewing. I dump my things in the dish bin, catching Neal's eye and giving her a cheesy smile on my way out. Okay, maybe I can be just a little bit of a horrid bitch today.

After I've showered and cleaned my teeth, I select my newest uniform, stick each of my patches on their Velcro strips and smooth everything down. At five seconds before o-nine-hundred, I knock lightly on the closed door of the colonel's office.

"Come in, Captain."

I open the door and throw a cracking salute, adding a perky, "Good morning, ma'am." Nice one, Sabs. Excellent false excitement.

Keane rises from her chair to return my greeting. "Close the door, please." My hand falls from the salute. Closed door. I'm fucked. I push it and give it a nudge to make sure it's shut. After it clicks, I turn and wait for an invitation to sit. She gestures to the chair then waits for me to get settled. I try to appear relaxed.

Have I been insubordinate? Well, yes, but only a little and she didn't seem to notice my sarcasm about marathon training. I tap my feet on the floor. Maybe someone did hear me mention Vic's name during the phone call. Fuck. This is probably about DADT. She's going to tell me I've been reported for homosexual conduct. That's why she didn't see me yesterday, she was gathering evidence. Oh shit. Keane shuffles through some files on her desk while I gaze around her office, trying to calm myself.

I've been in here before but I've never paid attention to Keane's things. She has a few military commendations, displayed alongside her diplomas and academic awards on the plywood walls. I squint, looking at the dates. Assuming she did undergraduate and then into medicine right after high school, she's about forty-three.

Eight or so years older than myself. I sneak a peek at her. Not such a big age difference. She does not look it. In fact, she looks amazing. If you're going to be disciplined under DADT then you should try not to act like such a lesbian, Sabine. I rest my hands in my lap and look at her desk.

Colonel Keane opens a file I recognize as mine. Even upside down I can see how young I look in my army identification photograph. She clicks her pen. "How are you, Captain?"

Easing me in. Good, good. I lick my lips. "I'm very well, thank you, Colonel." I leave out the clarification of very well *except* for the whole relationship breakdown, insomnia, lack of appetite and also the fact I'm shitting myself, trying to figure out why I'm here.

"If you need to talk about anything, I'm always available, Sabine." Keane's eyes search mine, but for what exactly I do not know. She has a way of looking at you that makes you feel as though you're the only person that matters. I've always found her gaze to be comforting but right now I am disconcerted.

"Thank you, ma'am. I appreciate that." Now please, tell me why I'm here before I dissolve into a groveling mess.

Thankfully she gets right to her point. "Sabine, at my discretion I've decided you're able to take some R and R."

Wait. That's it? Relief washes over me as I realize what she's saying. I'm not in trouble, but I am confused. This isn't how it usually works, shouldn't I be asking for it? I clear my throat. "Oh? I wasn't aware I was able to take leave now, ma'am."

"As I said, it's at my discretion. Technically, you're eligible." Keane gives me a patient smile. "Of course, it's your decision but a little time off base might be helpful." Her tone makes me feel I've been given an order, rather than offered a choice. "How about two weeks? Departing three days after Captain Boyd returns would be the soonest I can allow it."

I keep my face neutral, though my mind is racing. Go home to the house I shared with my girlfriend of nine years and try to sort through everything that went wrong. Look at our shared space. Rehash the way she cheated on me, moved out of state and took my pets while I'm working overseas and can't do a damned thing about it. Then, of course, I will see my family, which means we will examine it from every possible angle.

Well, I think all of that sounds just fucking awful, Colonel. I lean forward in my chair, ready to politely decline. She is watching me, the edge of her mouth twisted slightly and it highlights the dimples in her cheeks. Keep your eyes up, Sabine. Keane is right about one thing. I need to clear my head somewhere away from here. Away from her. It's too confusing trying to deal with my feelings about Victoria's betrayal and those I have about Keane, which have intensified out of nowhere. The breakup seems to have uncorked a bottle of lust in me. My response is a little too loud. "That would be...nice. Thank you, Colonel."

Keane leans back in her chair, looking relieved. How odd. She turns back to her laptop, leaving me to sit quietly while she types. "Will you be at your home address?"

Typical army, wanting to know everything. "Yes, and no doubt also in Ohio with my family, ma'am." Why did I say that? She doesn't need to know who you're going to be with, Sabine.

Keane consults my file and continues typing while I stare at my knees and run through the periodic table. When I reach Strontium, she prints the form and hands it to me, along with a pen. "I'll put this through right away, Sabine."

"Thank you, Colonel."

I check the dates and reach for the pen to put my signature and the date on the form. There is silence and I can sense she is watching me write. Don't look up, don't look up. I spin the paper around, sliding it back across the desk. Keane scans it quickly. When I offer the pen, she takes it and our fingers brush. I resist the urge to apologize. Brushing fingers isn't a thing to apologize for, you suck-up.

Keane adds her signature for approval and drops my form in a filing tray on her desk. "Is there anything else I can help you with, Sabine?"

I cross my legs. "Actually there is, ma'am. I need to change some personal details. Specifically, my Record of Emergency Data." The form designates who will be notified in the event of my death or an incident and details the breakdown of beneficiaries for my death gratuity. There's no need for Victoria to receive the news first, or any money from me now. She can find out from someone else or never, for all I care.

Keane's left eyebrow lifts. "Of course. No AOP change?"

"No ma'am," I respond instantly. My Arrears of Pay is anything due to me when I die after retiring, assuming I spend the requisite amount of time in the army. My sister is already the beneficiary for this. Keane spins in her chair and walks to one of her filing cabinets, rummaging through before pulling out the relevant form. I stand as she approaches and take the paper, flipping through the pages.

She doesn't move away from me. "There's very little I don't know about what is happening around here, Sabine. I would like to reiterate that my door is always open if you need a confidant."

I run my tongue over my teeth. There are so many things she could mean. She is standing a foot away, close enough to touch. Say something, Sabine. Say something or you're going to do something. "Thank you, ma'am. It was just a bit unexpected," I blurt before I think about what I should say. If I put a dollar in a jar every time I spoke without thinking, then maybe I'd stop doing it. Or I could buy myself a new car with all my hypothetical idiot jar money.

Keane watches me for a moment. "It often is," she says evenly.

The more she looks at me, the more I feel compelled to speak in order to fill the space between us. Don't do it, Sabine. "I would have preferred to know it was happening, rather than being bombed from across the world. Metaphorically speaking, ma'am," I clarify. I am mortified to be making this admission. Didn't I just tell myself to shut up? Will I never fucking learn? Why can't I keep quiet under her cool, silent stare?

Keane leans against the desk. She appears amused. "Do you think being prepared would have made a difference to the way you're feeling now, Sabine?"

It seems like a rhetorical question but I decide to answer anyway. "Yes ma'am. I could have formulated a strategy, or even gotten in first." I detect a hint of arrogance in my statement as though I cannot believe someone would dump me. How conceited. I'm walking a very thin line.

"So, your pride is also hurt," she says bluntly. "I'm surprised. I've never considered you egotistical." The way she says it makes it seem as though she's thought about it before.

I backpedal. "I'm not! I mean, I don't think I am. At least no more than anyone else, ma'am."

Keane tilts her head slightly, making a soft musing sound but she doesn't outright acknowledge what I have said. "I'll see you later this afternoon?" Today is our weekly team meeting. It feels like a brush-off.

I bite the inside of my lip. "Yes ma'am."

She nods. "Very good. Think about what I said. Dismissed Captain."

"Thank you, Colonel." I salute, wait for her to return it then turn sharply and exit her office. My head is full of what Keane said to me. Her expressions and nuances imply that she knows more about what happens here than she's letting on.

What exactly did she mean? Does she know about me, about Vic? She was so pointed as she said it. That must be it. Shit. Why didn't she say something? It's her job to act on those things. As I start my rounds I decide there's nothing she can do unless I say or do something, and I will not.

* * *

I'm a few minutes late to the meeting and I slide into a seat next to John, trying to appear inconspicuous. My RED form is filled out, ready for signing. Keane moves around the room as we discuss things, weaving through chairs rather than sitting in front of us like a boss or teacher. It appears we're ahead on survival rates and paperwork clearances this week. Go team.

I take careful notes for Mitch when he returns, keeping my head down as much as I can. I won't be able to concentrate if I see her smiling at my teammates or the crease beside her mouth as she listens to our concerns. I fidget on the hard plastic chair as the meeting begins to wind down.

Keane dismisses us, and the sharp sound of scraping chair legs as everyone stands cuts over chattering. I'm a little nervous about asking her to sign my form, given how she dismissed me earlier today.

Slightly off to the side and out of hearing range I wait for Keane to finish her conversation with one of the team. Her eyes flick to me, then away again and I stare at the floor to stop myself from looking at her. I became very good at standing still when I joined the military. Nope, staring at the floor isn't working. I shift my gaze to the wall so I can watch her surreptitiously. She's demonstrating something, gesturing as though she's replaying a surgery and she looks fucking adorable.

Stop it. Stop. It. You're just horny and feeling reckless after a breakup, Sabine. That's all it is. You've been self-servicing for too long. It's natural to be thinking about throwing your boss down onto the floor, especially when she's so hot, but this is ridiculous.

"Sabine. I apologize for keeping you waiting. What can I do for you?" Keane is in front of me and the room is now empty. Way to waste time daydreaming, Sabs.

I paste a smile on my lips and hold up the form. "Colonel, I'm sorry to bother you. Could you please witness this for me?"

She looks at the paper in my hand. "Of course."

I drop the paper on the desk, jamming my fingers down on it as it begins to flutter away. I pull a pen from my breast pocket and lean over the table to sign it. My stethoscope swings annoyingly and I hold it to my chest, using my elbow to stop the paper from moving. Keane laughs, planting her fingers on the edge of the form so I am not so contorted. She's so close I can smell the scent of her freshly laundered uniform and I have to twist so I don't bump her thigh with my elbow. There, it's done. Goodbye, Victoria.

"Thank you, ma'am."

Keane takes my pen to sign the form. "Shall I send this for you?"

"Yes, thank you, Colonel. I would appreciate that."

She's holding the paper by one corner like it's something precious. Keane gives me a sweet smile and walks off. How strange. Evidently I misread her earlier. It is only when I go back to the wards that I realize she still has my pen. I steal one from the nurses' area and flash my most charming smile to gain forgiveness when I'm caught mid-theft.

The wards are dim and I wander them for hours, checking monitors and having whispered conversations with any recovering soldier who is willing. After I'm done for the night, I pass Colonel Keane's office on my way out. The door is closed and the lights are off. She's gone. I keep walking.

CHAPTER TEN

Sleep eludes me for the second night in a row, leaving me staring up at the ceiling. My brain refuses to shut down. Since the phone call with Victoria I've been trying to pinpoint exactly when things started to go bad but I can't.

I run over and over a timeline in my head, back and forth, sticking on certain things. Big events. Arguments. Love. Vacations. More arguments. The only thing that keeps coming up is the army. When I came home from officer training, something had shifted but it was barely perceptible. I thought perhaps it was just me who had changed. I thought things would go back to the way they were before. They never did.

Vic and I argued about every aspect of my army career, from me joining to all the moving, from deployments to my thoughts about staying. It was gentle jibes at first, easy to ignore, but now I realize it became big without me even noticing. Was I really so absent from our life? Maybe I should have tried harder last deployment to take some R and R? But I was so caught up in work and the excitement of being *needed* that I didn't push when they said it would be hard to let us go home.

The room is pitch-black, thanks to the towel we roll against the door to keep the dim hallway light and noise out. Pity it also keeps noise in. Amy's snores echo off the walls, making the space claustrophobic. I push my blanket aside and lean down to grab my Ugg boots from the floor, slipping my feet into the soft sheepskin. For the briefest moment, I think about waking Amy and telling her about everything, just to get it out of my head. But I can't. *It's not allowed.* I'm all alone.

The hallway is empty but the low murmur in the lounge carries through the barracks. I turn away from the sound, pull my robe closed and shuffle along the hall. I pass Colonel Keane's private quarters and see no light under her doorway. By my watch it is just after two. I keep walking and spot some colleagues in the hall. Some have just finished surgery. Others are returning from calls with their families. There's a few who also can't sleep.

We nod to each other in acknowledgment as we pass, but nobody stops to talk. We know this is not the time. I find myself in the men's section and almost bump into someone as they come from the bathroom. "Sorry," I mumble and keep walking. I feel his eyes on my back.

I'm trying to find the logic in how my relationship ended. I can't. The past couple of years had not been smooth. There's no denying we have drifted from one another and were staying together simply for the sake of being together. We had pets, a shared home, Victoria's gallery and mutual friends. Staying was easier than dealing with a breakup, almost as though we both got comfortable in our discomfort.

The way we were going, I'm certain I would have initiated The Talk fairly soon. No doubt it would have led to this, but it would have been mutual. And I never cheated. Not once. I'm almost surprised when I reach a conclusion. Keane was right, my *pride* is wounded.

Victoria's actions ricochet around my head. The cheating. Moving so far away and taking our pets without telling me first. It's a total deviation from the woman I know. Or is it knew? Unlike the woman I love. Loved. Love? No, loved.

Perhaps she changed into someone completely different along the way and I never noticed it? Maybe it was me who changed so drastically. No, I would never do what she's done. I pass my bedroom door and keep walking. I just want to stop thinking, but I can't.

She *cheated.* That's what enrages me. She must have gone with Kate during my first deployment. Then I was home and she *still* did it. Maybe she cheated on me for our entire relationship. Stop thinking about it, Sabine.

After my first deployment, I was home for six months working at the Army Medical Center in D.C., then doing pre-deployment prep. Did she just tell this woman not to come by? No, I know Victoria. She would have been fucking her on the side while I was there. I lean against the wall for a few minutes and scrunch my eyes closed to rid myself of the image of her sneaking out to screw someone. How did I not know? I push off the wall and keep walking, past Colonel Keane's door again. The light is still off. Would I have acted on something if it were allowed? No. Never. Not while I was still with Victoria.

"Captain Fleischer."

I stop and spin around at the sound of her voice. Colonel Keane is standing in her bedroom doorway, dressed in pajama bottoms and a navy blue tank top. The tank clings to her body in ways no fabric has a right to and I have to force myself to keep my eyes up, away from her full breasts.

She peers at me for a moment then slips on a pair of black-framed glasses. I've never seen her wear glasses and didn't know she wore contacts. They change her face, making it more angular and emphasizing her cheekbones. I walk closer, stopping against the wall so I can't see into her private quarters.

"This is the second night in a row you've been walking the hallways instead of sleeping, Sabine." I tilt my head but before I can ask how she knows, Keane clears her throat and speaks again. "The footwear you insist on wearing as slippers make a very distinctive sound when you're pacing the hallways." She looks at my feet, pushing her glasses back up her nose. "This is also the second time this morning you've walked past my doorway."

I lift both hands in a conciliatory gesture. She's got me. "I apologize for disturbing you, Colonel." I keep my voice low.

"Have you been to sick bay to get something to help you sleep, Sabine?"

"No ma'am."

Keane pulls her glasses off and rubs her eyes. "Perhaps you should consider it."

"I will, Colonel. Consider it, I mean."

"Good, now please go back and try to sleep."

As if it was so easy. "Yes ma'am. Just another lap." I give her a smile and make a swirling motion with my forefinger.

"If I hear you go past my door again, I'm going to force you down the hallway and lock you in your room."

The thought of her trying to drag me down the hall makes me smile. "Yes Colonel."

She steps back into her room and closes the door, leaving me to make one more loop around the barracks. I will not disobey her. It's after three when I lie down on my bed. I'm in the exact same position, still awake when Amy stirs just before six. She rolls over, pulls her sleeping mask off and stares at me. "Lady, you look like shit."

Thanks.

We go to breakfast where I beeline to the coffeepots. My stomach feels too tight to handle two cups. If I cannot handle a decent quantity of food, breakfast needs to be something calorie-dense. I spread peanut butter and honey on the piece of toast I burned.

Amy kicks a chair out for me. "Not sleeping?"

I grunt and take a bite of cold toast, chewing and swallowing before my body can register it doesn't want it. My stomach turns but I force myself to take another. Amy wordlessly slides some melon over to me. I'm sure she knows what's happening, but in true Peterson style, she doesn't force me. In her odd, roundabout way she's just letting me know she's around if I need her for anything.

I do, badly, but we're friends and I can't put her in a position where she might have to make a statement under oath about my sexuality. Don't tell. I fork up a piece of melon and stuff it into my mouth. My stomach flips again.

"Why not get something? I can write a script for you." Amy breaks a muffin apart, dropping half of it in her lap.

Normally, I would laugh at her. Today, I don't. "Makes me groggy." I take a gulp of coffee. It's lukewarm and it tastes like shit.

She shoves a piece of muffin into her mouth, mumbling around the mouthful, "Groggier than zero hours sleep, Sab? No fucking shame in it. Everyone needs a bit of chemical help now and then."

Everyone isn't me. I swallow the rest of my coffee. "I gotta get going, Ames. I'll catch you later." She nods. I dump my half-eaten piece of toast in the muck bucket.

Halfway between the barracks and the main building, the incoming alarm sounds. I run across the base and into the building, rushing straight into the prep room to change. I scrub vigorously as John talks at me and have to ask him to repeat something he's already said twice. When I answer him, he looks at me askew. Oops, wrong answer? Guess I still didn't catch what he said.

The surgery is a blur. I shower. I go to chow and try to force myself to eat something for lunch, then throw half of it away. I go online and check our shared bank account—Vic took exactly half, as she's entitled to—then transfer the balance out into an account she can't access. I try to take a nap but end up staring at the wall instead.

What is it about me that made her fuck someone else? Was it anything more than just being apart? Why does it matter? You're not *really* unhappy about the actual act of breaking up with her, are you?

Yes, I am.

No, I'm not.

Remember how she's taken the boys? Remember how she cheated on you?

Yes, yes I am unhappy.

We have one day with no incomings and I try to force myself to sleep. I run laps and work out until my body is exhausted, but still my mind refuses to turn off and I lie on my bunk staring at the ceiling, the floor, the wall.

When I email my family, I hide how I am doing and make excuses about why I can't video call with Mom. Amy starts to make worried sounds, which I brush off. I can't even bother to be annoyed when someone comments on how tired I look. Their tone is always concerned, of course.

Even though I've barely slept the past two days I drag myself to our game of flag football. I drop an easy pass for a touchdown, and I'm so angry at my idiocy that I yell and kick the ball away before I can stop myself. It sails forty yards away down an embankment. When I go to fetch it, I notice everyone around me has stopped moving. They are all looking at me.

Their faces have that awkward expression people get when someone does something outrageously uncharacteristic and inappropriate. They don't know how to react. I run down the bank and retrieve the ball, my knuckles white as I grip the leather. I mumble apologies to my team and toss the ball to Bobby. He says nothing. I rush back and bend in formation with the tips of my fingers touching the ground.

I can tell everyone is still staring at me. My cheeks burn with embarrassment and the outrage of my stupidity. Colonel Keane's mouth is pressed into a thin line when she takes her place opposite me. I drop my head to avoid her stare, looking down at the rocky soil below my fingertips.

This is not me.

I am not this person.

I don't understand why I can't put this behind me and move on.

CHAPTER ELEVEN

The mark I leave on the bottom of the chart doesn't look much like my signature. I contemplate scribbling it out and trying again but decide it isn't worth it. My hand made the scrawl. It's good enough. John and Bobby burst out of the OR still chattering about our earlier football game. They don't mention my tantrum. Their conversation feels distant, like I'm underwater listening to someone talking outside the pool. I wash my hands, closing my eyes and willing the tiredness to go away. Like fatigue is something that can be reasoned with.

The loud ring of yet another incoming patient starts up as I toss the paper towel toward the trash. It hits the ground. Without a word, the three of us turn away from one another, sprinting to the bathrooms. My legs are heavy, almost drunk-feeling.

When I get back, I rummage through the uniform in my locker, hopeful of something sugary hiding on the shelf. Two pieces of candy. Bless you, Amy. I stuff both into my mouth, shrug into a fresh top and rush out to wait for the helo. "What've we got?" My fingers keep missing the holes in my disposable glove.

"Multiple hits in the vest and GSW left arm," says John.

I don't have a chance to ask anything because our casualty is rushed in. He's getting CPR. That's unexpected. The PJ squeezing the resuscitator explains breathlessly, "He literally just arrested, right as we were getting him out."

"Gotta be BABT," John tells me. He sounds a lot more excited now than when he was telling me it was just GSWs. "Tamponade?"

Behind armor blunt trauma. The armor vest stops the projectile but the energy of impact transfers to the body. I catch sight of large bruises on the soldier's left pectoral. With a high enough caliber and in the wrong spot, well…it's no wonder he's arrested. Pericardial sac is probably full of blood.

Stupidly, I glance at the face of the guy on the stretcher. He seems barely old enough to shave and the more I look at him, the more I think he looks like Vic's younger brother, Pete. Panicked, I look at the right side of his chest for a name but of course his torso is bare. I look at his face again. It can't be Pete. Pete isn't in the army. Is he? My tongue is thick inside my mouth and I can't ask the questions I need to.

Keane brushes past me with a clear declaration. "I'm leading this one. Sabine, take over compressions. John, get on the bag."

All I need to do are chest compressions. I can do that. I wait until the PJ has finished his compression cycle, confirm that there's neither pulse nor rhythm and take over. Words move through the space around me but I can't grasp them. We're moving to the theaters and with each compression I'm screaming inside my head at the heart. Beat! Beat! Beat!

A nurse takes over the bag so John and Colonel Keane can scrub. I keep doing my compressions. Beat…beat…beat. People swirl around me. Bobby swaps from the bag to oxygen and administers drugs, telling me what he's doing the whole time. Dumbly, I nod in response. Sweat inside my gloves squelches and slips. My scrub top is plastered to my back and sweat is dripping off my chin onto the casualty. I want to apologize for sweating on him. Not Pete. Beat. Beat.

I stop my compression cycle and do a vitals check. Nothing. I say a word I hate. "Asystole."

"Agree," Bobby confirms.

I start my compressions again. Keane materializes beside me, glancing up at the monitors. "He's been down for almost six minutes. We're doing a lateral thoracotomy. Get trays ready, please." There it is. She's made a diagnosis. Nothing to lose. "Kathy, take over compressions. Sabine, go scrub."

I finish my cycle and the nurse takes over from me. My arms tremble and I shake them out. I can't stand it any longer. "What's his name?"

The pause from everyone around me sits thickly in the air. Scalpel in hand, Keane answers, "Daniels."

It's not Pete.

Her eyes meet mine. Concerned. Querying. "Do you need to be relieved, Sabine?"

"No ma'am."

Keane is saying something else but I can't make it out through the ringing in my ears. She makes the first incision and I leave the room. At the scrub sink, I reach up for a pack, ripping at the plastic. It won't open and I fumble, tearing at it for a few seconds. The packaging finally gives and the sponge falls into the sink. I snatch at it and toss it toward the trash. It misses. Fuck, it can stay on the floor. The second one opens right away.

Inside the theater Keane is making quick movements to open the soldier's chest and remove the pericardial blood that's stopping his heart from beating. She is so confident. So competent. I finish my scrub and as I push into the theater, Keane pushes her hand inside the thorax.

I can't make out what they are saying over the blood rushing in my ears. Directives, observations, requests. Sarah steps into my line of sight. "Doctor."

"Hmm?" I respond inarticulately. She is holding a towel for me and I dry my hands hastily, then don gown, gloves and glasses as they are presented.

Above the strange thrum in my ears I hear Bobby muse, "Sucks when the thing that's supposed to save you is what might kill you."

"Not the time for speculation, Bobby," Keane says quietly.

"Nice sensitivity, Rodriguez," I snap. My feet won't move. I even glance down to see if I'm standing on something that's holding me in place. No.

"Focus everyone," Keane commands. "This is not good." She is so calm, it's as though she's telling us that it's a nice day outside and asking if we're ready for the next football game in a few days.

The tattoo inked across the soldier's ribs is now ruined by a gaping surgical incision. The thick black lines are another language, characters I don't recognize and now they will make absolutely no sense.

"Sabine!" The way Keane says it makes it clear it's not the first time she's tried to get my attention. "I need you over here right now."

But the more I try to lift my feet to get to the table, the more my muscles tense. I can shuffle backward but not forward. Why am I stuck? I can't do anything except offer, "He's been shot in the arm too. Why hasn't anyone done anything about it?" Suddenly that detail feels very important.

John stares at me like I've just stripped naked and jumped onto the table. "No shit. We've got bigger issues here."

This time Keane's voice is sharp. "Fleischer!"

"Yes?"

"Please step out."

"Pardon me, ma'am?" My voice is huskier than usual.

Keane's hands are busy and she doesn't look at me. "Leave the OR. You're relieved."

I…I've been kicked out. I'm not capable. She doesn't want me. Maybe my inaction just killed this guy. I keep my head down. If I look at Keane, I'm going to lose it. My legs obey me finally and I take a step back, yank my gown and gloves off and ball them into the waste receptacle.

Outside the theater I slump on the seat by the wall, resting my face in my hands. My biceps are still quivering from the CPR. Suddenly, I'm desperate to talk to my family, to hear about Jana's latest date and my mother's community project. I stand up and chance a look through the glass to see how the trauma is going. Keane looks up, her eyes meeting mine. She jerks her head toward the main door and I read her loud and clear. You're dismissed, Captain.

I rush outside, gulping in hot air. The sun is lowering in the sky, just starting to kiss the top of the mountains as I head to the track. Someone is running slow laps and I move to the very outside to avoid them. What the fuck just happened? You're tired, Sabine. You're tired and frazzled.

But sleep deprivation and stress are both a massive part of my life. Why now? During residency I worked ninety hours a week and somehow fit some sort of life around everything as well. Here, I've worked almost forty hours straight on trauma after trauma because I had no choice and I loved every moment of learning and honing my craft.

I'm trained for this. I'm not new at it, so why did I just act like a terrified med student? It has never happened before and I'm disgusted with myself. The worst thing is that I know she was right to make me leave. I'm not sure what frightens me more—my failure, or disappointing Keane.

I shuffle around the track, not even trying to push myself. I just want to move, I need to move to keep myself awake. I'm frightened that if I stop then I may have to think about what happened. Failure. It covers me like a suffocating blanket. After twenty minutes ambling in the late afternoon heat, I take a shower and am stretched out on top of my bed when Amy comes in.

My roommate swallows, licking her lips. "Sab, Keane wants to see you in her office. Immediately."

Since when is Peterson a personal assistant? I stare at her. "What for?"

"Just passing along a message, love." She pats my arm and slips back out of our room.

I'm in trouble. No surprises there. The emotion I want is sitting just out of my grasp. I think I want fear. Maybe sadness. Anger? I try to tidy my wet hair, but it resists all attempts at smoothing it. Oh, I never had it cut.

Keane's door is open and I knock on the frame to get her attention. She looks up and I salute. "Good afternoon, Colonel."

She rises slightly from her chair. “Come in, Sabine. Close the door please.”

Standing to attention in front of her desk I run my tongue over my lower lip. I watch her face, trying to find what she’s thinking but I can’t. Her face is a mask.

“At ease,” Keane says, almost absently as she sits down.

I move into the position and I feel anything but *at ease*. Behind my back I’m grasping my right hand so hard I feel the bones in my hand grating.

Keane turns a pen over in her delicate hands and utters a single, simple phrase. “We were unable to resuscitate.”

He died. Nausea grabs hold of my stomach. Please don’t puke on her desk, Sabs. People die. This isn’t new. Realistically, his prognosis was poor on arrival…but maybe my compressions weren’t good enough. Maybe if I had moved when I was supposed to and assisted Keane, it would have been a good outcome.

Finally, she looks me in the eyes. “Is there anything you’d like to say, Captain? Do you understand why I asked you to leave?”

I nod, understanding perfectly. “I—” That one syllable is as far as I get. I want to defend myself, or to explain but the words won’t come out. Don’t make excuses.

Her forehead is creased, the pen still moving through her fingers. “Sabine…I’m concerned about you, as are other people on this base.” Concerned translates to they don’t trust me. She thinks I’m a fuckup.

As I try to form a response, I notice her wedding band glinting every time she moves her hand. I can’t stop looking at it and I’m suddenly jealous, thinking of a faceless man who gets to put his hands and mouth on her. Don’t, Sabine. You have no right.

Keane opens her desk drawer, and pulls a file and an orange prescription bottle from it. She sets the bottle on her desk and opens the slim file. It’s my medical file. She passes a folded piece of paper across the desk to me. “Peterson told me she offered to write a script for something to assist you with your insomnia and you refused.” Keane is watching me, waiting to see how I will react.

I glance down at the sheet of paper. A prescription for seven Zolpidem tablets. Ambien. Ten milligrams. No repeats. Signed by LTC R. A. Keane. There is a dispensed sticker on it. My heart stutters. "Colonel, with all respect due, I didn't ask for this." I wiggle my toes inside my boots, trying to squash my rising indignation.

"I know, Sabine. But you will take one now and go back to your room immediately. Peterson will keep an eye on you. You're also cleared for one day of sick leave tomorrow, confined to barracks."

"And if I decline?" I blink. "Ma'am."

"Then I *will* have to give you a written reprimand, Captain. You may consider this an oral admonishment." When Keane continues, her voice is gentle. "Sabine, please stop arguing. You're exhausted, stressed and you need to sleep. Part of my job is ensuring that people under my command are fit and able to fulfill their duties. Anything less compromises the unit and casualty care. You're struggling. Please, let me help you."

I swallow the saliva welling in my mouth and the urge to cry is almost overwhelming. A nerve is twitching in my eyelid. Keane clears her throat and offers me my medical file. "Sign this for me, please."

I stare at the page. There's one day of sick leave marked for tomorrow. It is ambiguous, marked as *personal*. I pull out my pen, bending over her desk. Keane takes my file back. "Have you been to see psych, Captain?"

"No Colonel."

"I think you should. I believe talking would help."

I respond without thinking. "Are you going to force me to do that too, ma'am?" I close my eyes, well aware of how insolent I have just been. Nice one, Sabine. I force my eyes open again. "I…I'm very sorry, Colonel Keane. That was rude of me."

She ignores my original tone. "No, Sabine, I'm not going to force you. Not yet." Keane gets up and fills a paper cup from the water cooler in the corner of her office. She comes back around the desk to stand in front of me, holding a single tablet on her palm. I pluck it from her, take the cup of water and swallow the pill. She gives me a wry smile. "Do I have to check under your tongue?"

I crumple the paper cup in my hand. "Of course not, ma'am."

"Good. Now get going. I'll see you tomorrow afternoon, or later." Keane recaps the prescription bottle and gives it to me.

I shove it into a pocket. "Thank you, Colonel." My eyelid is still twitching.

She nods and moves to sit behind her desk again. I turn and exit her office without delay, heading straight to the barracks. It will take me at least five minutes to walk there. I estimate that I have fifteen minutes before I'm pretty woozy, and twenty before I fall over, face down, wherever I happen to be standing. At least she was discreet. She could have found me in a common area and made what she was doing obvious.

I reach my room in six minutes and push the door open wearily, then shove it closed with my foot. I leave a messy note on Amy's bed—I FORGIVE YOU, JUDAS followed by a big smiley face. She will see the humor in it. I fumble with my boots, lining them up at the end of my bunk then undress sluggishly, bundle my uniform up and stuff it in the laundry bag.

My eyes are starting to feel heavy. I tug my pajamas on, falling back on the bed to pull the pants up. I glance at my watch. Thirteen minutes to kick in, not a bad effort. A deep fog settles over my thoughts as I try to wiggle underneath the blank—

CHAPTER TWELVE

I wake, disoriented, my whole body aching. How long have I been out? My eyes are sticky and need to be forced open with my fingers. There's a patch of drool on my pillow. Nice, Sabine. Amy's bed is neatly made and I'm alone but I hear people moving along the hallway outside my door. I manage to drag my wrist close to my face and stare at the time. It's just after thirteen hundred hours. I blink hard to clear my eyes and look again.

I've been asleep for over seventeen hours. Or is it more? What day is it? Have I missed Mitch coming home? Fuck. I need to pee, but I'm so foggy that it takes me a minute to collect myself enough to get up. I slide off the bunk and lean on the wall as I pull my Uggs on, not bothering with my robe.

I stumble to the bathroom and almost fall into the stall. After I finish peeing, I remain sitting, drooping sideways until my head rests against the wall. I've no willpower to try and stand again until a loud noise startles me out of my daze. The stall door next to me opens and closes. Someone sniffs. I sigh and finish up, clumsily pushing my way out of the stall. The cold water shocks me when I splash it on my face and rub at my eyes.

Amy is strolling up the hallway and intercepts me shuffling back to our room. She smirks. "Hello, my monstrous creation. I was just coming to check on you."

I push our door open, giving her a weak smile. "What day is it?"

"Monday, seventeenth."

Thank you, universe. Mitch comes home tomorrow. The only thing acceptable for me not being his welcome wagon is if I was in surgery, or dead. Even then I imagine he would expect people to carry my corpse to greet him.

"How're you feeling?" Amy's question is slow and cautious, as though she's expecting me to snap at her. She settles on her bed, leaning back to rest against the wall.

"Like shit," I mumble. "Hungry. Groggy." My limbs feel jerky and uncoordinated, like I'm a loose-jointed puppet. I let myself drop back down onto the end of my own bed, falling backward with my feet still on the floor. The metal railing digs into the back of my knees. I don't care enough to move.

Amy clears her throat. "Wanna get some chow?"

I close my eyes again. "Gimmeaminute."

"Sabs?"

"Mmm?" I gurgle.

"Look, love, I'm sorry for telling Keane about the meds and stuff. I know you've got some shit happening. I'm just fucking worried, you know?" It sounds as though she's trying not to cry. I've never heard her like this before.

I open my eyes and turn my head. Her green eyes are moist, her mouth twisted and quivering. I know the look well, but I've never seen it on her. I'm the cause of the look. A flush of shame fills my cheeks. "It's fine, Ames. I get it and I'm sorry, yeah? Just can't quite get it together right now. I need a little time." I sigh and press the heels of my hands against my eyes. I wish I could just tell her what's wrong. My girlfriend and I broke up. She left me. She's a cheater. I can't. Every time I want to let the words out I will have to choke them back down.

"You know you can always talk to me, right?"

But not about everything… "I know. Come on, this is getting sappy. Let's go eat. I'm starving."

She waits for me to change and we head to the hall where I serve myself a few spoonfuls of yesterday's repurposed mac 'n' cheese, half a sandwich and a coffee. Amy tries to act casually, like she's not monitoring what I'm putting in my mouth. She'd make a terrible spy. I swallow slimy pasta. "Stop watching me eat, Ames."

She flashes me a wide smile. "I can't help it. You're so pretty."

"Your flattery is making me feel better already." I set my fork down. "Will you make a sticker chart for me and put a gold star on it for every good thing I do today?"

Amy laughs. "If you eat all that, you can have two stickers."

I pick up the sandwich and take an aggressive bite.

We're interrupted by an incoming call and she has to rush back to do surgery, leaving me to finish my meal and linger around barracks. I take a shower then spend the rest of my enforced day off reading and emailing my family to confirm plans for my leave. I don't see Colonel Keane at all and I wonder if she is staying around the operating rooms and wards so she can chase me off should I go near them.

Amy comes back in the early evening and we have dinner together. I sit with her at a full table of people while I eat a reasonable-sized meal and laugh genuinely for what feels like the first time in ages. I make a wisecrack and while we are all giggling like kids, I spot Keane on the other side of the room. She is watching me. I nod and raise my bottle of water to her. She smiles at me, smugly, inclining her head. Yes ma'am, you were right.

I'm ashamed that I was so outraged at people wanting to help me. Needing help doesn't mean you're weak, Sabine. You're an idiot. I watch Keane excuse herself and I have the urge to get up and run after her to apologize. My brain is already planning what I will say to her. I imagine calling out to get her to stop and when I catch up to her, I grab her by the front of her uniform jacket. Before I can stop myself, the scenario in my head ends with me pulling her close to kiss her. Whoa, what? That is not an apology, Sabine. You cannot even be trusted with your own thoughts. I turn back to the table's conversation.

I head back to my room where I lock myself away again. It is nearly eleven, early by most standards. I reach into the bedside drawer and drag out the bottle of Zolpidem, rattling the pills around. I'm still battling mentally, but physically I feel pretty decent now that I've shed the grogginess.

Take half each night until the rest are gone, Sabine. You know it works. I tap a pill from the bottle and push my short thumbnail against the score mark in the middle. I drop half back in the bottle then swallow the remainder and slide under the covers.

I sleep without waking until my alarm and notice the change as soon as I'm up and moving. It's as though the fog of exhaustion has burnt away and I'm standing on the edge of feeling normal. My morning is uneventful and when Mitch's helo sets down at midday, I'm waiting expectantly.

Mitch jumps out, his boots puffing up a cloud of dust as he lands on the ground. He rushes toward me, breaking into a broad smile. "Howdy!" My best friend drops his bags on the dirt beside us then scoops me up off the ground to crush me in a tight hug.

I wrap my arms around his back and squeeze him hard. Mitch sets me down, holding me at arm's length as we study one another. His tan seems darker, he looks relaxed and happy. I suppose the proof is right here in the pudding. Rec leave works. "How was your trip?" I ask.

"Delightful!" Mitch keeps looking at me and his grin fades a little. "Everythin' all right?"

I wave him off. "Mmm, just been having a little trouble sleeping." I omit the part where I was also having trouble eating and functioning in general.

"Have you been to sick bay?" he demands.

I don't want to ruin his excitement with my downer. There's plenty of time to talk later, so I stretch the truth a little. "Yeah. Got some Ambien and slept for a day. I'm fine Mitch, really I am. Just chugging along like the little Sab-engine that could." I pretend to pull a chain. "Toot toot!"

He grumbles incoherently and reaches for his bags, handing me his laptop. Evidently, I missed the memo where I agreed to be his computer carrier for the rest of time.

"What'd I miss?" Mitch asks.

I fill him in with a few work bits and pieces as we walk back into the main building. Nothing interesting, but things he will want to know before he starts shift in a few hours. Just outside the barracks I mention my R and R. "Keane thought I should take some leave, so I'm heading home in a couple of days."

"Did she now? You're going stateside? You lucky bitch. How'd you manage that?"

I shrug. "The Colonel organized it."

He gives me that trademark sly grin of his. "I suppose she knows best."

Apparently she does. I bump up against him. "Tell me about your trip."

Mitch turns his head to me, eyes wide and lips pursed. "Girlfriend, I *met* someone," he stage whispers as we step into the barracks. "But that's a whole 'nuther thing." He tilts his head, eyes sweeping the hallways. We are not alone.

"Yep. You and me at the running track before dinner. I want to hear all about it. Or mostly all about it. You can leave some details out."

He snorts as we stop outside his room. "You bet your ass you'll hear about it. I'll see you then, sugar." He's like a large puppy. Mitch pushes the door open with his butt, grinning at me as he closes it again.

I hurry out of the barracks toward the main building, hoping to find Keane in her office. I do a quick sweep of the wards and past the theaters, which are all empty. Way to go, troops. I'm mentally practicing what I will say to Keane. Apology, acknowledgment, acceptance. Psych buzzwords, ugh.

Colonel Keane's door is open and she is sitting at her desk in front of a large pile of reports. I stand quietly just outside the door, watching her. There's that crease between her eyebrows as she concentrates. My gaze drifts down to her hands as she methodically forms her signature. Like all surgeons, she is dexterous and I find myself wondering how nimble she would be as she unbuttoned my pants. Wow. Could you be more inappropriate, Sabs? This is getting creepy. I lean over to knock on the doorframe. "Excuse me, Colonel? Have you got a moment?"

Keane looks up, startled. "Of course," she says warmly. She sets her pen down and stands up behind her desk.

I step forward and come to attention. "I wanted to thank you, ma'am, and also to formally apologize for my poor attitude and unacceptable incompetence the other day. I assure you it will not happen again."

Keane studies me with her head canted to one side. "Thank you, Sabine. I accept your apology. How are you feeling?"

"Better, thank you, ma'am." I offer her a tentative smile.

She returns it openly. "You certainly look it." Keane opens her mouth, then closes it abruptly. I notice she is rubbing her thumb and forefinger together. "I'm pleased it helped, Sabine." Keane drops both hands to rest on her desk, looking at me expectantly. "Is there anything else you want to talk about, Captain?"

Suddenly, I feel awkward and shy. "No ma'am, I'll leave you to your reports." I salute and wait for her to respond with her own, then pivot and move to exit her office.

When I'm almost at the door she speaks. "Sabine, please remember you can come see me again if you're ever having any issues."

Everyone's offering to talk, but I just can't. They don't get it and of course, why would they? The army has made sure that I have to keep this inside, swallowing it down like poison. There's no way to discuss anything without giving myself away. *Don't tell!*

I stop and turn my head. "Yes ma'am. Thank you." The tips of my ears are warm. I could easily talk to her, which is the problem. I would say too much.

As I rush back to my room, I chastise myself for being like a stupid teenager with a crush. She's just being kind and doing her job, Sabs. Yes, but your attraction to her isn't new, you're just opening yourself up a little now that you're...single? I frown as I answer myself.

Yes.

Now that you're heartbroken?

Double yes.

Stop torturing yourself. It's never going to happen. Got it?

It is never going to happen.

CHAPTER THIRTEEN

The rest of the day is quiet, and Mitch finds me on the bench in the far corner of the grounds, right against the fence enclosing Invicta. It's a spot we all use when we want some quiet time and anyone who patrols the fence line keeps a respectful distance. I've sat here for nearly an hour, doing nothing except being alone with my thoughts.

Mitch sits down next to me, wood creaking as he settles. "Hey darlin'."

"Hey." I lean into him and stare out at the landscape, waiting for that perfect moment when the setting sun hits the top of the mountains and the brown turns to gold.

Mitch's voice is low. "How you feelin'?"

"Same old," I respond, grateful for his bulky comfort. "Tell me about this guy."

"Some other time, I wanna talk 'bout you for a bit. You thought about going to The Wizard?"

A joke, calling an army shrink The Wizard like they can magically make everything better. I shrug. "I did, but it's pointless. I can't tell them what's really happening and it just seems…wasteful to see psych but omit all the important things." It's an evasion and he knows it. Knows how much I loathe therapy.

Mitch grunts. "Fair enough, but I think it might help." He seems to be choosing his words carefully. "People talk, Sabs. I know what happened while I was away. I wish you had called me or somethin'. I'm just worried is all. Why haven't you said somethin'? I've been your best friend for longer than y'all were together, angel. I know you're drowning. Hell, I'm fit to be tied myself." He's rambling because he's distressed and not just on my behalf, but because he was friendly with Vic too.

I sigh loudly, rubbing a hand over my face. "You're right, I'm fucking upset. I'm upset and I'm hurt and I'm so fucking angry. And I can't understand what my problem is, because we knew it was coming, so who cares if she cheated. Right?"

"Hey…" he says softly.

"I just can't work out *why* she did that and the worst part of it is I can't even let myself really go, because if I do, then I'm scared I won't be able to pick myself up again and keep doing my fucking job!" I choke on a sob and stop talking so I can get myself back under control.

He pulls me closer, holding me until I calm down. "It'll be fine. You're okay. I love you, sugar-pie."

I grab his hand and squeeze it. "I love you too."

Mitch's arm steals around my waist and I feel his long exhalation. There's movement on the horizon and I have to squint to make out the figure coming toward us. Mitch sits up suddenly, letting me go as he leans forward. He lifts a hand to shield his eyes against the late afternoon sun. "We have a colonel incomin'. Promise you'll come find me for a chat later?"

"I will."

He pats my knee then stands, straightening his uniform. I clear my eyes with my palms and watch Mitch approach Colonel Keane. They stop to converse for a few moments, before Mitch walks on. Keane continues toward me. I stand and salute. "Colonel Keane, good afternoon."

She lifts her hand and returns my greeting. "Captain Fleischer, good afternoon to you too." Keane drops her hand and I count off three seconds before I do the same. She sits down on the bench gracefully, gesturing that I should too. "How are you?"

"I'm well, thank you, ma'am."

Keane pauses, seeming to consider what she is about to say. "Sabine, you know I'm required to ensure you're fit for work physically, but also emotionally." She turns to face me. "I would like to believe in the two deployments we've worked together that you think enough of me to talk to me if you had any issues. But so far you have not, even at my invitation." Keane leans back on the bench and crosses her legs.

She's right, I do think very highly of her. If it weren't for the separation of the command chain then I'm certain we would be as friendly as Amy and I are. "I do, ma'am. I mean, I think highly of you but I'm not certain I know what you're saying?" I rub my tongue on the roof of my mouth, trying to get some saliva to flow. I'm being deliberately evasive so as to not hand her anything.

She smiles patiently. "I know you know I'm aware of your relationship breakdown. You may or may not be aware that I also know some of the details involved with it."

I frown, jamming my eyebrows downward. "If I may ask, Colonel…how do you know?"

Keane smiles again. "The same way I know everything, Sabine." She leans closer, her smile turning conspiratorial. "People gossip." She glances around. "Nobody else knows specifics, if you're concerned, Sabine. But, certain things are obvious to people who know what those things are."

My pulse picks up as I take in what she is saying. Neither of us has said the word. I won't be the first. Keane looks to her right, past the fence before she turns back toward me. "I think we both know military life can make relationships difficult to maintain. After the recent upheaval in your life and other incidents, I just wanted to touch base with you." Her voice is a little croaky. Maybe she is getting sick.

"I appreciate that, ma'am. I'm fine." I watch my boots scuffing in the dirt.

We sit quietly together momentarily until she speaks again. "The nature of our job, having bad outcomes, these things can sometimes make us reevaluate what's important to us. The people who are important to us."

My teeth find my lip as I consider what she is saying. "My mom always tells me to let people know what they mean to you, while you can. You just never know when it'll be over, do you, ma'am." I turn to her and raise an eyebrow.

Keane smiles. "I think that's a fine principle to abide by," she says, her smile fading a little. "Sabine, I want you to know I value you enormously as a colleague." She falters. "However, beyond what I've just said, I also care about you a great deal." Her lips part and I cannot help but look at them. It's not as though she is being deliberately sensuous, yet all I can think of is kissing her.

This is the moment. No, this is our moment. If we were not where we are now. If there was no army, if there was no chain of command, no rules and no regulations, then I would lean forward and I would kiss her. Perhaps she would kiss me back. Perhaps not, but at least she would know. This is where it falls, one way or the other. Right now.

But I can't.

Don't do it, Sabine. Do not be so fucking stupid. Say something. Say it, before you do something stupid. "Thank you, ma'am." No, wrong response. I close my eyes. "I mean, I'm fond of you too," I state dumbly. Nice one, Sabine. Fond of. What are you, eighty years old? I open my eyes again, looking at her helplessly. I shouldn't have said it. "What I meant to say is I care about you too, Colonel," I assert. Nope, Sabs, shouldn't have said that either.

Her hand moves as though she is going to touch me but instead, she slides it back to rest on her leg, rubbing her forefinger and thumb together. She takes a breath, her eyes searching my face. I look away and ball my hands into fists to stop myself from touching her. Keane changes topic suddenly. "I notice you still haven't seen psych."

I'm pleased for the respite and let out a breath, my cheeks puffing out. "I had considered it, ma'am." My heart is still pounding after her admission and I am finding it hard to keep my composure.

Her question is immediate. "Then why haven't you been?"

The corner of my mouth lifts. "I didn't want to lie by omission, Colonel."

My response elicits a smile from her. "Understandable, but it is my strong recommendation that you attend."

I chew the inside of my cheek.

"Don't argue, Sabine," she tells me, still smiling.

"Yes ma'am."

Keane uncrosses and recrosses her legs. "You may find it will help. I'm confident you'll find a workaround for sharing the things you need to, but not things you don't want to."

Or I'll find a way to lie convincingly. Either way. I think for a moment, before I blurt, "My…my pets are gone. Taken out of state and I, uh, didn't even get to see them and I can't do anything about it because I'm here." I sound like a child and I flush, ashamed of my outburst, but I needed to say it. I want to verbalize this isn't just a relationship that's ended, but to make her understand something important was taken from me.

"I can imagine it must be very difficult for you to accept. Being helpless is an awful feeling," Keane says tenderly.

I nod, not trusting myself to speak. If I open my mouth again, I will cry. Keane clears her throat and lets out a long breath. "Sabine, when I was nineteen I became involved with someone. It was the start of my first real relationship."

Well, that's out of left field. I raise both eyebrows, unsure if I should respond. I've never had a superior share something personal with me. Should I say something? I decide to just listen and respond if appropriate, because she initiated it. She continues, "It was all consuming, as I'm sure you're aware things can be when you're that age."

She's right, I'm well aware of it. I smile, still silent.

"We were together all through most of our pre-med, then medical school and into residency where I went into surgery and…they went on to be a physician." Keane glances at me, as though she is waiting to see if I respond to what she has just said. They. Not *he*. They. I know what that neutral pronoun means. Oh boy.

"Anyway, the long and short of it is the relationship ended during my residency. After so much time spent defining myself by the fact I was with this person and having molded myself around the concept of being in a couple, I was lost. Completely and utterly adrift, even though I knew leaving was the right thing." Her voice has a soft, contemplative quality to it.

I nod to indicate I'm still with her. Keane laughs softly. "So, instead of dealing with my fears, I joined the army and here I am. I love my job but still, life could have been something else. The military can be difficult for those who are different."

I know exactly what she is saying and I sit, contemplating. *Those who are different*. She is telling me she knows I am and she is too. Why has she told me this? Is it just her demonstrating her incredible empathy, or is there an underlying reason? There's a nervous sensation in the pit of my stomach.

"If I may offer one piece of advice?" she asks, though of course I cannot say no.

I turn my head toward her. "Of course ma'am."

"Don't avoid problems and don't leave things unresolved. Tell people how you feel. Go home as I've arranged for you and finalize things so you can move on with your life, Sabine."

"Thank you, ma'am," I murmur. There's a slight hitch in my voice. Something has shifted between us and I sense the dynamic has now changed. The space between is still there, a by-product of years of military command, but in opening herself up and sharing something personal she made the space less dense somehow. She has humanized herself to me.

Keane shifts on the bench and begins to stand. I jump to attention before she is on her feet. "I trust what we've spoken about will stay between us," she insists.

"Of course, ma'am, I believe that goes without saying. I appreciate your candor and your concern." What I really want to tell her is that I appreciate her trust, but it's inappropriate for me to verbalize such a thing. To do so would acknowledge her sharing something with me. If I do not say it, then it has not happened. It feels as though we are both holding on tenuously to our thoughts of still being within the limits of what is allowed. Technically neither of us has asked, nor have we told.

Keane smiles at me, dimples slashing her cheeks. "It's getting dark, Sabine. Don't stay out here for too long." She leaves me before I can salute.

I sit back down and watch her walk away, my brain swimming. Most of all, I'm hyperaware to what she has alluded. I lean back, hook my elbows over the rear of the bench and allow myself to have a brief fantasy where something might come of it, or build into something more between us.

Then reality reasserts itself.

We are destined to remain as we are. Despite any feelings that may be between us, or changes enacted to policies in the future, we will be stagnant because one fact remains. She is my superior and there will be nothing more. There cannot be.

CHAPTER FOURTEEN

People move out of my way as I sprint over to the football field the next afternoon. Bobby cares for it lovingly, marking lines in the rocky dirt with a paint wheel and clearing it of debris. We play under the rules of a real game of gridiron football, except it's noncontact. Or supposed to be. Today I'm the last to arrive and I run around exchanging high fives with everyone and shit-talking as we all psych ourselves up. Someone hands me a stick of dark camo paint to smear under my eyes. This falls under official use, right?

Most games we have a crowd cheering for us and it's the same fourteen people playing each time, though we have a few reserves we can drag in if necessary. Major Conway, a general surgeon, is our timekeeper and referee. I've always found him to be fair, especially when the game is going my team's way.

There is only one standing rule. Mitch and I can never be on the same team. It was a unanimous decision, made a few games after we arrived on base years ago. Mitch and I do not play well on a team together. He's bossy. I'm stubborn. Apparently it's bad for morale when Mitch and I almost come to blows. The games always begin with Mitch and me stepping out while everyone from the group draws a piece of paper with either M or S written on it to decide what the teams will be. It's more than a little embarrassing.

In deference to rank, colonels Keane and Burnett, an orthopod who leads another of the surgical units, draw first. Keane picks a folded slip of paper with S marked on it and she moves up beside me. My first thought is to be thankful I don't have to risk accidentally touching her as I attempt a flagging. It's never bothered me before, but it now seems strange. I feel shy—I don't want to look her in the eye for fear of what I might see there.

Keane smiles, leaning toward me. "Last game before you go on leave tomorrow, Captain. Let's lock it down."

I force a grin. "Yes ma'am!"

My team is red, Mitch's green. I don't like red. The rest of the fourteen draws their team assignments and I end up with Bobby as team captain, Keane and John, surgeons Chapman and Soldano, and Stevenson who is my second favorite nurse. Mitch captains the green team of Amy and Sarah, anesthesiologist Bohler, Colonel Burnett, and two of the other nurses, Yoshida and O'Brien. We put on our flag belts and shrug into the team vests.

Bobby wins the coin toss and we go on the offensive. Red Team forms a brief huddle and I'm immediately conscious of Keane pushing in beside me. Everyone else is pushing, right? I glance around sneakily. Sort of, no not really. I keep still so I don't push back against her.

Bobby designates me as receiver, because I am the fastest and most agile on our team. He keeps Colonel Keane as tight end. She has an excellent set of catching hands and usually slips away from people trying to flag her. Bobby gives us all his serious eyes. "First play's a fake-out. Fleischer run right, I'll hand off to Chapman left. Keane, Soldano run left. Stevenson and me right." He looks around at all of us. "Got it?" We all nod and I try not to laugh at how earnest he is.

We have no linesmen and calls for play tactics mean nothing but we still call out to make it feel more like a real game. To add to our competitiveness, we award a prize after each game for the best, most inventive random call.

Everyone lines up and I manage to catch Keane's gaze. She widens her eyes at me and I roll mine in return as we get into position. Conway blows his whistle and I begin to sidestep back and forth behind the line formed by my teammates. "Set!" Bobby shouts.

The rest of my team drops down as I continue my movement. I stare at the opposing team, trying to get Mitch's attention. When he looks at me, I poke my tongue out at him. He glares and looks back to John, waiting for him to snap the ball to Bobby. Bobby clears his throat and instead of a usual number call, he yells a jumble of words at the top of his lungs. "Rudolph! Polymerase! Toothpick! Angina! Hike!"

Wait. Did he just say vagina? Focus, Sabine. John snaps to Bobby who feints and passes off to Chapman. I'm just before the twenty-yard line looking backward when the whistle blows. Bobby's been flagged. I start walking back. Mitch is glaring at Bobby, talking angrily. "You're guardin' your flag! Cut it out!" Mitch thinks Bobby pinned the flag against his hip with the ball, making it harder to remove. Knowing Bobby, he probably did. Mitch waves at the referee. "Did you see that, sir?"

Conway shakes his head and I laugh as I move back to my line. I straighten my vest, give Mitch an exaggerated head shake and mouth, "Temper, temper." His response is a middle finger. Bobby motions Red Team over. I bounce across the dirt and get back into position for a quick huddle. Bobby lowers his voice. "Same again, no fake. Keane, you run too. Sab you're it. Count to four and take the catch."

I make eye contact with him, but do not nod or give any indication I've been given a direction. Mitch will be watching us, trying to pick up clues on what's going to happen. John takes the ball and bends into position and out of the corner of my eye, I see him looking around as I begin to jog back and forth behind the line. Keane and I come together near where John is crouching.

"You got it?" she asks me as we pass one another.

"Always, ma'am," I respond cockily.

Bobby turns up the volume. "Set!" Everyone on my team drops down except for Keane and me. Bobby catches my eye and I run hard to my right, almost to the sideline.

His second call is equally nonsensical. "Watermelon! Cookie! Puppies! Prohibition Rum! Hike!"

My muscles coil in anticipation of my run. John snaps the ball to Bobby and I take off, sprinting. From the corner of my left eye I can see Keane on the opposite side of the field just behind my line. I'm counting as I run and when I get to four, I turn around ready to receive the ball. It sails toward me and I have to leap a little to catch it. Bohler and O'Brien are almost on me. I spin and pump my legs hard, making seven yards before they flag me.

Most of my teammates are around me, shouting jubilantly. Keane isn't among those huddled against me and I feel her absence like a missing ingredient. It's okay, but it's not *good*. We move up, huddle and set again. Colonel Keane catches a pass from Bobby while most of Green Team's defense is shadowing me. She makes a touchdown. We celebrate raucously and maintain the momentum for the rest of the game.

At four minutes before time, my team is up 30-18. I wipe sweat off my face with the arm of my tee and watch the other team huddling. They're screwed. I'm back a little because I can usually snag a flag if someone gets through the front line. Amy is ready to pass the ball off and she gives me an exaggerated snarl as soon as Mitch yells, "Set!"

I stand up on the balls of my feet, my eyes sweeping the other team before I fixate on the ball in my roommate's hands. Mitch looks around at his teammates. "Shaun of the Dead! Maverick! Salad! Pencil! Hike!" He catches the ball and I keep my eye on his hands as I bolt forward.

Everything moves slowly and with perfect clarity. Mitch fakes a pass to his right, then palms off to Burnett on his left. Burnett catches the ball awkwardly and I am almost upon him with my arm outstretched to grab a flag when he turns to run forward. He rams right into me and knocks me to the ground.

I land hard on my back, trying to roll so my skull doesn't hit the dirt. My roll isn't good enough and I crack the back of my head on the hard ground. The whistle blows long and loud. When I've finished tumbling, I look up to see a crowd around me. I move to roll over but am stopped by a number of hands and made to stay on my back. Come on, guys. I know how I fell and I'm fine.

I can hear Mitch and Bobby arguing as if it was a deliberate foul, and Burnett's frantic apologies. Someone speaks, "Make some space!" Yeah, you're all crowding me, and John you reek.

Amy's voice rises above everyone else's. "Sabs?"

"Yes Amy?"

"Can you hear me?"

"No Amy, which is why I just responded to you." My sarcasm goes unnoticed. I move my legs and prop myself up on an elbow, waving them away. Doctors. I pop up onto my knees, rubbing the back of my head. It's a little tender but still intact. My elbow stings and when I twist to look at it, there's a patch of bleeding gravel rash on it. Dirt sticks to the bare, sweaty skin on my arms like dusting on a cappuccino.

Keane is standing slightly back, staring at me with her mouth open. I fold my legs around so I can get up. Soldano offers his hand and I grab it to jump up onto my feet. "Ta-dah!" I resist doing jazz hands.

Most of the crowd laughs. Colonel Keane does not. Bobby and Mitch are still arguing and I look over at them. "Hey, stop it. It was an accident. Now come on, we've only got a few minutes and we need to cap our win with a penalty for Colonel Burnett's foul!" I clap my hands and start walking away without waiting for an answer, wiping my arms on my shirt.

My neck feels like someone is poking their fingers into the muscle and my elbow stings, but isn't bleeding beyond a trickle. Green Team moves back ten yards as penalty, are blocked repeatedly by our defense and unable to score again. Red Team runs an exuberant victory lap, complete with overenthusiastic leaping from Bobby.

Conway awards Green Team call of the game for "Methylprednisolone! Trimethoprim! Phenazopyridine! Hydroxychloroquine!" I think it's only because Mitch managed to pronounce each one. Smartass. We all shake hands, slap each other on the back and give out our customary shit-talking.

Everyone pulls off their flag belt and vest, giving them dutifully to Bobby who checks everything before putting it in his bag. He looks like a proud parent. We begin to gather our things and as the crowd disperses Colonel Burnett finds me to apologize again. He gives me a sweet smile, squeezing my non grazed elbow. "I'm very sorry, Captain Fleischer."

"Thank you, sir, but really, I'm fine."

Mitch comes up behind me. "You okay?"

"Perfectly. It was just a fall." We start walking back.

He glances at me. "Looked like he poleaxed you pretty hard."

I raise my voice. "Do I need to hire a skywriter? I'm fine."

He lifts both hands. "Okay, okay. So long as you're sure."

"I'm sure," I assert.

Colonel Keane appears on my left. "Fleischer, meet me at sick bay immediately."

I groan inwardly. "Yes, ma'am." She walks off ahead of me. When she is out of earshot I let the inward groan out. "Fuuuuck. Seriously?"

Mitch snorts. "Nice game, darlin'. Now go on ahead and get checked out by the good doctor." He winks.

I flick his arm and trot off to catch up to Keane. "Colonel Keane? Ma'am? I'm fine, honestly."

There is nobody around but she keeps her voice low. "I watched you fall, Sabine. You hit your head. You're getting checked out and you need that elbow cleaned. Don't argue."

I feel chastened, but when she looks at me her eyes are gentle. I exhale, trying not to make it too much like a sigh. "Yes, Colonel."

We walk silently together and when we reach the medical building, I open the door, following her through the hallway. The sick bay nurse, Liz Davies, looks surprised when we both walk in. "Colonel Keane. Captain Fleischer."

Keane gets right to it. "Liz. Sabine hit her head during a game of football and I'd like to check her. Can you grab her file for me, please?"

"Of course, ma'am." Davies scurries out of the room.

"Take your shoes and socks off please," Keane instructs me from across the room as she searches the shelves for some equipment.

I give the universe my silent thanks that I don't have smelly feet and tug at the laces of my boots. The paper cover crackles as I climb up and I have to shuffle so it's not wrinkled under my ass. Keane clicks the penlight on. "Any dizziness, nausea or headache?"

"A small headache, ma'am, but nothing acetaminophen won't fix. Maybe it's just from listening to Boyd complain about losing?" I wisecrack. There's a headache spreading through my temples and the back of my skull, but I still think this examination is overkill.

Keane lifts the corner of her mouth in a small smile when I mention Mitch whining, bringing the light up to my face. I open my eyes wider for her. Her voice is soft as she moves the beam between my eyes. "I was worried, Sabine."

I swallow and concentrate on the light, not her. Keane hooks the light in the neckline of her shirt and reaches out to palpate the back of my skull. As her fingers touch me I feel the pressure of her hip against my knee. Her body is warm against my skin. I move only my eyes, watching her.

"Any pain?" Keane turns so she is looking at my face instead of the side of my head. She lets her hands drop. I shake my head ever so slightly. She takes my arm and I don't resist as she lifts it to examine my elbow. The tips of her fingers are cooler than the rest of her hands. They feel nice on my overheated skin. "There's some dirt and gravel in there," Keane says softly and places my arm back down on my thigh.

I nod and my heart is pounding like I've just run a hundred-meter sprint. There's nobody here, it is just the two of us. It would be so easy to just…

Don't.

Don't.

I lean over an inch and she finally lifts her eyes to mine. Her pupils are dilated, just the barest sliver of blue showing around their edge. Keane's lips part and my eyes drop to them. She's so close I can almost taste her.

Davies rushes back into the room. "I have it, ma'am."

I start and Keane steps backward immediately, away from me. Davies is clicking a pen, staring at my file, not at us. My skin crawls. Thank you, universe. I look at the floor, taking shallow breaths. There's no question my cheeks and ears are pink.

Keane clears her throat. "Thank you. Can you scribe for me, please?" Davies flips pages of my file over as Keane lifts her index finger in front of me. "Follow it please, Captain." She is looking slightly to the side.

I follow her finger with my eyes as she moves it left and right in front of my face. I catch her eye and for a moment we look at one another. The truth of how close we were to something prohibited is all too clear in her expression. Just a fraction of a second and it would have been over. Keane avoids my gaze for the rest of her examination.

She checks my heart rate, which is understandably a little faster than normal. I feel like asking if she can blame me. I'm made to press my feet against her hands and do basic motor skills checks like finger to nose. She finishes by checking my patellar reflex. I laugh when my knee jerks uncontrollably. "Sorry ma'am." I laugh again. "It always reminds me of the time I kicked a doctor in the groin when I was a kid."

"I think we've all done that, Captain." She looks up at me with a tight smile, stretching her hand out to Davies. Davies bites her lip as though hiding a smirk when she drops my file in the colonel's hand. Keane writes a few things down. "You can put your shoes and socks on."

"I'm cleared ma'am?" I ask her hopefully.

"Yes. All fine."

"I appreciate the confirmation, Colonel." I slide off the table, leaning my ass against it as I put my boots back on. They both watch me double knot the laces. Maybe they still think I'm about to have a spontaneous brain bleed and fall over. Keane waves my file. "Can you take this back please, Davies? Also, would you mind cleaning up the graze on her elbow, please?"

Davies nods. "Of course, ma'am."

Keane casts her eyes over me one last time. "Enjoy your evening, ladies." She leaves abruptly.

I listen to the regular beat of her footsteps for a few seconds. There's a pause, silence, then she resumes walking. When I'm sure she's gone, I turn to Davies who is collecting items to clean and dress my elbow. "Can I have a couple of Tylenol please, Liz? I've got an awful headache."

She laughs and moves over to the dispensary. "Not such a tough guy after all."

"You know it."

Her back is to me and I lean against the table again, rubbing a hand over my stomach, as though I could somehow quash the heat building there.

CHAPTER FIFTEEN

The day after the football game is the day I'm due to fly home, and I spend my morning in the wards, doing rounds and talking to some of my patients. It doesn't take me long to pack my gear for leave: a few uniforms, some underwear, toiletries and my laptop. I find Peterson to say goodbye, promising to bring her back some things her husband has had trouble finding for her. Men.

Amy gives me a gentle hug, patting my back. "Have a good rest, Sab. I'll be jumping on your bed and playing with your shit while you're gone." Oh, I know you will, Ames.

I debate with myself whether I should seek out Colonel Keane to say goodbye. My transport will leave in an hour, so I decide to make one quick loop. If I see her, good. If not then I will have at least said goodbye to other people I see along the way.

She is not in surgery or doing rounds. The light in her office is off. I begin to argue with myself. Why is it so important I see her before I leave? Because it's polite and I am a polite person.

Yeah, keep lying to yourself, Sabs. She is not in the chow hall, or the gym. I don't see her on the running track and when I walk through the barracks I don't pass her in the halls. Her bedroom door is closed. I wander back outside and am strolling past the armory when I spot her exiting the shower block. Freshly showered. Oh boy.

I try to act casual, as if the last half hour of my afternoon hasn't been spent looking for her. Keane notices me and changes course, straight toward me. I fix my posture and quicken my pace. As she approaches, I stop and salute. "Colonel Keane. Good afternoon."

She smiles, returning my salute. Though her hair is pulled up, I can tell it's wet. "Sabine, good afternoon to you too. Aren't you supposed to be departing for leave?" Keane turns to walk back to the barracks and I fall into step beside her. She smells incredible, like strawberries in summer.

"Yes ma'am. I was just taking a walk before the transport arrives."

"Mmm, I see." She glances at me, then away again. "How are you feeling?" Keane asks.

"How am I feeling about what in particular, ma'am?"

"After your fall yesterday but also about going home."

"My head is fine, thank you." Truth time, Sabine. "May I speak freely, ma'am?"

"You may."

"I'm apprehensive," I say quietly.

Keane stops a few feet away from the entrance to the barracks. "I think that's a normal emotion in this situation, Sabine." She looks up at me, dropping the volume of her voice. "You recall what I said about moving forward?"

How could I forget? "Yes ma'am, I do."

"Focus on that and the rest will come to you." She smiles her dimpled smile, eyes creased against the light of the sun behind me. "Have a safe trip, and I'll see you in a little bit."

"Yes ma'am. Thank you."

Keane gives me another lingering look before she opens the door and walks inside. There's a tight knot in my belly.

Disappointment. I'm disappointed I'll be away from her for two weeks. I could laugh at the absurdity of wanting to stay here instead of going home, just because of Keane. Because you think you have some sort of connection with her, Sabine? Because you think something might happen under the nose of everyone around us? Stop being an idiot. I wait until she is out of sight then push the door open to find Mitch and collect my bags from my room.

Mitch carries my bags across the base to the helicopter, imparting wisdom along the way. "Now, darlin', no drunk mopin' around the house. It's so cliché," he deadpans. I give him a placating nod and he lowers his voice. "Also, it probably wouldn't hurt if you found yourself some lookers for a little, you know…" He clucks his tongue like he's trying to get a horse to move.

"Way ahead of you. I'm going to have some epic rebound sex." The words are layered with enthusiasm I don't feel.

"There's my girl." He gives me an approving nod and passes my bags up into the helo. "Have a good rest, angel. Say hi to everyone for me and thank your mama for the book she sent."

"I will. Try not to burn the place down while I'm gone, okay?"

Mitch pulls me in for a hug. "Enjoy. I'll see you in a coupla weeks."

"Sure thing," I agree. He releases me, and I climb up into the only spare seat and glance toward the front. "Fleischer, Sabine." I'm the last person to board and as soon as my headset is on, we lift off. I wave at Mitch and blow him a kiss. He makes a crude gesture and I laugh before turning away.

* * *

After a quick hop to Bagram, I settle in to wait for a Space-A flight. Space Available basically means you get what you're given when you're given it. I sent in my request for a spot the day Colonel Keane told me I had to go on leave, and it's a fairly standard five hours before my name is called.

It's a little after twenty-two hundred when I'm herded in the cargo compartment of a hot, noisy C-17 along with thirty or so other troops. After stuffing my earbuds in, and swallowing five milligrams of diazepam it's easy to nap until I'm shaken awake for our landing in Al Udeid.

We disembark and mill around while they refuel, unpack and repack supplies and equipment, and do whatever else they need to. I eat, freshen up as best I can and after a couple more hours of waiting, we're called again. I make a quick call to Jana to let her know I'll be arriving in Baltimore around five in the afternoon then walk out to board again. The cargo area seems especially cavernous in the early morning darkness.

After takeoff, an unspoken signal goes through the plane. We slip out of our jump seats and jostle for the best spots for sleeping around the cargo. Everyone is inflating air mattresses and unrolling yoga mats for the long haul back to the States. I unpack my pillow and blanket, stretch out on my mat and sleep most of the way.

When I walk out into the blissfully cool early evening air in Baltimore, Jana is waiting for me, looking around at the arrivals. I stay back, watching surreptitiously as her face lights up each time she catches sight of someone who resembles me. Her delight-then-disappointment cycle makes me smile. When I can stand it no longer, I stride out from behind my vantage point. She notices me sneaking, bursts into a run before me and we crash into each other. She laughs. "You bitch."

I grab her, hugging her fiercely. "I've missed you, Jannie." I speak into her hair, around the hard lump in my throat.

"I've missed you too. What a mess, eh? You look fucking awful. You've lost weight. You shouldn't have." Her words are muffled in the fabric of my uniform jacket. Nit-picking is a ritual repeated at family reunions everywhere. My sister pats my back and we hold each other for a full minute.

I can't help but compare this pickup to the last time I came back. It's the same place, yet so different. Victoria and I groped each other the whole way home from the airport and only just made it through the door before we tore at our clothing and devoured one another in the hallway. We spent days rediscovering each other, never leaving the house.

She had a new tattoo. I had a new scar from tripping and cutting my shin on the brick edging around the hospital garden. I wonder now if she was acting, given Kate was waiting in the wings. I push the thought from my head. What's the point in thinking about it? Jana grabs my laptop, leaving me to pick up my kit bag. As she drives out, Jana turns to look at me, her eyes wide. "Ready for the onslaught, Sabs?"

I laugh, knowing exactly what she means. My father makes dissection of a failed relationship his hobby, though he always comes to the same conclusion: his daughters were treated unfairly. I've only had to listen to this for myself twice before but my sister has been on the receiving end more times that I can remember.

"I suppose I'll have to deal with it sooner or later," I say matter-of-factly. My tone covers the truth. I'm dreading it, wanting nothing more than to crawl into a bed and sleep for a week. Tomorrow, we will fly to Ohio to spend a whirlwind eight days with my family. Then I will come back to try and sort out my shell of a home, and face the remnants of what is now my old life.

I drop my head against the headrest, relishing the comfortable seats. It's the little things you miss, like traffic lights, burgers, booze and a bed you can sprawl across. I'm startled by the long blast of a car horn. My sister gives a pointed middle finger to the idiot who cut her off and flashes her lights. "Fucking asshole." She changes lanes without indicating and zooms off. I haven't missed her driving.

I look over at her, a sudden fondness rising in my chest. "I love you, Jana."

She smiles at me, road rage forgotten for now. "I love you too, Sabbie. I'm so glad you're home."

Almost an hour later we turn into my neighborhood and I press my nose against the window to watch the houses rush past. There are a few people walking dogs and running along the sidewalk. It all seems so different, but it can't be. Everyone's front lawn is neatly mown, including mine and the flower beds are immaculate. Vic must not have canceled our yard guy.

Jana and I sit together in the car on my driveway and she passes me my car keys, all my new house keys and garage remotes. "Do you want me to come in with you?"

Silently, I look through the windshield at my house. It's dark, except for the sensor lights that came on as soon as we drove up, and looks exactly as I remember it. Oddly, I feel the same excitement as when I drove up for my first inspection, thinking of how it reminded me of houses I saw in Germany as a kid. My house is a beautiful Tudor of gray stone with blue and white contrast on the second story. It has two symmetrical gabled dormer windows at the front, the hedges I hate but Victoria loved along the side and a backyard big enough for an exuberant Doberman.

The excitement is tempered by sudden sick dread. I cover the feeling with false confidence. "It's fine. I'll be fine." The thought of walking through the front door and confronting what's inside has me terrified, but I don't want Jana to see me break down. I want to process it on my own first.

My sister nods, her eyes soft. "I get it." She reminds me about our flights tomorrow, then waits in the car for me to unlock the front door and flip the light on. I wave at her and watch her speed off into the darkness. The house smells different, like it's already become a musty, unused dwelling.

I leave my laptop on the kitchen table then wander through the house with my other bag slung over my shoulder, taking stock of what's missing. No scrabbling of claws on the floor. No sounds from upstairs as Vic moves around, painting and blaring horrid techno funk music. The sound of nothingness.

Most of the artwork is gone. It makes sense. A few photographs have been removed, though those of us remain. I pick each one up and dump them all in an empty drawer of the filing cabinet, noting right away that Victoria has taken her files. Taxes, commissions, personal bills. Of course. Why would she leave them?

Except for the basics of milk, coffee and bread that Jana kindly put in the refrigerator, the kitchen is empty of food, but all my appliances, pots and pans are still there. Vic always hated to cook. It seems she left most of the cutlery and crockery behind. Thanks for being so thoughtful, Victoria. I guess they want to have their own, new stuff.

I turn on more lights, sliding the curtains aside to try to see into the backyard, but it's too dark. I don't want to think about the chewed tennis balls and plastic mice with no tails that used to hide in the grass. I close the curtains and climb the stairs. The room she used as a studio has been stripped and repainted. All the color splashes I loved on the walls are now gone, replaced by a single hue. I close the door on those memories.

The door to our, no *my*, bedroom is open. I flip the lights on and drop my bag just inside the doorway. As instructed, my sister had a bed and mattress delivered and it's already set up with new linens. I don't know what Jana did with all the old stuff. I hope she burned it.

I expected it to feel different in here but it doesn't. Aside from the new bed, it looks just the way I remember. Except Victoria's side of the closet is open and empty, and all of her things are missing from the top of the dresser and her bedside table. My finger trails along the wall as I walk into the master bathroom and drop my toiletries onto the counter.

The bathroom cabinet is open and completely bare. Nothing of mine ever stays here unless I'm on a down cycle. It is logical she would take things but she's also taken most of my makeup, the bitch. I push the cabinet door closed and catch sight of my reflection in the mirror.

My face appears unchanged which is ironic given everything else has. I wrinkle my nose and pull a funny face. No, I am still me. I floss and brush my teeth then pull my clothes off and leave them in a pile on the floor. The pipes groan as I turn the faucet, water stuttering out of the showerhead for a few moments before it settles to a steady flow. When I step under the hot spray my jet lag seems to evaporate like steam. The vast emptiness of my house is smothering me. I need to get out.

CHAPTER SIXTEEN

Where should I go? I think of my old haunts, pulling on a lacy bra and thong. The satin against my skin feels good, soothing almost. I doubt it's known on base that my underwear preference is for scant and very feminine, but I learned early in my first deployment that the dirt and hard water in the washing machines ruins nice things.

I use the old mascara and eyeliner Victoria kindly left for me. It's not enough, but it's better than nothing. At least all of my civilian clothes are still here, a closet full of things she bought me. I settle on skinny jeans and long boots paired with a clingy tank top. The cab honks from the driveway and I shrug into my leather jacket and race out of the house.

The driver takes me to my favorite bar on 17th Street, the one Mitch and I came to on our free weekends after we both moved to D.C. I wait outside in line, fighting a sudden pang of nostalgia when I realize how much I miss doing things like this with him. I miss our giggling, pointing out all the hotties while we danced and cavorted. At the end of the night he would invariably leave with some guy and I would rush home and jump my girlfriend, because the night of drinking and writhing with strangers had ignited my lust. Vic hates clubbing which is part of the reason why I'm here now.

The heavy beat carries outside, each thump increasing my nervousness. It's been almost sixteen months since I was in a club. The song is unfamiliar and I'm fretting about what will happen when a voice catches my attention. "Do you always look so upset about the prospect of a great night in a club?"

I turn and look into the eyes of an attractive, dark-haired woman. My smile is charming. "It's been a while. I thought perhaps protocol had changed." I lean closer to her. "Back in the dark ages you had to look sad or they wouldn't let you in." I grin facetiously and take a few steps to my left as the line moves up. The stranger follows me.

She laughs at my lame humor, offering her hand. "Andrea."

I take it, shaking it softly. "Sabine."

"A pleasure," Andrea says. "I haven't seen you here before?" It sounds like a question. The line moves again and we shuffle up. This time she stands a little closer. Even with my heels she's taller than me, maybe five foot ten. My brain ticks over, thinking of Keane and the way she looks up at me.

I shake my head, both to disagree with Andrea's statement and to dispel the image of my boss. "It's been a while. I've been out of town."

She raises a shaped eyebrow, studying me. "Oh? Work?"

"That's it."

"Where do you work, Sabine? If you don't mind me asking?"

"I don't mind. Afghanistan."

A flicker of unease crosses her face. "Military?"

"Yes. Army."

She opens her mouth and it's a few seconds before she speaks. "I lost my brother over there. Two years and four months ago."

I frown. "I'm sorry to hear it." And I am. It's everywhere. I can't get away from it. Something that started as casual flirting has come full circle back to my work. I wonder if I operated on him and almost ask her his name.

She clamps her lips together. "Part of life, I suppose. Anyway I'm sure you don't like talking about work while you're home." I recognize instantly what she's really telling me. It's not her thinking I don't want to talk about it, but that she doesn't. Andrea gestures to my left. "You're up."

I give her a soft smile and turn away, stepping forward a few paces and fishing in my pocket for some cash. I pull out a few bills and my ID, offering them to the bouncer. He looks me up and down then gives me back my license. I glance back at Andrea. "I might see you inside?"

"Sure."

I pause. "I really am very sorry about your brother."

The atmosphere grabs me the moment I step through the door and I move through a sea of bodies with the beat pounding in my chest. It no longer matters that the song is unfamiliar. The smell makes my stomach clench—a mix of healthy sweat, cologne, perfume and booze. My face splits into a smile. Oh, I have missed this. Bodies brush mine as I make my way toward the bar that spans the length of back wall. Someone touches my ass. I smile even wider but don't turn back.

There's a fairly even split tonight, and a number of women catch my eye. Before I make it to the bar, a woman beckons me over from one of the tables near the stairs leading to the upper floor. It takes me a moment before I recognize her and I change course to rush over excitedly. She pulls me in for a hug. "Sabine?"

"Beth! Holy shit, it's been ages!" Of course it has, you've been away, Sabine.

She's changed her hair since I saw her last, now shorter and peroxide blond instead of dark waves to her shoulders. We've known each other for years and never hooked up, but after a glance down at her tight dress and heels, I wonder if I might try to change that. Beth grabs my arms, her blue eyes wide. "What are you doing here? I thought you were still over…" She lets a hand go to wave it around, "in whatsit."

I grin. "I am. Just home on leave."

She drags me away from the group. "I heard about you and Vic. Fucking awful. Fucking bitch. Everyone thinks so." Beth sneers, eyes narrowing.

I tilt my head, giving her a *what are you gonna do?* shrug. I'm pleased Victoria's actions seem to have earned disapproval from our circle of friends. Golden Girl Sabine lives on to fight another day. Beth barrels on. "How long are you here for?"

"Fourteen days or so, visiting family tomorrow for a bit, then back to sort a couple of things out."

She nods furiously. "For sure. Hey, if you're free we'll have coffee, yeah?"

I wink at her. "I'll see what I can do. I'll be finished in a few months, anyway, so we'll catch up then?"

"Of course." Beth squeezes my biceps. "That stupid bitch, who would cheat on arms like this?" She pulls me in for another hug. "Hang out and dance with us for a bit. What are you drinking?"

I stay with Beth and her friends for hours, losing myself among them. I am nobody, just one insignificant person in a sea of many. We mix with the boys and I think of how much Mitch would be enjoying himself if he were here with me. Beth's friends are all funny, charming and excellent company, and accept me like I've been part of the group for years. Beth makes the rounds, offering me up as though I was an auction piece. I am just drunk enough that I'm not bothered when she tells them I am "Newly single and only home from the wars for a week, so snap her up, ladies."

We laugh and before long, I've kissed all of them and have several phone numbers, which are, of course, useless to me once I go back to Afghanistan. It's not like I can call them for a quickie and why would they want a girlfriend who's in Afghanistan? Beth pinches my arm as she introduces me to one of her friends. Nicole. She's late twenties, a little shorter than me with a quick smile and a magnificent set of tits. "Nikki, please," she tells me as she leans in to kiss my cheek.

I turn my head slightly so the kiss lands on the edge of my mouth. "Nice to meet you." I suppose she will do, it's just sex, right? I'm almost ashamed of myself for my thinking, but both of us know this is not going to move beyond tonight. She stays with me as I drink and dance with reckless abandon, enjoying the beat, writhing bodies and people grabbing me constantly. I'd forgotten how sexual dancing is and it's not long before I am squirming with desire.

It's past two in the morning when Nikki leans in, keeping her hands on my hips. "I think you need dusting off, Sabine."

My pulse picks up. "I suppose you think you're excellent with a duster?" I ask, raising an eyebrow.

She laughs. "I am, as well as with other things…" She trails off, moving her eyes up to mine. My gut twists, knowing something intimate is imminent. I tilt my head to consent and she breaks into a smile.

I bite my lower lip. "I'll just say bye."

When I find her to say my farewells, Beth holds me tightly. "She's a good one, enjoy the rest of your night," she says slyly.

"You're a pimp." I kiss her cheek.

"That I am, but it's for the best. You need it. Take care of yourself, Sabine, and call me if you've got time for a coffee before you go."

Nikki and I leave the club hand in hand and for the entirety of the short ride home she runs her hand along my inner thigh, teasing me. I am so desperate for the touch of a woman that it's all I can do not to take her in the backseat. I pay for the cab then follow Nikki upstairs.

I duck into the apartment, watching as Nikki locks the door and fits the chain. The thought of having another woman's tongue on me has me practically turned inside out with hunger. We don't waste time with precursors and we almost crash together in our frantic desire.

She pulls my jacket from my shoulders, tossing it onto a chair as we kiss furiously. Her tongue slides into my mouth, probing softly and mine reaches to meet it. We're stumbling around her apartment like tipsy tango dancers. Nikki pauses to pull her top over her head and then she grabs at me again. Her hands are everywhere, yanking my tank top over my head and unbuckling my belt. I let out an involuntary groan, aware of the heat in my groin and the curl of anticipation in my stomach. She begins to walk backward, pulling me with her, leading me to what I can only assume is her bedroom.

I stop to push her against the wall beside the kitchen, and she is still for a moment as I unsnap her bra and let it drop to the floor. I waste no time, putting my mouth on her, kissing her full breasts and running my tongue over her nipple. Full breasts, bigger than Keane's. Stop it, Sabine. Nikki holds the back of my head, her fingers massaging my scalp.

The sensation pulls me away and to Colonel Keane doing the very same thing as she checked me after the football game. I groan, trying to dispel the image and be present in what I'm doing but Nikki seems to take the sound as a cue, grasping a handful of my hair and tugging. This only intensifies the image in my head. I scrunch my eyes closed as I find her nipple again and bite softly. This elicits a soft gasp from her and she takes her hands away from my hair.

My tongue trails along her breast and up her neck while Nikki reaches down to unfasten my jeans and slip a hand inside my panties. I brace myself against the wall and my breathing catches when she hits her mark. We look at one another and I speak for the first time since we got into the cab at the club. "Fuck me," I say roughly. We don't make it to the bedroom.

CHAPTER SEVENTEEN

"Keep the change," I mutter. Some asshole has locked the passenger door in a special way and I fumble with it until the cab driver leans over to release me. He gives me a knowing look. Yep, guilty and unrepentant. I left Nikki lying stretched out in her bed after we snatched a few hours sleep. She rolled over, smiling lazily as she waved goodbye then closed her eyes again. It was perfect. Thanks for the sex, please lock the door behind you and catch you never.

Considering my lack of sleep and the amount of alcohol I consumed last night, I feel pretty good. I'm squinting in the sharp morning light and it takes me a few attempts to get the key in the lock. On second thought, perhaps I'm not quite as together as I thought. I shoulder my front door open.

The sex was good, borderline great, but I don't feel as rejuvenated as I'd imagined. The raw physicality and the pleasure of having someone so close again helped, yet I don't feel everything is now magically all right. A childish hope, to think everything would be fixed if I could just move on physically. Maybe it's because it wasn't the person I wanted.

I unzip my boots and leave them by the door. My jacket and keys go on the kitchen table and I empty my pockets of a handful of coins, my license and debit card. My mouth feels like a desert. A desert with gin-tasting sand. I reach up, open one of the cabinets and pull down a glass. The glasses are sitting haphazardly, not in their respective groups. Wineglasses, water glasses and small tumblers. They are all together, but they should be separated so I don't have to waste time trying to find the right kind.

Irritation tightens the skin on the back of my neck as I pour myself cold water from the fridge. Fuck it, I need to fix them. I leave the glass in the sink, then pull all of the remaining glasses out and set them on the counter behind me. I fling the cabinet beside it open and snatch at the coffee mugs, setting them out as well. All Victoria's favorite mugs are gone.

The shelves are dirty, so there's no point in putting things back until I've wiped the surface down. I wet a dishcloth and climb up onto the bench underneath the cabinets and clean them out. While I'm up here, I may as well wipe out the next cabinet over where plates and bowls are. It snowballs from there.

After an hour, everything is out and spread around the kitchen, on the table, the benches and even the floor. At least the pantry is empty, so all I need to do is remove the thin layer of dust. It seems sort of pointless given I won't put anything in there for a few months, but I do it anyway. I sort and rearrange things into piles ready to be put away again but get no further than that. I'm sitting cross-legged on the floor, surrounded by stacks of crockery and cooking utensils when motivation exits my body as suddenly as it came. I stay there for five minutes, waiting to see if it returns. It doesn't. Oh well.

I leave the contents of my kitchen strewn everywhere and move around the house aimlessly. I'm still dressed in the clothes from last night and don't care. Some things need repairing, like one of the window latches in the spare room and the back door handle. From the window facing the backyard, it looks like the gutters around the shed are coming apart at the seams. Thanks for keeping the house in good order, Vic. Her words echo in my head. *Your house, your problem.* It makes me want to throw a chair through the window. I need to go out and buy supplies to fix up *my* house. Later.

I drag my clothes off and dump them in the laundry then clump up the stairs and flop into the bed, climbing naked under the covers. I set an alarm for three thirty.

* * *

I'm momentarily confused by my alarm cutting over the sound of cars on the street below me. Light streaks through my window and hits me in the eyes. My body is uncooperative and stiff from sleeping, or maybe it's from last night. After all, it has been a while. Something crunches in my neck when I roll over. Shit. Thought I'd wake up way before my alarm. Jana will be here in forty minutes to collect me and I haven't packed, showered or eaten. I panic, kick off the duvet, roll from the bed and rush to the shower.

There's commotion from downstairs, and the sound of someone running up the stairs. My sister is early for what may be the first time in her life. I finish drying myself and hurriedly put underwear on. "Sabine!" Jana bursts into my room as I'm reaching for my jeans.

"Yeah, I know. You're early. Can you check the doors and lock up, please? I'll be done in a sec." I toss toiletries, underwear and a random assortment of clothing into a bag. Maybe it's enough, maybe not, but I can always buy things in Ohio. I rush into the kitchen and shift a stack of cutlery aside to get my card and license.

My sister gestures to my jacket, on the table, half covered by pots and pans. "Did you go out last night?"

"I did, yes." I stuff my cards back into my wallet.

She gives me a shrewd smile. "Have a good time, Sabbie?"

"It was rather enlightening." I can't stop my smirk.

Jana scrunches an eyebrow. "Interesting way to describe it. Still, I suppose it could be worse," she chirps. "You could be paralytically drunk in a pile of your own vomit, listening to ballads and burning all your photos of her. Instead, you're fucking and rearranging!" She ends the sentence with an upward inflection.

I laugh and grab my jacket. A pot falls to the floor. "Come on, we don't want to miss our flight."

* * *

I stare out the window as the plane lifts off, trying to ignore my anxiety. I'm torn, because I'm desperate to see my parents and grandparents but on the other hand, I need some downtime. I need some time to do nothing, to not have to make small talk with cousins I haven't seen in over a year. The short flight to Dayton is spent trying to steel myself for the eight days.

This visit was so hastily put together that there are no real plans, except some quiet family meals. No constant orgy of food and alcohol and I'm grateful for this small mercy. Usually there would be a little more advance notice for leave and we would plan a combined celebration for Thanksgiving, Christmas and my birthday. Something to satisfy all the occasions I miss while deployed, or stuck on base back home.

On my last trip home I felt like a museum display or royalty sitting around while people came to see me. I don't have the energy to cope this time. I just want to spend a week cocooned with my parents, sister and grandparents. Opa doesn't drive much anymore, so I promised him we'll be there after dinner tonight. Jana and I hire a car and drive out to our parents' place, singing along with crappy eighties music blasting out of the speakers.

My father crushes me in a tight hug the moment I am in reach and Mom pretends she's not crying as she grabs Jana and me together. I hug my parents tightly, feeling like a small child again, and we end up in a weird four-way embrace on the sidewalk. Seeing my parents after so long is indescribable. Happiness, joy and comfort, but with a tinge of sadness because I know I'll have to leave them again.

I smell evidence Mom has been cooking for most of the afternoon, and she ushers us straight to the kitchen to taste test something for her. A proud matriarch, she is always delighted whenever one of us comes home, but to have both of us together seems to have pushed her over an excitement precipice.

Daddy grills outside and I set the table then go chat with him, a beer in my hand. Jana is helping Mom in the kitchen and their inane chattering filters through, something about couch patterns.

"Did you turn the grill off, Gerhardt?" Mom calls when she hears him placing a platter on the table.

"Yes, yes," he grouses. My father turns to me. "Leave it on one time and you never live it down." He winks. I grin and close the sliding door, peeking to make sure the grill is off.

"Well you *did* leave it on that one time," my mother admonishes him.

In a family with three women, my father knows which battles to pursue. He sits down with his mouth closed. Jana grabs my arm and pulls me out of earshot of our parents. "I hope you're hungry, Sabbie. It's time to get fattened up for slaughter." She widens her eyes at me but before I can respond, Mom orders us to sit.

We settle in our customary places and begin passing things around. I butter a piece of bread. "How's work, Jana?" If I get in first I can deflect the conversation away from myself.

"It's good, busy. I've been spending a lot of time in court. Plenty of people getting divorced," she says sweetly, dishing up salad for herself. She just had to mention the D word. The bitch does it on purpose, though I *did* set myself up asking my divorce lawyer sister about her work.

My mother sets her fork down. Here we go. "Sabs. How are you after Victoria's bombshell? Have you found someone to watch the house?" She looks around the table. "Awful, just awful after so many years! I never would have thought she had that in her."

I bite off a mouthful of bread, narrowing my eyes at my traitorous sister. I take my time chewing, stalling. "I'm fine, Mom. It wasn't really unexpected. Things hadn't been good for a while." I kick Jana's shin under the table. My sister grunts.

"Well, I do wish you had said something to us beforehand," my mother frets.

My response is firm. "I wasn't aware it was going to happen like this, Mom, otherwise I would have. Can we maybe just eat now and talk about this later?" Or talk about it never.

Daddy finally speaks up. "I always thought she was strange. How do you trust a person who voted for—"

"Dad!" Jana cuts him off, but she is smiling.

My father grins and reaches for his beer. "Well, it's true. And she cheated on my girl."

I can't handle a deep discussion about what a horrible person my ex is. I try to be diplomatic. "I know, Daddy. I just want to move on with my life now." It's such a cliché but it seems to appease him.

My father nods emphatically. "You're right, Sabine." He never shortens my name. "You have work and the army to focus on, you can think about partners later."

Or, I can think about the potential of one right now and how she is at work and completely out of reach. I eat so I don't have to speak and my thoughts drift back to last night with Nikki. I was hoping the encounter had taken the edge off my desire for Keane, but it's done the opposite. The comparisons come easily and Nikki cannot compare. It's not her fault that her eyes are hazel, not a deep ocean blue. Nor that she has no dimples. No blond hair. No high-pitched laugh.

"Sabs?"

I look up at my mother. "Yes?"

"You're not eating. Aren't you hungry?"

"Oh. Yeah. I was just thinking about something." I pick up my fork again. "Sorry."

"Are you okay, honey?"

The lie falls off my tongue. "Just a little jet-lagged, Mom."

Jana nudges my foot under the table and when I look up, she mouths, "Liar" at me, followed by what I can only imagine is her impersonation of an orgasm face. I kick her again under the table and she retaliates with one of her own, catching me on the knee.

When Mom is done forcing dessert on us, I excuse myself to go upstairs to sleep. My room is like a time capsule, except there's no dust and the bed is freshly made. Mom finds it hard to accept that her daughters are grown up and gone from her house. Faded posters from when I was a teenager are still stuck to the walls—prints of bands I once cared about and women I thought hot. Trophies and ribbons are stacked and hung neatly everywhere. There's a soft knock on my door. I glance up. "Yeah?"

The door opens slowly, the light flicks on and a pillow is lobbed through the open space, landing on the floor next to the bed. Oh, piss off. "Pillow fight, Jana? Really? Aren't we twenty-five years too old for that?"

She bursts into the room and jumps on my bed. "Never too old!"

"Did you take drugs with dinner?" I grunt as her elbow digs into my hip. "Fuck! Ow!"

"No!" She drapes herself over me to grab the pillow from the floor.

"I don't believe you."

"Ha!" Jana stops fidgeting and settles, leaning against the wall with her legs over mine. "Tell me about your one-night stand. Gory, juicy, toe-curling details."

I raise an eyebrow. "There's not much to tell, Jannie. Friend of a friend. We fucked, I came home."

"So you got back on the horse and all that shit."

"Yeah, I guess." I lean back against the headboard. "But, what if the horse I wanted to get back on isn't the one I rode?"

My younger sister is watching me keenly. "So you got a cow pony, not a racehorse. Who cares? Isn't a ride a ride?"

"No, of course not."

Jana's eyes widen. "Was she untrained?"

I laugh softly. "Definitely not."

She holds my gaze, her lips twisted in a grin. "Something's going on, Sabs. I can feel it. You're never this thoughtful."

"Thanks."

"Do I have to tickle it out of you?"

My body tenses. "You wouldn't fucking dare."

Jana dives on top of me and I flinch, batting at her. My sister sits up on her knees, leaning forward. "You're safe. For now. But don't think I'm going to leave this alone." Mercifully my ticklish spots are left alone as she gives me a full body hug before she rolls off the bed and skips across the room. Jana stops at the door. "Sleep tight!" Her expression tells me she's going to launch another attack, and soon.

I tuck my hands under my armpits. "You too." After she leaves me in the dark again and closes the door, I get up to lock it. Just in case.

There's a little moonlight sneaking through the blinds, keeping me awake. You're a transparent idiot, Sabine. Nice job hiding your feelings. I want to tell Jana about everything and dissect it from every angle, but of course I can't. What would I even say? Oh yeah, I'm sort of in love with my boss and miss her like crazy but it's so against the rules it could get me discharged, and give Daddy a heart attack? Of course not.

Keane. Now that I'm away, I miss her and all the little things that I hadn't even realized I was paying attention to. Our conversations about cases and the way she watches me with her head tilted while I give my opinion. She celebrates a football touchdown with a little skip-heel-click. I miss her compassion, watching her talk through a loss with my workmates. Her smile. I miss catching her looking at me and how she bites her lower lip as she looks away again.

I lie alone in the darkness with my thoughts set loose. There are no constraints, no facial expressions needing to be hidden. I slide a hand down over my breasts as I think of Keane exploring my body. My nipples are hard points between my fingertips, sending a sharp current sliding through my stomach to my groin. When my fingers find my slick clit, there is nothing soft or sensual about the pleasure I bring myself. I am desperate and needy, almost frantic as I buck underneath my fingers, which are coated with my arousal. Imagining Keane's tongue flicking against my clit pushes me over the edge and I have to bite my wrist to stop myself from crying out when my release comes.

* * *

The rest of the time in Ohio passes in a blur of family events. My days are filled with sympathetic faces and voices as we eat, drink and talk about nothing. Inevitably, the conversation turns to Victoria. I make appropriate noises then pass the conversation on to my sister so I don't have to talk about either my ex or what I've been doing in the war.

I bring Oma and Opa over when the family has barbeques or potluck dinners. Oma mutters unhappily in German that I am *too thin, too thin* and keeps ordering my sister to bring me food. Everyone bustles around and I move through them, making appropriate sounds and trying to blend in. Jana makes intermittent runs at me, like an aircraft failing landing after landing.

"Who is it?"

"Do I know her?"

"It's not Mitch is it? Ew, please no. You guys haven't been turned?"

"Is she pretty?"

No. No. NO! Yes...

Eventually, Jana gives up after every prod is met with my silence.

I catch a break when she flies home after four days for a court appearance that couldn't be rescheduled. On the plus side, it means no more constant questions and sideways looks. But her leaving means there's nobody to run interference when my family wants to talk about Vic and work and wars.

I engage dutifully and the moment I stop talking, daydreams about Keane sneak into my head. I dissect our conversation on the bench over and over. My brain replays our moment in sick bay and I run over every look and touch, trying to see if it's all in my imagination. I don't believe it is. There is something between us. I'm certain of it.

CHAPTER EIGHTEEN

The day I'm due to fly back to D.C., I drive into Dayton in the morning to pick up a cake Mom ordered for our final family lunch. I enjoy the feeling of concrete sidewalks underfoot and the way people bustle around knowing nothing about me. Not my past or my secrets. They don't know I'm thinking about Rebecca Keane.

I walk past a hair salon, take another few steps then turn around and push the door open. The girl at the desk is young, with bottle-blond hair and murky green eyes that gleam hazel as they catch the light. I smile broadly. "Hi, sorry, I don't have an appointment. I'm heading out of town today and just thought I could sneak a haircut, if you have any spaces?"

She takes her time perusing the appointment book. "Can you wait fifteen minutes? I can fit you in then."

"Perfect, thank you." I take a seat next to a stack of magazines which all follow the same theme. Dating. Dieting. Divorcing. I'm reading a tedious piece of gossip when a woman about my age appears in front of me.

"Hi, I'm Amanda." She offers a smile and her hand.

I shake it lightly. "Sabine."

We make small talk and I avoid specifics about what I do, settling for telling her I'm a medical professional. I'm often tempted to flat-out lie and say I'm an accountant, but the fear someone might ask me something about their taxes always stops me. When my hair is shampooed and I'm settled in front of the mirror, Amanda asks me what I want done.

I don't know why, but instead of telling the hairdresser to just tidy it, I find myself saying, "Something different, short." Put a dollar in that think before you speak jar, Sabine.

Amanda raises both eyebrows at me in the mirror. "A big change, hey? Let me guess…" She fluffs my shoulder-length hair, folding the ends up. "Relationship break-up."

I tilt my head in acknowledgment. "You got me."

"It's the natural progression of things, sweetie. You need a change. Leave the old you behind. Changing hair is usually the first thing people choose. Do you have anything particular in mind? Color? Though, if I had hair this dark, I'd never change it." She smiles and combs my hair out.

This is very spur of the moment. Maybe it's a mistake. I haven't thought about it and the army requirement is clear. I catch her eye in the mirror. "No. Something practical, but it still needs to be feminine." I pause before I come clean with, "I'm in the military."

Amanda nods and begins to pin long sections of my hair. "I know just what you need for your fresh start. Leave it to me." She picks up her scissors.

I watch her transforming my hair while we talk about my job, her kids and her bastard ex-husband. I leave the salon with an armful of styling products and pixie cut I love, which also fits into military grooming regulations.

After lunch, I break down crying when I have to say goodbye to Mom and Dad, then Oma and Opa. Goodbyes are always tearful and difficult, full of promises and regrets. It doesn't matter that I will be back soon. A goodbye is a goodbye. I'm weighed down by sadness during the flight home and, mercifully, the flight attendants realize the hunched over woman in 15D doesn't want to be bothered.

Jana collects me from Dulles, only twenty minutes later than when she said she'd be there. It appears she got the hint during our few days apart and she gives up after whining, "Come on. Why won't you tell me?"

When we pull into the driveway the sensor light comes on, as though someone lives inside this husk and cares about a car arriving. Jana hands me my jacket. "Do you want me to come by tomorrow?"

"Sure."

She pulls me in for a hug. "The hair really is something else, Sabs. Hot. I'll stop by around lunchtime."

"Sounds great." I hold her tight.

She lets me go, jumping back into the car to speed away. I stand on the driveway and watch her leave, then let myself in and stand in the kitchen among all my appliances and crockery. Being inside my house is loathsome. It feels too quiet. Too calm. My body feels like it doesn't belong here anymore.

I need to go to the store but awkwardness found me while I was in Ohio and refuses to go away. It makes me question my interactions with strangers, the processes behind purchasing things and making conversation. What am I going to do when I come home after this cycle? I open my fridge, stare at its emptiness and close it again, to crawl up to bed.

CHAPTER NINETEEN

When I wake it's drizzling lightly. By the time I've decided I need more than coffee and stale bread, the rain is heavier, making the roads slick and confusing. I find a drive-through, get takeout burger and fries and make a quick stop for alcohol. Fuck you, Victoria. You're not the only one who likes scotch, remember? I add a case of beer I probably won't finish, drive to the hardware store and toss some gutter sealant, a handle for the back door and a window latch into my cart.

On a whim, I wander into the paint aisle and add everything needed to change the color of my bedroom. I rush back to my trusty pickup, safe in the noisy cab and speed home. I wonder who will love it when I'm gone again, as Vic used to turn it over from time to time. The world disappears as the garage door slides down, enclosing me safely within my house again.

I take the painting supplies straight upstairs to my bedroom then stack the entire case of beer into the fridge, jamming the bottles close together on their sides so they won't roll around. There is still no food in the fridge or pantry. I pour myself three fingers of scotch with a handful of ice and carry it upstairs where

I spread drop cloths around, draping the floor and furniture in a macabre white. My sander is probably still here, but I haven't been out to the shed, so I just bought a new one, along with all the other bits and pieces. You're avoiding, Sabine. I fit a dust mask over my mouth, slide on safety glasses and organize earplugs.

I've finished over three quarters of my room when I hear a loud call from the doorway. "Sab!"

I turn the sander off, set it down and drag off my protective gear. "Coming!" I call out loudly. My sister mimes pulling something out of her ears. Ha, of course. I tug the earplugs out of mine and set them down as she turns to go downstairs. I brush dust off myself and bounce down the stairs with my empty tumbler. My hands feel strange without the vibration of the sander moving through them.

My sister has brought more groceries. Real food. Bless her. She glances around, taking in everything still spread over the floor, table and counters from before we went to Ohio, pushes a stack of plates to the side and lifts bags to the countertop. "Repainting?" She pulls open my fridge door.

I wiggle my jaw back and forth. "Yeah." There's a headache starting behind my eyes.

"Shouldn't you have tidied all this shit up already?" She sweeps an arm around and starts to pack fruit and vegetables into my fridge around all the beer. "Got enough booze? Christ."

I step over the mixer and place my glass in the sink. "There's only a few days left to reach my quota, Jannie, then it's back to sobriety."

Jana reaches for a bag of apples and I snag one before it makes it into the crisper. I bite into it, licking my lower lip to stop the juice from running down my chin. It's delicious and so fresh. I take another few bites, watching my sister put things in my pantry. She turns around and stares at me. "You didn't wash that. It's probably covered in wax and toxic chemicals."

"I'm in the army. Nothing I eat is fresh and I'm pretty sure most of it is full of chemicals." I toss the apple core, grab a box of crackers and pull it open.

Jana shrugs. "Fair enough. Maybe they're secretly trying to mutate you all into super soldiers or something."

I laugh, choking on the mouthful of cracker.

"Lovely. Say it, don't spray it. Here, I made you these dinners. Just toss them in the oven." Jana shows me some foil containers, with the contents written on top. She puts them into the freezer.

I cough, trying to clear the dry cracker from my throat. "Thank you."

She waves me off and grabs a beer from the fridge, offering it to me before she gets one for herself. "I guess you want me to help you finish sanding your room?" Her question is monotone, as though she hopes I might say no.

I take a casual sip of beer, nodding as I swallow. "Can you please go to the shed and get the tall ladder?"

She looks out the window and I can almost see her mental processes working. Jana sets her bottle down. "I remember the lock combination, back in a minute."

* * *

My sister has a blind date and as the sun begins to set she leaves me with a hug and a reminder to have more for dinner than booze. Optimist. I gather our empty bottles and carry them downstairs to the recycling tub.

I open another beer and grab one of the meals from the freezer without bothering to look at the label. The oven isn't ready yet but I slide the tray in anyway. While it heats, I put everything back in the cabinet and cupboards. Tidy kitchen, tidy mind? I almost transfer the food to a plate but I don't because then it'll just need to be washed. There's no point in watching television because Vic canceled the cable. I grab a book and eat dinner one-handed, leaning against the kitchen counter while I read.

My cell vibrates on the counter, skittering across the surface. It's a text from Jana: "CALL 10." This is an old code of ours. Her date isn't going well and she wants me to call her with an out in ten minutes. We used this code when we were younger, though it was always her needing to be rescued more so than me. On the odd occasion when I needed a bailout, my sister excelled. For some reason, she could always play the part brilliantly, pretending there was some real family emergency.

I was never so considerate. Once, I told her our pool was on fire, then listened as she ummed and ahhed, trying to hold a one-sided conversation as I casually asked her how to put out a water fire. I hit her number and imagine her holding her phone up to show her date. *Oh, it's my sister. Sorry I have to take it, she's just back from Afghanistan, her girlfriend left her. I have to make sure she's okay.*

Jana answers with the perfect amount of concern in her voice. "Sabine, what's up?"

I pitch my voice high. "Hi, is this the parakeet rescue service?"

"No, I'm just out to dinner with a friend."

"It is? Excellent. I've got a problem with my parakeet."

"Really? Are you sure?" Her voice is so calm. Good for her.

"He's in the toaster and I can't get him out." I snort.

"No, no it's okay, Sabs. Just give me twenty minutes or so?"

"Do you think I should push it down then pop it back up again and see if he jumps out like toast?"

"Will you be okay until then?" Jana's voice lifts half an octave at the end of her question. She's struggling. I've almost got her.

"Okay. I'm gonna do it."

"I'll...be there soon."

She hangs up and I laugh until my eyes are tearing. She should get an acting award. My phone rings a few minutes later. I hear Jana's car as she speeds away from her poor date. "You fucking bitch!" she exclaims while I guffaw in her ear. "That was so hard, trying not to laugh."

"Think of it as payback for the dinner with Mom and Dad, Jannie," I tell her sweetly, reaching for the scotch.

She grunts. "You're horrible."

"So, no second date then?"

"Ha! No. He was horrible too. So arrogant and fucking boring. What a waste of a night." There's a long blast on her car horn. "I'll see you the day after tomorrow at six for airport duty." She hangs up on me.

I giggle again and pour another drink. As I'm putting the bottle back, the moonlight through the rear windows catches my eye. I look out into the semidarkness for a while until I cannot bear it any longer. The scotch goes down in one burning gulp and I go upstairs, hoping to sleep. It's a lot better and I can only hope it continues back on base. Perhaps I am moving on a little in my own way. Thank you, brain.

I wake before dawn and lie in bed trying to decide how to fill my day. There is so much to be done. I'm tempted to stay in bed and do none of it. I fly out tomorrow evening so between now and then is the only time I have. I slide out of bed reluctantly, dressing and slipping my feet into an old pair of Uggs, one with a hole in the side.

I open the coffee Jana bought, shove my nose in the package and inhale deeply. It would make good currency, maybe I can smuggle it back to work. Swap you a cup of great coffee for midnight rounds? I glance out the window to see the sun just peeking over my back fence.

There's a rope tug toy lying in the long grass. I make a mental note to tell the yard guy that the dog is gone so he can add the backyard to his mowing. He'll collect everything that's lying around. For a moment I'm angry at Vic for leaving some of Caesar's things behind. Don't be stupid, Sabine. They have pet stores in Colorado.

I remember when we first got the animals. I picked out Brutus from the shelter because he was the only one awake as I wandered past heartbreaking pens of abandoned felines. Because I'm a lover of Roman history and because he was the runt, I thought it amusing to give him a name implying he was a brute. After we brought Brutus home, Victoria decided we should get a dog too.

Vic being Vic, she wanted a purebred. She researched breeders for weeks before she chose a Doberman because her family always had one while she was growing up. Tail and ears undocked, naturally. Caesar arrived on a plane when he was fourteen weeks old, all paws and floppy ears. Vic suggested his name because she thought he would grow up to be regal and powerful, plus it fit in with Brutus's Roman theme. Caes grew up to be dorky and always subservient to the cat, which amuses me. Amused me. I begin to cry.

I lean against the fridge letting out great hiccupping cries. I can't stop myself. There is no hysteria, no throwing myself down to beat the ground with my fists. I just cry. I don't know how long I stand there with my hand over my mouth, sobbing, but I'm left spent, my face itchy from dried tears. There's nothing left.

I wonder how I would be if they were human children. Fucking unbearable. I'm embarrassed, but at least I managed to touch the hurt held so deeply inside. I don't think I fully knew how to feel about what Victoria did before now, before I was here in my house to see it. I wash my face in the kitchen sink, lifting my shirt to dry it off. The burden of it all seems lighter but I'm not sure if it's because I understand, or if I am simply more accepting.

* * *

I spend the day napping, sorting through paperwork, fixing the door and window then undercoating my bedroom walls. The main coat will have to wait until I come home from deployment. No matter how hard I try, I still can't make myself go into the backyard. The shed guttering will have to wait too. Maybe in a few months I'll have moved past my shit enough to be able to deal with what's out there. I almost want to laugh at the absurdity of avoiding dog toys and memories.

Late afternoon, I toss my sister's lasagna into the oven and trudge up to my room to fold the drop cloths into a tidy pile in the corner. I take hot shower, wash my hair and spend ten minutes under the spray watching water drain between my feet. The dinging of the oven timer breaks me out of my water wastage.

I eat standing at the kitchen counter, not tasting my meal. I realize I haven't had any reflections on my life with Vic all afternoon. Until now. Shit. I reach for the scotch and don't measure my pour. Fortified by a slug of the amber liquid, I decide it's time to start sorting through some clothing.

I've been organizing for an hour and two more scotches when my phone startles me. I slide across the smooth wooden floor on my knees to pounce on it. An unknown number. Telemarketing? Wrong number? No thank you, not tonight. I tap the screen to decline the call and drop the phone on the floor so I can resume my methodical sorting of all my accumulated crap.

It feels cathartic to be ridding myself of these things. My eyes stray to a top Vic gave me one year for no reason at all other than she saw it and thought it would look good on me. I hold it against myself for a moment, then throw it to the "maybe" pile. I sit cross-legged, sipping my drink and sorting through one portion of my old life. I'm actually enjoying myself. Yes, no, maybe.

The piles of clothing around me grow and another thirty minutes passes before I hear the doorbell ring. I pause with a hideous skirt in my hand. Why is Jana back and why didn't she just use her key? The bell rings again. Calm your tits, I'm coming. I pull myself up using the bed frame, grab my drink and toss the skirt onto the "no" pile.

I hop down the stairs and leap over the final two to land lightly on the balls of my feet. Not a single drop spilled. Well done, Sabine! Should have done a backflip. "I'm coming!" I set the glass on the kitchen counter and rush to peer through my peephole, expecting to see a sheepish sister.

Oh, shit.

Double shit.

Why? Or more importantly…how?

I reach down and fumble with the locks. Standing on my doorstep, with her hair damp and curling from the drizzle, is Lieutenant Colonel Rebecca Anne Keane.

CHAPTER TWENTY

In my hurry to open the door, I fling it back a little too hard and have to grab the wood before it hits the wall. My right hand moves automatically before my brain registers we are both in civvies and there's no need to salute. I drop it again. "Good evening, ma'am."

I wait for her response and force myself to stand up straighter, though it's tricky when I have a slight whiskey lean. Words echo in my head. Fraternization. Discharge. There's now a lump in my throat and I try hard to swallow it.

Keane inclines her head slightly, her hands clasped in front of her. "Sabine." She adjusts her glasses. "May I come in?"

Why is she here? Do you want her here, Sabine? Yes. Then stop holding a silent monologue with yourself and let your boss come in. I step backward, holding the door open. "Of course, yes ma'am." I move back further to allow her inside. "May I take your coat, Colonel?" I take a quick look around outside before I close and lock the door.

"Thank you." Keane looks around my house as she unbuttons her trench, and her scent floats from the fabric as she passes it to me. She is wearing a fitted blouse and a tight skirt accentuating her shapely legs. Her hair is loose, wavy and falling past her shoulders. I've never seen her without her hair up. She's immaculately made up. Maybe she's been out somewhere before coming here. She looks incredible. Oh, help.

Keane turns to me, a smile playing on her lips. "We're not at work," she says and the words feel charged with meaning. "There's no need for ma'am or Colonel. I'd prefer it if you called me Rebecca."

"Rebecca. Of course." Remember, Sabs. Rebecca, Rebecca, Rebecca.

"You cut your hair. I like it."

My hand strays unconsciously to push hair out of my eyes. "Thank you."

"I called your cell. About forty minutes ago." Her gaze seems deeper somehow, as though she's trying to tell me something with just this look.

I am trying very hard to look her in the eyes and not let my own stray to places they shouldn't. "Oh, right. Sorry. I'm just, well I'm just sorting through some things. I didn't recognize the number, so…" I smile. The words sound weak.

She gives me a knowing grin then turns to walk away, the heels of her pumps sharp against my wooden floors. I find it unsurprising that the confidence she displays at work would carry over outside of it. The confidence to look up a personal address and phone number, then come over without warning. The confidence which gives her no issues about walking through my house. The confidence I find so compelling.

"This is a beautiful place—have you lived here long?" she asks, but doesn't wait for me to answer before she strides toward the kitchen.

I follow her. "Almost six years." Fighting the instinct to call her ma'am makes my words clumsy. "Can I offer you a drink, or something to eat?" Like myself, perhaps. Stop it, Sabine.

Keane places her hands on the granite countertop. "Thank you, I already ate but I would like a drink." She gestures to my glass, still on the counter. "Whatever you're having, Sabine." The

French lilt she places on my name seems far more pronounced now.

I reach up for a tumbler and set it on the counter. "Ice?"

"Please."

The ice cracks sharply as it breaks from the tray. I add a generous splash of scotch and pass it to her. Her fingers brush against mine as she takes the glass. Rebecca takes a careful sip, a slight smile twisting her lips. I drop a handful of ice into my own glass, more to stop myself from staring too obviously at her than out of need for a top up. I still don't know why she is here and I don't have the courage to ask.

Evidently, my expression gives me away because she smiles, the laugh lines around her eyes creasing. "I'm sure you're curious about why and how I'm here."

The grin I give in response feels lopsided. "I am, yes. Very curious actually." We are standing on opposite sides of my kitchen bench and I am now feeling very sober. There's a strange sensation creeping over my arms, like someone is blowing on them and I rub my hand over my forearm, trying to dispel it. We're not at work. There is nobody here but us. Nobody to see us. Or stop us. I cross my arms and tuck my hands into my armpits as though it could hold in my panic. She's caught me, in my house after a few drinks and I'm afraid I'm going to slip and give myself away.

Rebecca dips her head, looking over at me. "Sabine, I came here because I wanted to talk to you, away from eyes and ears, and…regulations."

I raise an eyebrow. "You planned this overlap! That's why you were so specific about when I was to take my leave." I untuck a hand to gesture between us.

"Yes," she says instantly.

Things are beginning to fall into place. "I wondered how you managed to have my R and R approved so quickly."

She smiles again. "There are some benefits that come with rank, Sabine. Also, I was owed a rather large favor by someone higher up." The smile becomes a grin, cheeky and confident.

"Why?"

Rebecca lifts the drink halfway to her lips, her grin fading as she murmurs, “I think you know why.” I’m beginning to think I do, yet I’m too afraid to say it out loud. Rebecca continues, “I know you fly out tomorrow night.”

A simple statement of fact and I catch on immediately. Tomorrow, I will go back to the base and we will go back to the state of flux we have existed in for the past few years. It’s tonight, or not at all. My boss takes another sip, swirling the glass to settle the ice before she finishes it.

She’s left lipstick on the rim and I stare at the mark, feeling my heart rate increase as I think of what may happen, what I want to happen. I want to drag her down onto the floor with me and spread her apart. Imagining what she would taste like starts an insistent throb between my thighs. We are not at work and we are two consenting adults. Flimsy, Sabine.

I lift my eyes. “Another?” I’m already reaching for the bottle when she holds the tumbler out to me. The lack of wedding band draws my eyes to her finger like a magnet.

She follows my eyes to her hand, waiting until I’ve refilled her drink and added another splash to my own before she speaks. “I’m not married, Sabine. I never have been. I thought that might have been obvious.” Rebecca pulls the glass back toward herself, peering into the depths of the liquid. “I wear it at work to imply things about myself. Things which aren’t true. Things to make it easier for me to do my job the way I need to, without people looking over my shoulder all the time.” She takes a sip of scotch. “Do you understand what I’m saying?”

“Yes.” I understand very well.

“Good.” Rebecca sets her glass down, lifting her eyes to mine. “I’m so tired of pretending, Sabine. You have no idea how close I’ve come, so many times, to just giving in.” Her voice is soft, almost sad. “In the examination room, I thought that was it and I would finally let go, rules and policies be damned.”

I take a steadying breath. There’s a sudden, almost overwhelming rush of relief as I realize I really haven’t been imagining things, or projecting my own needs.

She wants me, just as I want her.

Yes, this is happening. Rebecca pulls her glasses off, drops them on the countertop and moves around to me, her gait steady and certain. I turn to face her, my hip bumping against a handle on the drawers as she approaches me. Ice cubes clink against the glass when she takes it from my hand and leans around to place it on the countertop. My pulse is pounding in my ears, adrenaline tingling in my fingertips. She steps toward me, reaching for my belt to pull me closer and I let out a soft gasp as I'm tugged forward. We are now inches apart.

I can't move or say anything because all I can think about is how close her hand is to the wet, swollen heat between my legs. There's piles of clothing all over the floor upstairs and my bed isn't made. Shit. This is happening. It's happening. In all the fantasies I've had about her, the way I felt in each of them is nothing like the way I feel right now. At least my sheets are barely slept in. Fuck, stop it! It doesn't matter, Sabine.

"What are you thinking?" she asks me, voice low. Her hand is still on my belt, holding me in place and she brings her other hand up to rest on my waist.

"Nothing. Nothing important." It's a lie, but I can't tell her how desperate I am for her to unzip my jeans and slide her fingers inside my panties. It's too forward, too soon.

The tilt of her head and sly smile tells me she doesn't believe me. "Then why are you chewing the inside of your cheek?" She's right. I sweep my tongue around the inside of my mouth, feeling the raggedness where my teeth have been. Rebecca continues, "You do it whenever you're contemplating something. You're not as good at hiding your feelings as you think you are, Sabine." The words are softened by her slight smile.

I exhale and lean back against the counter, wondering how often she's watched me without my noticing. "I'm thinking... everything. All at once."

"Do you want to know what I'm thinking?" Rebecca lifts her eyes to mine, not waiting for my response. "I'm thinking about how I've wanted to kiss you ever since the first time we worked together." Her voice is throaty, delicious. If we kiss, then it's over. What will we do afterward when everything has changed?

My fists clench with the effort of trying to stop myself from grabbing her. The prospect of what is about to happen has my stomach tightening in anticipation. I take a deeper breath, trying to calm myself but my heart ignores me and keeps up its frantic pace. With her heels on, she is almost the same height as me. I am a statue, disciplined into stillness. I will not make the first move, though every cell in my body is screaming for me to kiss her.

In the bright white light of my kitchen, her dark blue eyes have an even darker ring circling them. Rebecca waits, eyes searching mine as though she's looking for any sign of hesitation. She will find none. My want of her causes an almost unbearable heat, spreading downward and I'm almost trembling from the effort of holding myself back. I nod slightly, lowering my eyes to watch her as she leans in and presses her lips to mine. Her hands tighten on my waist, holding me in place.

The kiss starts slow at first then builds, carrying my arousal along with it. I let her guide us, wanting her to be sure, but I needn't worry. It's her tongue that breaks past the borders of our lips and as soon as I feel it against my lower lip, I am set free.

My hands break rank first, reaching for her and I hold her face and let my tongue meet hers. We're testing each other, giving and taking as everything is released at once, all our years of want and denial. Rebecca pulls back and I instinctively follow, leaning forward to seek her out again. She places her hand against my shoulder to stop me. "You taste exactly the way I always imagined," she murmurs, eyes seductive.

I study her, smirking a little. "You thought I had a secret stash of scotch somewhere in my room?" I keep eye contact, my heart knocking against my ribs so hard that I'm scared she can hear it.

This makes her laugh. "No. I may have sought you out earlier if I thought that was the case." Her hands are on the move, the one on my shoulder coming up to grab the back of my neck, the other sliding around to cup my ass. She runs her tongue up my neck and over my earlobe before she whispers in my ear, "You taste like desire."

I groan and she arches up into me as our lips meet again and we are soon dueling with one another. I smell her shampoo against a soft undercurrent of the perfume I love, fruity and floral. We taste one another with my back jammed into the hard countertop and she is almost frantic as she reaches to grasp the bottom of my shirt. I lean away from the counter so the fabric can slide easily up my torso and our lips break contact to allow her to pull it over my head and toss it away.

Rebecca runs her nails over my stomach, pausing at the small scar just above my right hip. "Appendix?"

I nod and she continues trailing her nails up over my breasts before she reaches around to unhook my bra, letting it swing from a forefinger before she tosses it away. I look at those small, feminine hands, each nail short and perfectly shaped. Hands I've seen hundreds of times doing so many things, but never exploring my body. Rebecca unfastens the button of my jeans and slides my zipper down, her knuckles brushing against me.

Her head is bent, her words barely audible. "That is not what I expected, Sabine." She raises her eyes to mine and lets her hand brush over the black lace of my thong before it continues upward. "It's incredibly hot." Her voice is low and sensual, dripping with desire.

I force myself to be still while she explores me with her fingertips, leaving goose pimples everywhere she touches. A tremor moves through my legs and I give a low moan, thinking of her hot tongue against my nipples and running circles over my clit. She holds my jaw, her thumb gently brushing my lips. I can't deny myself any longer. "Kiss me again," I demand.

Rebecca complies without hesitation, and I pull her even closer, trying to ignore the deep throbbing threatening to overwhelm me. My fingers are deft as I unbutton her blouse and slide it from her shoulders, letting my fingers brush along her collarbone. She reaches around to pull her bra off, dropping it on the floor. Full breasts, hard nipples, creamy skin. I run my hands down to cup her, letting my thumb play over her nipples. I think of my mouth on her skin, my fingers inside her and my arousal floods my panties.

"Sabine..." Rebecca's voice is raspy with need.

For a brief, terrifying moment, I'm so overwhelmed that I don't know what to do. My desire and arousal are foreign in their intensity and I want everything. All at once. I want to pick her up, drop her on my kitchen table and taste every part of her. I want my mouth on her nipples, hands tangled in her hair. I'm desperate to put my fingers inside her, to lick her until she comes in a flood in my mouth. I can't, I need to wait. I need to find a lower gear, somewhere more tolerable where I can think enough to do everything I want to. Everything I need to.

She moans when I bend to kiss her neck and along the curve of her breast and I take a moment, just inhaling. Perfume, lotion and the unmistakable scent of arousal. Rebecca pulls away and kicks off her shoes. I start to tug my jeans down but only get them just under my hips before I see what she's doing and am stunned into stillness. She unzips her skirt and hooks her thumb in the seam of her panties to slide them off, her eyes locked with mine.

I look away first, taking in every delicious inch of her. Oh, help. Rebecca Keane is naked in my kitchen and I feel like a dumbstruck cliché, staring at her with my mouth agape. She is so fucking beautiful, slender and full of delicious curves.

"Rebecca, I...Christ." I'm practically stammering like a virgin.

She smiles, like she knows exactly what I'm thinking and twists around, hopping a little as she places her hands on the counter behind her. Rebecca hoists herself up, opens her legs and pulls me closer. I'm desperate for contact on my aching center but I ignore it, sliding her forward and using my hipbone to press against her as our lips meet again. There is now a new kind of urgency to our foreplay. This is not a good idea. This is going to cause problems. We can't be together. Shut up, Sabine.

Rebecca has fistfuls of my hair as I tease her. I hear her gasp as I gently suck on her nipple and her nails find my shoulder. She is grinding herself on my hip and her need is obvious, wet and hot against me. My thighs clench in response, giving in to try and release some of the pressure of my clit. I relish the taste of her, exploring with my tongue, listening to the sound of her rough inhalations. Her scent. Those desperate sounds. The way she tastes and feels. There's an electric current running under my skin, sparking all of my nerves. We don't speak. We are too busy devouring one another.

This will not do, I need more. Something more than fucking her on my kitchen counter. I wrap my arms around her waist, drag her down and lead her up to my bedroom.

CHAPTER TWENTY-ONE

Rebecca wakes me with hands on my breasts and a line of soft kisses along my shoulder. I feel like I only just fell asleep and don't even know what time it is, though I soon forget about it as her fingers trail down my belly to reignite me. "I got tired of waiting for you to wake up," she whispers against my ear.

"I can think of worse ways to be woken up." I roll over and pull her close. Again, I'm struck by the differences between us. The contrast in our skin tones, her milky complexion set against my tan. I'm lithely muscular and while she is slender and fit, her body curves and swells under my hands as they explore her. This foreplay is nothing like last night where we were raw and frantic with one another. Now we are slow. Indulgent. Our kisses gentle and sweet.

Dusky light seeps through to fill my room, casting muted light over her face and I keep my eyes open, taking in everything she has to offer me. I can't believe that after all the times I've looked at her and thought her beautiful, I've never really *seen* her. Things I didn't notice in my desperate need to consume her last night now seem glaringly obvious. The chickenpox scars on her back. The fire engine red of her toenails. The smattering of freckles over her shoulders.

I slide my hands around to her ass and roll her over, pinning her beneath me, my hip against her wetness. When I press forward, she inhales sharply and wraps her legs around my ass, forcing me closer. Rebecca pulls me down to kiss her and I oblige briefly before my lips leave hers to travel over her face and neck. Somehow, after last night's marathon a trace of perfume remains near her ear and as the scent hits me, I'm consumed by hundreds of thoughts all at once. The most prevalent is an almost overwhelming desire to taste her again but I deny myself and take my time exploring her. My tongue roams over a breast before I settle to suck on an engorged nipple. She tastes like sweat and grapefruit lotion. Sweet and salty at the same time.

She is whimpering as my finger circles her clit, slow and soft. Those sounds, her desperation is like pouring gasoline on my arousal. Her nails dig into my shoulder as I reach down and slip inside her cavern. Rebecca gasps, tightening her grip when I curl my fingers to stroke her slick walls. She squirms, letting out another groan. A hand tangles in my hair. "Please, please," she begs me. Her voice is husky, needy.

I pull away and inch my way back up her body, leaving a wet trail as my tongue marks her. I deliberately withdraw all contact with her and lift myself up to look down at her. "Please what?"

She is flushed, her hair loose and strewn over the pillow like a waterfall of spun gold. Her legs squirm underneath mine and she lifts her head slightly. "Please Sabine. Let me come."

I drop my body down gently, arm sliding under her waist while I lick and suck at her neck. "Not until you beg me," I murmur against her skin.

Rebecca tries to grind herself against me, but she can find no purchase. I keep myself away, denying her contact. She groans again. "Please. Fuck me. I need your tongue on me." She digs her fingers into my shoulders, trying to push me down, but I hold myself taut, resisting.

My teeth lock into her neck and I roll over onto my back, pulling her on top of me. Rebecca lets out a frustrated moan, until I slide down to position myself underneath her glistening sex. I part her slick folds, slip two fingers inside and lift my head to lap at her engorged clitoris.

Rebecca responds with a loud cry. When I glance up, I see her rolling a nipple between thumb and forefinger. This beautiful act of self-gratification mixes with the raw animalistic sounds above me to make the throbbing in my groin almost unbearable. My own arousal is hot and wet when I reach down to touch myself. There's fire in my belly, fanned by the scent and taste of her above me. I never want it to go out. My fingers find my clit, making lazy circles as I drive her closer and closer to her release.

"Sabine. Don't you dare," Rebecca gasps, reaching down to grab my wrist and pull my hand away. She puts my fingers in her mouth, sucking my juices from them and I feel her tighten around the fingers I have buried deep inside her. Oh God. I jam my thighs together.

Her cries reach a crescendo as I flick my tongue against the underside of her clit again and I'm rewarded with a flood of her sweet juice in my mouth. Rebecca bucks and shudders above me, her breathing loud, erratic and so fucking sexy. I wait for her to go still then press kisses over her thighs until she unclamps herself from my shoulders and edges down to straddle me, pausing to cup my face. She kisses me softly, sweetly then keeps making her way down, the hard bullet points of her nipples trailing over my stomach.

I prop myself up on my elbows to watch her but she pushes me back down and grabs my hands. Her dominance excites me even further and my wetness overflows, thick and hot. Rebecca slings a leg over mine, spreading me apart with her thigh to press against my throbbing center. She takes one of my nipples in her mouth, biting hard then soothing it with a gentle sweep of her tongue. I groan and she does it again, teasing me. Every touch of her teeth and tongue sends another throb straight to my clit.

My hands are being held above my head, her grip on my wrists firm. I could still pull away if I wanted to. *If* I wanted to. She kisses me again and I moan around the kiss, my hands balling into fists as her lips leave mine to travel down my neck and to my breasts.

She increases the pressure on my throbbing clit, releasing my wrists and leaving me squirming. "Please." I lift my hips again, desperate for some more contact, some friction, anything.

Rebecca ignores me and moves down my body, the silken softness of her hair against my skin as her lips seem to find every inch of me. She settles between my legs, nails digging into my thighs and holding me in place. Her tongue is everywhere, running over my hipbones and sweeping across my stomach. Her tongue is everywhere but where I need it. Where I want it. I bite the inside of my arm in frustration. "Please," I rasp again.

"Please what?" she asks me devilishly, biting my hip hard enough to make me flinch.

"Lick me," I beg.

"Now who's begging?" She looks up from between my legs, those gorgeous lips twisted into a seductive grin. I can't even answer, and when she drops her head and her tongue finds my clit, my knees quiver. Her hands are on my breasts, thumbs playing softly over my nipples, which are so hard they are aching.

Rebecca slows, her tongue light and rhythm steady, holding me just outside of reach. She's playing me expertly, bringing me to the brink and then pulling me back again until finally she allows me to come. I almost feel like I'm levitating as I let out a guttural sound, crying out as the waves of my climax ebb with my toes curling against the sheets.

The aftermath of my orgasm settles deep inside my belly, spreading through me like tendrils curling to touch every cell. I feel almost whole again, as though we are now in the place where we were always meant to be. She kisses the inside of my thighs and props herself up to look at me. I lie there, weak and boneless, for a few moments then stretch a little. "Do I still taste of desire?" I ask, lifting my head to look at her.

Rebecca laughs, showing the tiny chip on one of her front teeth. "Yes. And what about me?" She runs her tongue over her lower lip. "What do I taste of?"

I move to prop myself against the bedhead, buying time to consider it. My mouth is dry as the options run through my head. "I'm not sure yet," I say finally. "Something illicit maybe?" I hold eye contact with her, watching her lift a fine eyebrow.

"You've never done anything you shouldn't have?" Rebecca sits up and swings her legs to drape over mine. She reaches for the duvet, pulling it around herself to keep the morning air off her bare skin.

"Of course not!" I exclaim but feign horror, giving her a little wink. She laughs, which takes the edge off my feeling of doing something wrong. I gently change the subject. "So, Colonel. You've wanted me ever since the first time we operated together?" My question is coy.

Rebecca laughs and plays along. "More or less…Captain. Do you remember? You repaired that tricky liver laceration. Then you made a stupid pun about how he was going to live-r."

"I remember." It was stupid. I was new, nervous and so awed by her. My standard in such situations is to blurt something ridiculous.

She laughs again. "Then you flushed and gave me that helpless look, like you couldn't believe what had just come out of your mouth."

I shake my head, but I'm laughing with her. "You've always made me nervously verbose. At first I thought it was just a case of hero worship, then I realized it was actually the huge crush I have on you."

She smiles at my revelation. Rebecca slides her hand along the sheet and grabs my calf, raking her fingernails along my bare skin. "What about you?" She studies me with her head tilted.

I pretend to consider it, though I know without thinking when she first appeared on my radar. "Probably." I draw the word out. "Our first flag football game. You were so different, as if you had a whole new personality. Lighter somehow. It was intriguing." I feel heat in my cheeks. There's a slight smile on her lips. The heat moves down my spine.

It's so clear to me now that the thing between us has always been there, hidden from view but there nonetheless. The undercurrents and the denial. A friendship teetering but never being able to fall into formation. This attraction. We have always been on this path, but I've shied away from it because I was attached, afraid and it is not allowed. Yet here we are. Things are the same and they are so different. How will we deal with it when we are back at work?

"You know this has changed everything," I say carefully. What was once a thought is now reality. I am not the slightest bit regretful, but my feelings are a mix of confusion and uncertainty tinged with a hint of fear. The consequences of what we've done, things I should have thought of before, are now rushing toward me. This could be very bad.

Rebecca nods. "I'm well aware of it, Sabine."

I lean over and gently take some of her hair, winding it around my fingers. "What are we going to do? This isn't sustainable. Not back there." I cannot help but let out a sigh.

"I know." She glances away and I see the tautness in the muscles of her jaw.

Before I can help myself I scoff, "So it's longing looks across the OR? Hand brushes in the hallway? Maybe we can sneak a shower together and hope nobody catches us. Otherwise it's waiting until we can try and get on leave together. Or better yet, we can wait four years until I've finished my service obligation and hope they don't care that a Lieutenant Colonel is fucking a reservist! Though by then you'd probably have made Colonel which is even better." The volume of my voice rises with my indignation. It dawns on me that by giving in, I may have made things even harder for myself and also for her. Stupid. You're so stupid, Sabine.

"I'm not sure. I don't have an answer." She is quiet, as though she is trying to keep this from becoming an argument.

An argument after less than twelve hours. Nice start, Sabine. I take a breath, trying to keep my tone level. "I can't risk it, Rebecca, not even for you. I'm contracted to the army. If they find us together then I'll be discharged and I'll have to repay my HPSP debt. I'll have to repay it with a job I won't be able to get because they'll probably court-martial me and then it'll be a Dismissal." The Commissioned Officer's version of a dishonorable discharge. My father would probably cry.

"I think you're being a little dramatic. They're not going to court-martial you, Sabine."

"Really? Aren't we supposed to guard and suppress all dissolute and immoral practices, Rebecca, not indulge in them? And while we're talking about rules, I'm pretty sure what we're doing is also conduct unbecoming an officer." Despite DADT, our relationship could still be cause for disciplinary action because she is my boss, and it would be seen as having the potential to affect the chain of command.

She looks at me, her expression relaxed, but the tension around her eyes makes it clear that it's forced. It's an expression I've seen before. "Calm down, Sabine. You've gone straight to worst-case scenario before anything's even happened." Rebecca takes a deep breath. "Look, I care about you a great deal. I just don't have a solution. Not right now."

I have a sudden and completely irrational feeling that perhaps she is only here to try to help me move on, not out of any actual desire to be with me. I blow rudely through my nose. I know I'm being unfair, but I can't help it. I can tell I've gone too far when Rebecca stares at me, her body rigid with annoyance. "It's my ass too! You don't think I know this isn't allowed, and it could get me severely reprimanded? You don't think I'm not…" She grasps a fistful of air as she searches for the words, "disgusted with myself for being so weak?" She rolls over, swings her legs off the bed and stalks into the bathroom. The door closes softly. I was expecting a slam.

Perhaps my assessment of her motives was incorrect. I rub a hand over my face. This is a clusterfuck of epic proportions. Of course nothing can ever just be simple, there is always a trade-off. The question we will need to ask ourselves is if the trade is worth it?

I toss the covers aside and climb out of bed. "Rebecca?" The morning is cool. I bend over a pile of clothing on the floor, and tug on a pair of sweats and my high school senior year shirt emblazoned with my graduating year along with a list of all my nerdy extracurricular activities. "Bec?" I try experimentally. "I'm sorry."

The toilet flushes, followed by running water and a few moments later the bathroom door opens. She seems a lot calmer, as if moving away has given her room to settle down. "My aunt called me Bec."

I flash an apologetic grin. "Sorry, it just slipped out."

"Don't be. I've always liked it." She is smiling at me. God, those dimples. "Is there enough food in this house for both of us to have breakfast, or do we have to go out?"

"If you're happy with booze and my sister's frozen meal, then we can stay in."

"Pass. Let's go out." She looks me up and down. "Nice shirt. It reminds me of how much older I am than you." She is still smiling as she moves past me and I assume she is going to retrieve her clothing left in the kitchen last night.

I watch her naked form walking away then go to the bathroom myself. I'll need to shower if we're going out. I undress again, turn the shower on and step in, angling the spray downward to wash my face. As I'm rinsing it, the glass shower door opens. I turn and wipe water from my eyes. Rebecca steps into the shower with me. "I'm feeling a little dirty too," she says provocatively, closing the door behind her.

I bite my lip, eyes wandering over her body. "After hearing what comes out of your mouth, I can believe it."

Rebecca shakes her head, moving even closer. "Can you blame me?" She presses me against the wall of the shower. I don't get a chance to respond before her mouth is on mine and she has a hand on my breast. Our tongues find each other again, like old friends. Though we spent all night and most of this morning making love, I still don't feel satisfied. Every time she touches me or looks at me, I feel my stomach curl and the insistent tug between my legs. I groan and pull away. "Bec. If we start this again, we're never going to leave the house."

She exhales and leans her forehead against my shoulder, breathing shallowly. "You're right. I just can't help myself."

When we leave the shower, the bite she left on my hip earlier has turned a lovely shade of purple. She uses my toothbrush and deodorant before twisting her wet hair up and securing it with one of the bands I have left over. I stand behind her, drying myself and catch her smug expression in the mirror.

She turns around, leaning in to kiss me before she exits the bathroom. I towel my hair, watching as she stares at the piles of clothing dotted around my floor. Rebecca bends to pick up the skirt I tossed hastily onto my "no" pile last night. "Please tell me you're not keeping this," she says emphatically.

I snort. "No. I'm not keeping it."

CHAPTER TWENTY-TWO

Rebecca takes a few minutes to retrieve sunglasses from the glove compartment of a dark blue Audi convertible parked in front of my house. The top is up but I can easily picture her driving with it down, her hair loose as she negotiates winding roads. I open the passenger door of my pickup for her, tilting my head toward the Audi. "Great car. It's very…you." Elegant, sophisticated, sexy.

She grins. "My one luxury. A friend keeps it safe while I'm away." She glances at the convertible as we drive away. "It's the second thing I miss while I'm deployed."

"And the first?" I ask, though I'm fairly sure I know the answer. My thoughts are confirmed when her hand glides up my thigh.

Rebecca's hand caresses mine as I drive into town, the touch of her fingertips leaving a warm trail on my skin. The rain starts up again as I park, realizing too late that we have no umbrellas. We rush down the street into a small café. She chooses a booth in the corner where we can watch people through the full-length window.

The young man who shows us to the booth mumbles his introduction and sets menus down on the table. His eyes are red-rimmed and I smell last night's alcohol seeping from his pores. Poor kid. I've forgotten what it's like to work with a hangover. He pours coffee with an unsteady hand. I smile up at him. "May I please have milk? Whole."

His eyebrows knit together for a moment. "Milk?"

Rebecca turns her head away but not before I catch the dimpling of her cheek and her pinching her lower lip. What's so confusing about milk? "Yes please. Milk," I repeat.

"Like, a glass, or…?"

I lift my cup. "For coffee. Instead of creamer."

"Oh." He walks off on his complex mission.

Rebecca settles next to me with her thigh pressed against mine. She reaches for sugar and trickles a spoonful into her black coffee. "You and milk."

"It's how my oma and opa taught me to drink coffee. I've always drunk it that way." Her reference to me and milk makes me realize how closely she's been watching me at work. A gentle swell of pleasure sits behind my sternum.

She tilts her head. "You call them by their German names?"

I nod. "Mhmm." It's not an intimate question but it makes me feel shy and I'm not sure what to say, or if I should elaborate. Rebecca waits, possibly to see if I'm going to say more. When I don't, she opens her menu and studies it. I study her.

Our server returns, setting a small jug in front of me. His lips are set in a thin line, his Adam's apple bobbing at irregular intervals. I catch his nametag. Aaron. I top off my coffee with milk and stir slowly. "Thanks."

Aaron flips open his order pad. "Ready to order, ladies?"

Shit, no I'm not. I open the menu and point at the first thing on the list. That'll do. "Pancakes. Uh, a side of fruit salad too, please. And bacon, please. Thank you."

Aaron scribbles, raising his eyes to Rebecca. "For you?"

She folds the menu and passes it up to him. "French toast, no syrup. Side of bacon and sausage, thank you."

"Sure thing." He shuffles away with the menus tucked under his arm. You can do it, buddy.

Alone again, Rebecca turns back to me. "Tell me more about your grandparents. You speak German with them?"

"*Ja, natürlich.*"

"What's it like?"

I smirk. "Speaking German?"

She pinches my thigh softly. "Your family."

"Loud. Crazy. Wonderful." I swallow the sadness sitting in my throat.

"Tell me about them."

She listens ravenously as I talk, prodding me into detailing what feels insignificant to me but seems like oxygen for her. Aaron returns to set our plates down, refills our coffee and places another small jug of milk in front of me. Bless him. I drag my plate toward me. Good food, I'm going to miss you. I cut and fork up a piece of pancake. "What about you? Parents? Siblings?"

She shakes salt over her plate. "No, I'm an only child."

I swallow my mouthful. "Where do your parents live?"

"They don't."

It takes me a moment. "I'm really sorry."

"Don't be. I was only five. I've got very few memories of them, honestly."

I want to ask what happened, but this dynamic is still so new. "Where did you grow up? Who raised you?"

"My aunt. In a one bedroom in New York." She spears bacon and French toast together.

"New York? I never would have picked that."

"No? You know for a while I wanted to do musical theater. Broadway and all that stuff."

I can't picture it at all. "Why didn't you?"

"Turns out, I can't sing," she says drily.

* * *

Breakfast stretches to lunch. I learn she lives even closer than I do to our home base in D.C., in what she refers to as her *starving artist's studio.* "I'm hardly ever home, and we both know they could move me at any time," Bec rationalizes. "I never saw the point in buying or renting anything bigger than a one-bedroom apartment."

She tells me about college. We swap stories about med school and our differing experiences. Me with Mitch and our scholarships. Her, alone at Johns Hopkins. Our questions back and forth are endless—we saturate one another with details. Her humor, so similar to my own, is on full display and I'm treated to her quick wit.

Rebecca tells me more about the relationship that prompted her to join the army. "She wanted white picket fences and this big American dream. I got scared, thinking eventually she'd maneuver me into being a housewife who gave up her career to bake or something. I didn't want that, so I broke up with her and ran to hide in the army." She laughs. "I admit, it was a little extreme."

I stir my already-stirred coffee, trying to tamp down a rising unease. She doesn't want the thing I want—something stable, someone to build a life with. "Are you still hiding?"

"No." Rebecca reaches across the table and clasps my hand. "After so many years in the service my perspective seems to have changed." She looks up, grinning.

"Anyone you've considered testing this change of perspective with?" I ask, somewhat cheekily.

"I've had my eye on someone." Bec pauses, eyebrows coming together. "Do you think it's too soon, Sabine?" I know what she's referring to. She wonders if she's a rebound. She wants to know if I'm still hung up on my ex. No and no. This thing between us isn't new. It's just never been addressed. Until now.

I choose my words carefully. "No, I don't. Now, I feel like this was always going to happen. We aren't strangers, Rebecca. This is just another layer." Our eyes meet briefly. We do not speak of it again. It seems as though we are coming together as we were always meant to. The timing feels right but more than anything, I need to get back to myself and I want her there when I do.

After we finish lunch, regret creeps into my voice. "I need to leave and get everything organized to go back. I don't want to risk missing my flight and getting into trouble with the boss."

She laughs softly. "I'm quite certain she won't mind."

"If we leave now, then we might have time for a proper goodbye."

She raises both eyebrows and I flag down our server for the check. I peel off a few large bills, leaving them in the folder. Buy some electrolytes and something for that headache, pal. I hold the door of the café open with my foot, shrug my jacket on and pull the collar up against the light rain.

We walk the damp streets back to my truck, ducking under awnings to avoid the rain. As we wait on the sidewalk for a crossing light, she slips her hand into mine, interlacing our fingers. My stomach does a small flip and I tighten my grip. How quickly our relationship has turned into something I never dreamed would actually happen, and that feels so right.

We drive home in silence but it is not a tense one—more contemplative. Her hand finds mine again, her thumb playing over my skin. I pull into the garage and by the time my keys are in hand she is already around at my side. I open the door and the moment she's through it, our bodies meet again. We don't make it out of the laundry room before we are tearing at one another's clothes, kissing furiously and bouncing off doorways and walls on our way through the house.

I know what we are doing. We are gorging ourselves in the hope it will carry us through until whenever it is we might get the chance to be lovers again. I want her so badly that I feel I could spend months exploring her and still not be satiated. This is too slow. I need her right now. I wrap my arms around her waist, hoist her just off the ground and carry her toward the stairs.

Her lips are on my neck, breath hot against my ear when she tells me, "No. Here. Fuck me here." She wriggles free of my hold and pulls me to the floor on top of her. Lust floods through me as I cover her body with mine, and if I'm a little too rough with her, she doesn't complain. Rather, she matches me equally, leaving stinging scratches on my skin and bite marks on my shoulder to fan the fire in my groin.

After such a short time together, she reads me better than any lover I've ever had. She knows my sounds, when to press and when to pull back. She knows what I need. Her mouth is hot against mine as my hand slides down to stroke her and she gasps when I slip back into her familiar warmth. How am I supposed to be without this?

Rebecca hooks her legs around my ass to roll me onto my back, then settles astride me, guiding my fingers back to her slippery depths. I sit up, aching for more contact and pull her closer with my free hand. Our bodies are damp with sweat, breasts pressed together as she grinds against my thumb and I feel the tension in her body, her delicious trembling as her cries hit the note I've been waiting for. She slings her arms over my shoulders and bites my neck, shuddering into her climax.

Her pulse throbs under my lips when I trail kisses over her neck, tasting the salt on her skin. "You are so fucking sexy," I murmur against her. The raw sounds she emitted have driven me almost to the brink myself and I feel like I could come the moment she touches me.

Rebecca waits a short while, collecting herself before she reaches down for my hand and brings it to my mouth, giving me a look of pure, unrestrained lust. I taste her on my fingers and cannot help but let out a low moan. "Don't tease me, I can't stand it." I grab her hips and rock her backward.

She smiles slyly before she reaches down between us to finish me off. I want to say something but as soon as she touches me, every coherent thought departs. Rebecca presses her forehead to mine. "Come for me, Sabine." Fingers glide over my clit, sending me over the edge. The sounds of my climax are silenced by a deep kiss and I have the strangest sensation of carrying her along with me. Our kiss turns sweet, almost chaste and I'm suddenly all too aware that this will be the last time we make love for months. I almost manage to stifle my choked sob, but the end of it sneaks out.

Bec pulls back, blue eyes wide. She cups my face and runs her thumbs over my cheekbones, her eyes softening. "It's okay, it's okay."

I swallow and reach up to take hold of her wrist. "This is so fucking unfair, to give you to me for less than twenty-four hours and then take you away again."

"I know," she says quietly. Rebecca kisses me again then releases me so I can drop back to the cool wooden floor. She slides off my lap, lies beside me and hooks her leg over my trembling one.

I turn my head toward her. "We could always go AWOL together."

"We could," she agrees, tracing her fingertips over my skin. "This is almost worth it." The edge of her mouth is lifted in the beginning of a smile.

"Almost?" I ask with mock indignation.

She laughs, leaning over to kiss me. "How would we pay our bills while we're running from a court-martial, Sabine?"

I grin. "A minor detail." Along with all the other *minor details* in the way.

Rebecca laughs again, kissing my nose before she disentangles herself and gets up to find her clothes. I sigh. This is really it. My post-orgasmic bliss is marred by anxiety. I allow myself a moment of self-indulgent wallowing before rolling over to grab my jeans and panties. I can't find my bra or shirt and I'm certain my jacket is still on the floor of the garage next to my truck. I zip my jeans and glance around trying to spot my missing clothing.

Rebecca returns, buttoning her blouse and holding my bra and shirt under her arm. "I found these on top of your dryer." She holds them out to me. I lift an eyebrow. Evidently she flung them a little farther than she thought. I take my clothes and finish dressing with her eyes on me.

I don't know what I should say to her. Thank you? It doesn't feel as though there are any words to express how I feel. Before I can speak, she closes the gap between us and her arms wrap around my waist. I hug her tightly, feeling that awful fluttering in my chest. I don't want it to be over. Her breath tickles my neck as she speaks. "If you want it to, it'll all work out. We don't need to decide anything right now, Sabine."

I drop my head, burying my nose in her hair and inhaling. I want to remember the scent of her, the way she feels in my arms and how she tucks her nose in against my neck. I need to remember, because I don't know when this will happen again. Rebecca relaxes her grip, standing up on tiptoes to kiss me. "I'll see you when I get back in five days. Have a safe trip." Her mouth stays open as though she wants to say more but she closes it abruptly and takes her hands off me.

I open my front door for her, and watch her walk down the stairs and along my pathway with her head ducked down against the rain. She gives me a little wave from inside her car and the engine starts as I return her goodbye.

I stand by myself in my doorway and watch her drive away. I pack my things and shower, then walk through the house one last time. This is different to my arrival home almost thirteen days ago. There's no more sadness, anxiety or guilt. I feel renewed. Rebecca Keane has made me new again.

CHAPTER TWENTY-THREE

While Jana pumps gas, I go in to pay and buy some gum. A guy, maybe ten years older than me, looks up as I pass and he straightens immediately with his hands down at his sides. It's obvious the guy is a veteran. I smile and give him a small nod. What else can I do? My combat uniform attracts attention. Attention makes me uncomfortable. I never know what to say when someone thanks me for my service, wants to buy my coffee or mentions someone they know who is deployed, and all the while calling me *ma'am*. The encounter makes me feel out of sorts and the back of my neck is tight when I slide back into the car for our drive to the airport.

The waiting area is only half-full of personnel and family, which means at least we can talk without raising our voices. Jana and I settle to wait for my Space-A flight back to Afghanistan, spending the time playing card games and drinking bad coffee. We don't talk about me leaving. We talk about mundane things like her keeping an eye on my house, mail collection, bill paying and turning my car over. We talk about our grandparents and how healthy they both look. We discuss presents for our parents' thirty-sixth wedding anniversary in January and what we both want for Christmas. Then names are being called and we can't put off the inevitable with the inane any longer.

I hate this part more than almost anything. I hate the children crying and screaming and clawing when they realize that a parent is leaving. All around are husbands and wives trying to be brave for their children and spouse. I hate the haunted look in those men's and women's eyes as they try to say goodbye to their family. Those who are new to the process don't do so well but the old hats are good actors and I almost believe them when they say *I'll be fine*. I see parents saying goodbye to their soldier kid and know they are wondering if that kid will come home again.

I stand, brush my jacket off and raise both hands helplessly. "Well, I guess this is it."

My sister bites her lower lip and throws herself at me. I don't bother trying to be brave, it just makes it harder. Jana and I both cry, holding one another tightly, not talking. I can feel eyes on me and I wonder what people are thinking as they look at us in our tight, tearful embrace. But we look so obviously alike that it should be clear she's my sister. I want to speak up and make some self-righteous speech about who cares if we *were* lovers not sisters and fuck the rules. Great thinking, Sabine.

If Bec was seeing me off, I wouldn't be able to kiss her the way the couple to my right are doing. It's not fair. If my lover was here, we'd have to settle for a hug and a polite, "See you when I get back, yes I promise I'll be fine." I've done it before and it's sterile and awful and so unfair.

Jana wipes her eyes. "Call me when you're back on the ground, Sabbie."

All I manage is a choked, "Yep."

I hear my name called again and my sister throws herself into me for another hug. "I love you, Sabs, please be careful."

"I love you too, Jannie. I gotta go. I'll see you in a few months. Mid-November, remember? Back for Thanksgiving." I give her a wobbly smile then disengage from her, rush away and cry quietly until the plane moves out over the ocean. I'm not the only one crying.

The flights back to Afghanistan are long and tedious, my thoughts fluctuating between what I'm leaving behind and what I'm flying toward. I spend a lot of the time trying to find a real solution. How do you solve a problem like Rebecca? I don't know. What am I going to do? How am I supposed to go back to the way we were?

As the journey unfolds, I read, listen to music and struggle to eat with my nerves building. I'm tired, but can't sleep and I can't palm a couple of diazepam because my shift will start a few hours after I get back. I need a clear head. As clear as it can be with everything that's happened.

I'm so afraid. Can I stop my eyes from straying, now that I know what lies under those clothes? Can I stop myself from touching her when I've explored each curve of her breasts with my tongue? When the sound she makes when I run my tongue over her hard nipples is burned into my brain?

I toss and turn on my mat, annoying the people trying to sleep around me. After the sixth exasperated sigh from the guy on my left, someone hisses, "Take a fucking pill." Fine, all right. I dry swallow half a diazepam and try again to be still.

I glance at my watch. It is o-one-twenty-six. I should land at Bagram in about six hours, maybe more depending on how long they hold us in Al Udeid this time. I stretch my legs out as much as I can, reflecting upon how something, no someone, can become so consuming.

What was at the back of my mind is now sitting firmly front and center. Her shift from my boss to my equal came without effort, as though she's been waiting for the right moment to make the change. I've rehashed the memories of her over and over, reliving every touch, look and conversation. I know now in my gut I want her, but the fact there's no real way to make it work makes it worse than ever.

I close my eyes and think of *her*. Thoughts tumble around my head like clothes in a dryer, but none of them manage to stick. I want to talk to Mitch about it, even though it will lead to a heated discussion about my stupidity and the many consequences of our actions. I wouldn't want it to affect his working relationship with Rebecca. He'll be upset about me breaking the rules but no doubt excited otherwise. I hope.

Though he may not have a solution, he will help me calmly work through the problem the same way we have done for each other so many times before. I need him to understand because he's the only person I can talk to.

* * *

We're told to prepare for approach and knots in my gut tighten tenfold. The plane makes a sharp descent, landing short and rough. Welcome to Afghanistan. As soon as we are cleared, I fling off my seat belt, grab my bags and rush out. We are ushered through into a large building where my ID is checked. "Welcome home, Captain."

The heat reflecting off the tarmac is awful, a stark contrast to the cooler weather of the past two weeks. Sweat dampens my armpits and makes my uniform clammy. I board a helo and stare out at the familiar landscapes as we fly forty minutes to make the first drop-off. When we land, the pilot is concerned about some oil pressure issue and instead of being flown back to my doorstep I have to go the rest of the way in a troop carrier. Joy.

The guys have all stopped for a pee break so I leave them and jog in the dry heat toward the group of three armored vehicles that will take us in convoy to our bases. I clamber into the back of the one in the middle, make my way forward and crouch on the floor beside the gunner's feet. "Captain Sabine Fleischer."

The corporal in the driver's seat glances at my name patch and writes something on the paper clipped to the lapboard. I slide into the back corner and fish in my pocket for my iPod and earbuds. The battery is almost dead. Great. I sit with my bags jammed between my ankles. More personnel board, shuffling past me to report in and get settled. I nod but don't speak to them.

I run my tongue around the inside of my mouth to try and conjure up some moisture. Dry mouth nerves. Nerves about

Rebecca. Nerves about seeing her. Nerves about not seeing her. Stupid. I still have four days before she returns, so maybe a solution will be dropped in my lap by then. But probably not.

Being lonely makes you do stupid things and I've done one of the stupidest things of all. I'm a stickler for rules. I like regulation, order and to know where lines are painted. Now I've stepped over them as if they didn't exist. No. We've *both* stepped over them. I don't know if I'm going to stay on that side with her or climb back over to where it is safe. I know what I should do but also know it's not what I want to do. I want to be with her. I want it so badly that my chest has had a dull ache ever since she left me standing on my doorstep. It's interesting how losing something and wanting something gives you the same sort of feeling.

People around me converse, their noise cutting through my music. My stomach growls audibly. The soldier sitting next to me laughs, but before I can respond with something self-deprecating there's movement from the front. I glance up. The driver is doing a quick final head count, marking his list before clipping himself into the harness. I belt myself in and scrunch my eyes closed, hoping I can block the headache building over my left ear. No such luck.

"Nobody's going anywhere until someone sings 'The Wheels on the Bus'." The driver is deadpan. I open my eyes and thumb the screen to stop the music, looking around to make sure I heard him correctly. Everyone looks slightly alarmed, so it appears I did. The gunner snickers.

I peer around the dim interior. There are six passengers and two crew. With the exception of the young corporal at the wheel each set of lips is clamped closed. He seems to be enjoying himself. I wonder how many choruses he wants. I'm not interested in playing chicken with someone over a song, so I take a deep breath and sing the first four lines in clear soprano.

Our driver spins in his seat and begins to conduct me grandly, his graceful hand and arm gestures made funnier by the fact he is in combat uniform with a helmet and vest. I stop singing. There is silence. The driver gives me a slow clap. "Our medical corps, gentlemen. Patching us up and entertaining us as well."

He pulls his shades down and winks at me, clearly approving my rendition.

The gunner is laughing and I grin, despite myself. The rest of the troops clap furiously before they join me for the second chorus. The armored carrier begins to move and we stop singing to cheer as we pull in behind the lead vehicle. I drop my head and start my music again, smirking at the ridiculousness of it.

The drive to the first drop is half an hour or so. I almost doze off, lulled by the constant gentle bump of the wheels over rough, unsealed roads and I force myself to think of anything but her. It doesn't work. Every time I push her from my thoughts it's just like holding a fishing bobber underwater. She always pops right back up again.

I give in and indulge myself a little, recalling the feel of her under my fingers and her scent. How she tasted, the way she left scratches on my shoulders as she begged me to let her come. I feel a little warm and sneakily open my eyes behind my shades to see if anyone is looking at me. No. Good, because I am probably flushed. I close my eyes again and drop all pretense of self-discipline.

The engine growls as we roll down gears and pull into a base for the drop off. I sit up and watch as the others gather their kit bags. We exchange goodbyes. "Have a good one, hope I don't see you again, Doc." It's the usual sentiment. Ha-ha. Yeah, because that would mean you've been shot or something. As if I've never heard that one before. I wave them off and make it the rest of the way to Invicta.

CHAPTER TWENTY-FOUR

Mitch is almost vibrating with excitement when he sees me. "Girl, your hair. Holy shit, it is fuc-kin' gor-geous. You look amazin'. In a sorta quasi-dyke way of course, but amazin' nonetheless." He pulls me up for a hug. "I missed you, lady."

"I've missed you too, Mitchy." I kick my legs back as he lifts me then sets me down again. He picks up my bag and I hand him my laptop bag as well. Two can play the pack mule game, Mitch.

We start back toward the barracks with Mitch swinging my bag back and forth. "How was it? Did ya'll get things finalized?"

"It was good. Busy, but yeah I got a lot of things sorted out." And then I gave myself another problem.

"That's good. Plenty of time with the family?"

"Mhmm, yep."

His eyebrows dip. "Was it bad?"

Mitch's hands are full of my bags so I open the door for him. "No, just tiring. I'm glad I went." We step into the cool building, moving toward my room. "What's been happening?"

"Nothin' much. Bobby twisted his ankle last game. We were one down and couldn't keep up."

I giggle. "I'm sure Bobby's ankle is the reason you lost, Mitch."

He gives me his *Bitch, really?* look. "Oh and Keane left. We had to sub in. Liz is a great nurse but she's fuckin' useless at football. It's like she has hands made of butter."

I feign ignorance. "What do you mean, Keane left?"

"She's on rec leave, due back in a few days."

"Oh. So not gone for good. Who's been watching you kids then?" My question is calm with just the right amount of curious employee in my tone.

"Burnett." Mitch grins and lowers his voice. "But don't you worry, Sabs. She'll be back soon and ready for oglin'."

"You're terrible." No, I'm terrible.

I should drag him somewhere private and tell him about Rebecca, but now I'm scared of what he will say. I am desperate to discuss it and I'm going to have to tell him eventually, so why am I stalling? Maybe by keeping it all to myself, it makes the issue less real.

Mitch has to rush off to rounds. I spend ten minutes unpacking, leave Amy's gifts on her bed then head to the main hospital building where I greet everyone cheerfully. We chat about my leave, my hair and I give them news about what was going on back home.

There's always a wistful quality to people's questions about home. I know I've done the same thing when talking about someone's time away, as though you could absorb some fragment of being there by talking about it. I find Amy scrubbing out of a surgery and the moment I'm in range she grabs me tightly by the arms.

"Sabine." She drags my name out. "My God. You are the absolute best fucking thing I've seen all year." She is shaking me furiously, emphasizing each word with a jolt. I grin as my head jerks around. When she's done pretending I'm a martini, Amy hugs me. "You look fucking amazing. So much better. How're you feeling?"

"Wonderful."

"Ready to get back to it?" Amy releases me and pulls her cap off.

"Absolutely." I itch to get back to work. I need to put my hands on a patient. I need to fix something and most of all, I need a distraction from my jitters.

"Good. You can help me do rounds then maybe I can eat some fucking lunch."

The afternoon sees an influx of casualties and I slide right back into work, filling the days until Rebecca's return. I'm pleased it's busy because I know that if I stop to really think, then despair about our fledgling relationship will creep in. The bite mark on my hip has almost faded, as have the scratches. I hope it's not a metaphor of what we had fading away. Don't be ridiculous, Sabine. Stop trying to make everything have some hidden meaning. It's your skin healing and nothing more.

* * *

Mitch and I manage to work out a few times and he finally fills me in about the guy he met while he was in Qatar. He has received a number of emails from him and they plan to get together again when they are both stateside. I'm so happy for him that I cry and he laughs at me, but I can tell he is touched. He lacks friends outside of our immediate circle here and even if nothing romantic comes of it, this will be such a boon for him.

"What's his name again?" I ask.

"Mike," he says proudly.

I snort. "Mitch and Mike. It sounds like a really shitty sitcom."

He flicks me.

I almost tell him my secret a number of times, but something always makes me swallow the words. Perhaps I don't want to step on his new friendship, or maybe I'm afraid to verbalize and admit how important this thing with Rebecca is to me. How important she is to me. She gave me back the lost piece of myself and I'm frightened if I open my mouth to let him know, it will somehow be taken from me again. Such a stupid, irrational thought.

The night before Rebecca is due back, I sleep surprisingly well. I have already decided not to go meet her transport when it comes in because under ordinary circumstances I wouldn't, and I have to pretend everything is still ordinary. Another small group of patients comes through early in the morning and I spend the day trying to save the life of a soldier injured by an IED blast.

Both John and Amy are with me, three sets of hands jostling for space and hurriedly controlling the hemorrhage. We leave him in the best shape we can, but he will need to go under again tomorrow or the following day for another round of surgeries before he can be moved on. Amy signs his chart. "I am fucking starving," she grumbles, handing it off to me.

Her blunt declaration makes me smile. I glance at the time. It's nearly half-past one and we still haven't eaten a real meal today. There has been no sign of Rebecca. Keane. Colonel Keane. Get it into your head, Sabine. "I'll come with you." I flip through the pages, sign my name and stretch out to pass the chart over to John.

"Sold." Amy pops a gun finger at me. "So long as you find me an orange." She barges out of the theater with me in tow.

I know Keane is back. I catch sight of her walking past the doorway while I'm typing reports but she keeps going, looking straight ahead. She's had a few days, maybe she regrets it. Maybe she has changed her mind. I feel as though I'm in an elevator with a broken cable, the floor falling out from underneath me. I try to dispel my doubt. Her words and actions were clear. It's your insecurity, Sabine. Stop thinking about it.

We don't speak until later in the afternoon. She joins me outside where I'm running solo laps, trying to work off nervous energy. I stop, come to attention and wait for her to approach me. "Colonel Keane." I put just the right amount of respect into my greeting and congratulate myself for keeping my eyes on her face. You can do this! You are strong, capable and you just looked at her tits. You suck, Sabine.

"Captain Fleischer, good afternoon. May I join you?" Rebecca smiles as she asks the question, knowing I could never decline.

"Of course, ma'am, but I'm afraid I was just going to start a cooldown lap."

"That's fine, Sabine. Honestly, I'm a little jet-lagged," she admits in a tired voice. She begins to walk and I fall in beside her, careful to keep distance between us. I glance sideways. The corner of her mouth is lifted and I see her cheek dimple. She finally turns her head, flashing a cheeky grin. "How was your leave, Captain? Did you manage to resolve anything?"

My heart stutters and I respond with a broad smile. "Yes ma'am, as a matter of fact I did." I keep eye contact and raise an eyebrow. "May I inquire about yours? I heard you took a break. Did you enjoy your time away?"

"Indeed, thank you. It was very relaxing and also quite informative."

We laugh at our private joke and some of my anxiety settles. At the far corner of the track away from the buildings, Rebecca turns to me without breaking stride. "I missed you, Sabine," she murmurs.

I pause, aware of the lump in my throat. "I've missed you too."

We exchange a tender look and instantly I know all my doubts and fears are baseless. There's so much I want to say but before I can open my mouth, she tells me regretfully, "I do have to get in. I've got a meeting with Burnett but I just needed to see you. In case I don't talk to you during work tomorrow, I'll meet you here at the same time and we'll talk."

"Yes ma'am."

"As you were, Captain." She winks at me then peels off, leaving me alone. She walks across the dirt and into the building. My eyes are on her ass the entire time.

* * *

The days blend together as we reconnect. We run every afternoon, discussing everything from surgery to books and movies. She asks about my family and I oblige with details of Jana's latest dating disasters. All the things we ran out of time for in the short time back home are now laid out bare. The more we expose ourselves to each other, the more I find myself falling in love with her. We haven't said it yet. I'm afraid to. Afraid to admit it when we are still so fragile.

We keep at least a foot between us at all times but when we stop running each afternoon and I see her, sweaty and panting, I think of the way she looked each time we made love and I'm desperate to touch her. My body aches with my desire to hold her, to make her scream my name again. Judging by her pained expression as she watches me watching her, it would seem she feels similarly.

Each run ends with us no closer to a resolution than when we began and I have to take myself to the showers to relive her touch over and over again. We do not touch at all, not even when I am called into her office and the door is closed.

"You drawin' pictures on your reports?" Mitch asks me at breakfast.

I look up from my plate. "What do you mean?"

"All them meetin's with Keane. You gotta be doing something wrong, Sabs."

Shit, shit, shit. I take a bite of toast, trying to think of a lie. "Oh. No, uh…I saw a thing about those trials they did earlier this year. You know, the different clotting preps? Thought she'd be interested."

He looks at me like I've suddenly sprouted a second set of ears. "Since when were you interested in clinical trials?" The incoming alert saves me from having to say anything further.

If Keane and I operate together she is cordial, almost standoffish. I recognize the way her fingers always twitch to rub thumb and forefinger together whenever she is cold toward me. It's the same thing they did in the dusky light when we spoke on the bench. I catch her looking at me during group meetings and across the lounge.

Despite our physical distance I've never felt closer to her, yet we still have no solution. We contemplate a number of options—like asking for a unit transfer for one of us, sneaking around and risking getting caught, being discharged, waiting my service obligation out and being miserable under DADT, and everything in between.

I drift to sleep trying to think of ways I can fix this and I wake up empty. The whispers about changes to Don't Ask, Don't Tell are becoming louder but Rebecca and I agree that even if it comes into effect before I leave service it will do us no good. She will always be my superior. Unless I ask for that transfer. And then we will be apart.

We even discuss my idea that I would extend my contract—the very same thing I fought about with Vic. But there's still no certainty there, either of us could be moved at any time. Even if we aren't, both of us staying in the military means we will have to deny our feelings and that is a miserable idea. Everything goes around and around in circles. There is no easy or good solution. I know I'm being selfish and childish, wanting everything to work out without any of the hard or annoying things in the way. It's just so hard not having a game plan, or one that makes any sense.

Rebecca listens as I work through my thoughts out loud but doesn't push me one way or the other. Put simply it comes down to deciding what's worse—a year apart every deployment, working in different locations, or working together knowing we're breaking the rules and trying to act like we're not lovers.

I force myself to be upbeat. "Maybe I should just stand on the table at breakfast and shout 'I'm gay!' Problem solved."

She laughs. "I'm sure that will end well." Then she hints at a possible solution. "You know, I could leave the army. My obligation is long over."

I stumble, almost tripping. "Really?"

In the end, both of us agree that's not a good solution right now. Despite our feelings, everything is too new, too unsure. We agree I need to fulfill my contractual requirements to clear my college debts and we can start properly when I am out. Perhaps she will also retire then.

Rebecca lets out a helpless groan. "I just cannot think of a way around it. Not one which won't risk our jobs and reputations, or disappoint your family."

"I know," I whisper.

When we get home in a few months, we'll talk more in a neutral place away from the thing that's causing the issue. Maybe it'll bring some clarity. I've made it clear that for me, leaving things the way they are feels like the better of a bunch of bad options. I don't think I could stand being transferred away from her. But then the thought of at least four more years pretending there is nothing between us fills me with distress so deep that I wonder if I can do it.

Rebecca meets me just before sunset one afternoon, inside the running track where I am stretching. I jump to my feet. "Come to help me with my hamstrings, Colonel?"

She smiles wistfully at me. "If only. Are you ready to go?"

"Always." I pull my cap on to keep my bangs off my face.

We run silently for almost four laps before she speaks. She is distraught. "I wish I could make this work. I'm so sorry, I've tried. We've both tried. I've barely thought of anything else, Sabine."

I swallow, trying to think of something to say. I can't. I look at the ground as I run.

Rebecca's voice cracks a little. "I hate it," she spits out. "I hate not touching you and pretending I'm annoyed with you, because if I don't do it this way, then I'm scared I might slip up. Every night I go to bed thinking about you, Sabine. The way you taste and feel. Every look and every touch. It's driving me fucking crazy."

She slows and I stop jogging to walk beside her. My chest feels tight and it has nothing to do with running. I rub my palm over my sternum. "Do you want to forget it all together?" My voice is soft. I can't look at her because I'm too afraid if I do then she might say yes, it's all too hard and she wants to throw it away. My heart beats sluggishly.

"No," Rebecca says immediately.

I let out a breath. "Me either."

"I just want it to be different. The way we know it can be. The way it will be." She looks sideways at me and I catch her eye. It's getting dark. We begin to walk off the track toward the barracks. "It can be, Sabine, but we just have to wait and try to find some way to make it through together."

She is right. The only way is to wait. Can I do it? Every moment without her, I feel as though something dims within, like a few of my cells dying off. Not such a big deal now, but if I lose enough will I lose myself all over again?

As we stroll I stare at the ground. There it is. We've made a choice. We wait years, hiding under DADT and army expectations, and hope we can make it. My family and our careers are facing off with our life together. What is more important? There is such an awful taste in my mouth. This is a fucking horrible decision to make, and a horrible situation to be shoved into because of *policy*. I swipe my palms over my eyes. I feel completely defeated.

CHAPTER TWENTY-FIVE

I rise before dawn after a restless night, waking constantly to think about Rebecca. Knowing she is in bed so close to me but untouchable is torture. Today I'll go to Fermo, a nearby camp, and spend the day stabbing the arms of soldiers with their yearly influenza booster. It's easier for one of us to spend a day there, than for them to transport troops back and forth to the hospital. A nurse usually administers vaccines, but I asked Rebecca to let me go this time. I need to think about something other than our relationship, and I imagine a day with a little bit of distance will help.

I leave without saying goodbye to anyone. The halls are quiet. Everyone is most likely asleep after our late surgeries last night. When I pass Rebecca's door, I almost knock but I don't know what I would say should she open it. I hoist medkit and cooler bags up onto my shoulder and walk outside into the surprisingly crisp September morning air.

Our room was too dark to see when I left and I didn't want to wake Amy by turning on the light. I give myself a look over, check my rifle and sling it back behind me. It bumps against my ass and I keep wanting to turn to see what's touching me. We always carry our pistols, but our rifle is required as well when we're moving outside the wire. I tug my pistol from its holster, double-check the safety then reholster it. Everything is in order. Not a bad effort for a night op.

A single vehicle arrives at o-five thirty as the sun begins to show in the gaps between the mountains. Apparently the quick errand of running me back and forth to the base doesn't need a second escort vehicle. While the Humvee pulls around, I stare at those beautiful mountains, watching the arresting beauty of the sunrise. The sky is cast in pink and orange, settling a strange glow over the dusty ground and reflecting back at me through the valley.

The ranges seem endless, as though someone spent a lifetime with a carving tool making perfect gullies and ridges in the red and brown rock. At the start of my deployment the ranges were snow-capped, their beauty increased by a hundredfold. They are bare now and I probably won't see the snow again before I leave. No matter what we are doing or who lives at Invicta, the seasons continue to cycle and every one of them is gorgeous.

As I approach the Humvee, the rear doors fling open and the gunner leaps from the back. "Good morning, Captain." He snaps a sharp salute.

I return his salute, glancing at his insignia patch. "Good morning, Specialist. Thank you for the ride."

He nods. "Our pleasure, ma'am. Might I ask instead of fare payment, you go easy on both of us with the needle?" He is beaming, clearly in high spirits despite the hour.

I lean in, trying to make out his name patch. "I forgot my wallet so I suppose that's an acceptable trade, Richards."

He laughs, seemingly pleased I am playing along. "Thank you, ma'am. I sure would appreciate it." Richards takes all three bags from me and places them in the back under the bench seat so they don't slide around. He offers a hand to help me climb up into the back of the vehicle. "Should only be twenty minutes, Captain," Richards says cheerfully as I settle on one of the seats and belt myself in. He pulls the rear doors closed. "We're set, Elliot."

The driver shifts into gear. "Copy that."

Richards slides up next to the turret and stands slowly, wiggling to get through the gap in the top. I settle under the hunched, turtle-like roof and lean back, listening to them talking and butchering songs as we drive.

When we pull in, Richards squirms down from the turret and opens the doors. Before I can pick up my bags, he grabs the handles and carries them into the main building. I've been allocated space in the large mission briefing room, and there's a desk and a fresh pot of coffee waiting, along with some pastries. Thank you, soldiers, for your hospitality. A small refrigerator for the vaccinations is attached to what seems like a mile of extension leads.

"You know where the latrines are, Captain?" Richards asks politely.

"Yes I do, thank you."

"I'll see you when it's my turn, ma'am. You remember our deal?" he asks me, eyes wide.

I grab the least stale looking doughnut and smile at him. "I do indeed, Specialist."

He salutes and walks away, whistling to himself. I shrug out of my ballistic vest and set it and my helmet on a spare chair then glance at my watch. Seventeen minutes until we are due to start. I take a bite of doughnut and unzip my bags.

The soldiers will come in alphabetically with their sleeve rolled up and ready for their shot. Whoever is allocated to assist me will take the code from the vaccine and stick it into their medical file. Barring any issues, each member should take ninety seconds to receive their vaccination from the moment they walk through the door.

It's all about coordination and as long as they keep moving through I will be done at about sixteen hundred, factoring in a few bathroom breaks and half an hour to eat lunch. The sound of soldiers massing outside grows louder. Hurry Sabine. I shove more doughnut in my mouth and unpack boxes of vaccinations from their cooler bags and stack them into the refrigerator.

A young soldier rushes into the room pushing a large trolley stacked with medical files. She stops a few feet in front of me, saluting enthusiastically. What is it with these kids? They are all so damned chipper.

"Good morning, Captain Fleischer! I'm Private Jeffries, your assistant for today," she informs me loudly. This one has some extra zeal.

I cannot help but smile as I return her salute. "Good morning, Jeffries. As you were." I unzip my last bag and pull out gloves and alcohol swabs. "Do you know what you have to do?" I ask, lining up the boxes.

Her nod is repetitive and vigorous. "Yes ma'am, I've been briefed."

"Okay then, why don't you get set up? It seems everyone is beginning to come in." I wonder if I'll become annoyed by her fervor.

As she stacks the files, I give her a quick rundown of what I'll do and what I expect from her. Jeffries assures me she is capable and confident in her ability. I have to press my lips together to stop myself from laughing. I know girls like her. My first year in the army, when everything was fresh, I *was* her.

The first troops are five feet away, the rest waiting in a long snaking line out of the building. It's amusing to listen to them fret and to watch large muscular men sweat and go pale at the thought of getting a tiny needle. I stuff a piece of gum in my mouth and pull on a pair of disposable gloves.

The first soldier approaches and I smile at him, to help put him at ease. His voice is barely audible and his hands are shaking as he pulls his left sleeve up a little higher. "Abbot, Patrick."

I peel the barcode from the syringe and pass it to Jeffries. When I turn back to the soldier, his face has drained of color. Oh come on, kid, it's just a little needle. "Are you okay, Private?" I place the syringe on the table, opting to leave the cap on the needle for now.

"Yes ma'am." He nods, wavers for a moment and crashes into the man standing behind him. A few of the troops grab at him and manage to stop him from hitting the ground too heavily. The sound of laughter is cut short by a barked order from the side of the room.

I kneel to check on poor Abbot. Yep, he's unconscious but he didn't hit his head so he should be fine. I check his pulse and wait for him to come to. When his eyes flutter, I reach up and grab the vaccine corresponding to the code which is now in his file. "Can you hold him there for a moment please, gentlemen?" It takes me less than ten seconds to rub a swab over his arm and stick him with the needle. There. Done. I stand up and toss the spent vaccine in the sharps bin. I wish I had a smiley sticker to put on the front of his uniform, proclaiming *You Tried!*

I point to a spot on the floor. "Just put him down over there on his side, where I can keep an eye on him, please." They manhandle Abbot ten feet away and lie him down. He groans. Poor baby. I give the assembled soldiers a wide grin. "Right! Next!"

* * *

Everything else goes fairly smoothly. I have twenty-seven fainters in a group of three hundred and eighteen soldiers. Not bad. I'm surprised at Jeffries's efficiency. When it was time for "Jeffries, Lauren" she barely broke stride, leaning over to offer her arm while simultaneously putting the sticker in her own file.

When the last arm has been stuck, Jeffries helps me pack my things and seals the sharps bins ready for disposal. She says goodbye as brightly as she said good morning, then gives me a salute before she pushes the cart of files across the room with her back straight and head high.

"Jeffries?" I call after her.

She stops near the doorway, pivots and stands to attention. "Captain Fleischer."

"Thank you for your assistance, you were invaluable. I've enjoyed working with you."

She bites her lower lip, but it doesn't hide her smile. "You're welcome, Captain."

I put my helmet and vest on again and carry my own bags out to the transport home. Richards and Elliot, my crew from this morning both step from the Humvee and greet me with a salute, which I return. "Specialist, Corporal. How are your arms?"

Elliot's frown is exaggerated as he rubs his left arm. Richards leans to the side as though the arm I stuck him in suddenly weighs a hundred pounds. "Not sure I can hold my rifle, Captain," he jokes.

I grin. "I'm sure you'll manage." I lift the now considerably lighter bags up into the back of the vehicle. Richards reaches down to pull them all the way inside for me. I grasp his hand and climb in to settle on the bench seat, wedged into the rear right-hand corner of the cramped cabin. I fasten my seat belt just before Elliot drops the clutch and bunny-hops forward. The laughter tells me it's intentional. Jokers, all of them. Facing the middle of the vehicle, there's nothing to hold on to and I'm jolted to my right. Perfect.

"Another twenty-minute trip, traffic pending, Captain," Elliot calls back to me, looking in his rearview mirror. He laughs to himself. *Of course* there is no traffic. He's still snickering as he drives away from the base. Everyone's a comedian.

Well, here it is. I've just completed one whole day without worrying about Rebecca. How many do I have left? I refuse to do the math. My body armor is digging in under my armpits. I tug at it. Vests never sit right on women and the official word on a female-friendly version is *Soon*. A typical response which means *Maybe we'll start thinking about it in a few years.*

I loosen the straps around my torso a little so I can breathe without being jabbed by armor plates. It's so fucking hot in here. I'm tired. I lean forward and pull my rifle sling over my head, leaving the weapon sitting across my knees. We haven't driven ten minutes when the radio buzzes with static and a calm voice cuts through the silence. "Transport Blue, do you copy? Over."

Elliot snatches the radio up. "Transport Blue. Over."

"Looks like you have hajji en route. Three units. Over."

He pauses. "Roger that. Over."

"What's your ETA? Over."

I sneak a peek at my watch. It is sixteen thirty-nine.

"Eight mikes. At least. Over." Elliot's voice is now pitched slightly higher. Eight minutes.

"Make it sooner, or you're going to be TIC. We've got a couple of Humvees coming out behind you. ETA intercept with you in six. Over."

"Copy that. Over out." Elliot hooks the radio mouthpiece back into its cradle. "*Now* they can spare a couple of teams for escort. Typical," he mutters.

TIC. Troops in combat. My skin suddenly feels too small for my body, tight, as if it's being stretched somehow. Adrenaline floods through me and I feel sweat dampening my armpits. It's probably nothing, right?

"Ass pucker factor, Spec?" Elliot is looking back in the rearview mirror again. I pull a small first aid kit from one of my large bags and shove it in a pants pocket. I want it with me, not out of reach if things get hot.

Richards drops back down into the Humvee and blows through pursed lips. "Five out of ten. It's probably nothing. We're single vee, not a convoy. Not fuckin' worth their time." Still, I catch him absently patting his chest. He is checking his tags. He tilts his head to study the ammo stack for the fifty caliber gun in the turret then turns around and glances down at me. "You dressed, Captain?"

"Yes." My hands are trembling as I check the chinstrap on my helmet. My hands never tremble.

Richards climbs back up through the hole to the turret gun and calls down to me, "How about you get your rifle ready, just in case we ne—"

CHAPTER TWENTY-SIX

Time lengthens, pushing everything past me at half speed. The first thing I register is a sudden increase in heat. I am so hot. It washes over my body as though I'm being tumbled through a wave of boiling water. There's a complete lack of noise and a swelling pressure in my ears.

Then an explosion bursts through the cabin and my upper body is thrown backward, my shoulder and head cracking against the frame of the vehicle. I cry out as the belt bites at my waist. My eyes are jammed tightly closed and I flail wildly, trying to find something to grab to stop myself from tumbling. It's no use. The vehicle is moving underneath me. I am strapped in and being taken along.

The last thing I register is pain as time contracts again. We stop rolling and settle, creaking, in the dirt. I'm lying on my back, still belted to the seat. The vehicle has tipped over onto its right side. I can't hear anything through the intense ringing in my ears, but I feel the remnants of the explosion in my chest. It vibrates, low and resonant. I open and close my mouth, trying to clear my ears but it does nothing. The cabin is filled with smoke and dust and I wave my hand in front of my face, as if I could clear it away.

Am I alive? You're thinking, Sabine and also breathing, so I would say yes. Yes, you're alive. Step one of checklist complete. I try to pull my sunglasses off but they catch under my helmet. I tug harder and manage to unsnag and toss them aside. Acrid smoke stings my eyes and they begin to tear up.

"Corporal? Specialist?"

No answer.

The metallic tang of blood fills my mouth. My tongue sweeps around my mouth and stings whenever it touches something. I must have bitten it. I swallow my bloody saliva and begin to check myself, fearful of what I might find. There's pain in my right leg, near my knee. My stomach tightens. No, please. Please let it still be there.

There's a sharp pain low in my torso when I lean forward against the seat belt. Raw fear rushes through me as I reach to gingerly touch my leg and I let out a shaky breath. My leg is still there but there's something embedded in the side of it just below the strap of my holster. The feel and scent of blood is as familiar to me as my own face.

I do a quick extremity check. Things are moving which should be movable. Good. That's good. I'm okay, but I'm certain I'm covered in cuts and abrasions. My breathing is quick and shallow. Panic breaths. I try to slow my respirations down. We just got blown up. *Someone blew us up.* I reach up to touch my head, making contact with the hard surface of my helmet. Of course.

There's pain from where my head made contact with the side of the vehicle and my face feels like a horse kicked me. I probe my temple and cheek carefully. It's just a small laceration. My hand comes away bloody. Both my hands now have my blood on them. I notice the unmistakable scent of viscera. My throat constricts. I slide my hands under my vest and pat my torso. There's pain, I assumed from the belt snatching at me, so I didn't physically check there. There are no wounds. The smell is not my viscera.

I try again. "Corporal? Specialist?" My voice is croaky and I cough, trying to clear the acrid explosive residue sticking in my throat. There is no answer from either of them. The air inside the cabin is still smoky so I can't see much. After a few moments, the ringing in my ears clears enough for me to catch the unmistakable sound of a bullet pinging against metal. Instinctively, I duck my head. Oh shit. Please, no.

Another bullet hits the metal to the right of me then ricochets away. I flinch, like a rabbit zigging away from a fox and cough again to try and clear my airways. Oh fuck. The smoke has dispersed enough for me to see some of the interior. It fades into view, like movie credits. Light streams through the hole in the left side of the vehicle, which is now the roof, allowing me to see that something has cut a diagonal path through the cabin.

The hole starts just behind where the driver sits and exits a few feet to my right. How did that happen? The floor is intact so can't be IED? RPG? No...not powerful enough. It must have been a HEAT. High explosive anti-tank device. How'd they get that? Why did we flip? Did Elliot swerve? It doesn't matter, Sabine. Stop thinking about unimportant shit. Dirt has spilled through the gap in the side of the vehicle just beside me.

If I was sitting two feet to my right.

If I had leaned forward to speak to the driver.

If he was traveling just a little faster.

I shut my brain down before it can start up any more what-if scenarios. A low moan catches my attention from the front of the vehicle. "Elliot? Richards?" I rasp out. Elliot's soft, slurred murmur is the only answer I get.

"I'm coming." The belt buckle sticks and I have to wrestle with it before it gives and releases me. I start to crawl along the side of the vehicle, letting out a sharp gasp as I move my leg. The pain radiates from my right knee up into my hip, sharp and electric and I have to pause to catch my breath. I'm on my hands and knees, trying to calm myself when I notice a large pool of blood in front of me.

Blood. Blood is comprised of erythrocytes, leukocytes and thrombocytes. The average-sized male has a blood volume of roughly five and a half liters. A person can lose around fifteen percent of their blood before things get tricky. What is fifteen percent of five and a half liters? This is more than fifteen percent. How many liters do you think it is, Sabine?

Stop it.

Richards was in a direct line of the explosive device. The lower half of his body is against the side of the vehicle, which is now technically the floor. The rocket has cut through him high up on his torso, leaving the bottom part of his body dangling by nothing more than a small amount of muscle and skin. His spine is not…it's not…it's not there. It's not there.

We were just joking. He's so polite. This morning he did a one-man rendition of "The Bohemian Rhapsody," complete with falsetto and the beat drummed on the top of the Humvee with his hands. His eyes are a really beautiful caramel brown and he snorts when he laughs.

The top half of his body has been twisted around and is now wedged in the turret so I cannot see his pretty eyes, or reach his neck. Organs hang in slippery, bloodied clumps still attached by tissue. Blood drips, joining the pile on the floor. I choke on saliva at the back of my mouth. Do not get sick. You will not get sick. I forbid it. This is your job.

More saliva wells in my mouth as the bile rises up my throat, despite my command. I have to turn my head so I do not vomit on the remains of Richards. You're not weak, Sabine, and it's okay. You're okay. I try to spit the taste from my mouth. The only reason you just puked is because of shock. You're not weak.

Evisceration. Exsanguination. Emesis.

I reach up to touch him. This isn't survivable. If he isn't already dead it will not be long. When I press the tips of my forefingers to his wrist, they leave smears of my blood on his still-warm skin. I wait with my eyes closed, trying to drown out the sound of bullets as I feel for a pulse. Each time a round makes contact with the vehicle, I flinch. I reposition my fingers to check again. One site will have to do, because I can't reach up to confirm or deny he has other vitals. I wait another fifteen seconds, counting them off in my head.

One-one-thousand.

Two-one-thousand...

He's gone. I make no judgments about his luck or lack of it. I look at my watch—sixteen forty-one. I speak, but to nobody. "Time of death sixteen forty-one." I peer around the interior, trying to find my rifle. I dropped it. I need my rifle.

Even if I were to move Richards...the remains of him, the turret-mounted gun is pointed in the wrong direction anyway. I realize that I actually never trained how to use or load a fifty so this whole fucking thing is just more wasted thoughts. I look again for my rifle and spot it a few feet away, jammed against the underside of the seats.

There's not enough room to stand in here so I drop to my belly and stretch for it, snagging the edge of the stock with my fingertips. I flick my fingers to bring it closer and manage to get a grip on the stock as a bullet hits the side of the vehicle. I snatch my hand away, but I have the rifle and I lift a middle finger toward the side where the round pinged. Fuck you. Fuck. You.

From the driver's seat there's movement and a slightly more coherent string of words than Elliot's last attempt. My pulse drops by a few beats per minute. "Corporal! You okay?"

His response is a mumbled, "Yeah."

"I'm coming. Just...wait." My skin tingles with adrenaline. I jam myself against the bench seat and eject the magazine. Full, just like it was this morning. I reinsert it and make sure the weapon is still on safe. Then, I begin to crawl backward toward the front of the vehicle, dragging my right leg. There's blood all over the interior and as I move through it coats my uniform, seeping through to dampen my knees. I glance at my watch—sixteen forty-two.

The cut on my tongue has stopped bleeding. See? It's not all bad, Sabine. With the rifle clutched firmly in my hand I keep scrambling backward past Richards's dismembered body. Bullets ping over the sound of air hissing from a punctured tire, but their echo inside the armored car makes it hard for me to decipher their originating direction. Left. Right. Behind?

I flatten as best as I can and move up to the space beside Elliot then drop back to sit, wedged against the dash and the gearstick. Now I'm in a safer place, I can get a better look at my leg. The bleeding around the embedded metal is not excessive.

Elliot's head lolls and his eyes find mine. "Captain?"

"I'm here. Can you hold a weapon?" I'm racing frantically through memories of my training but my mind goes blank when I try to grasp details.

"Affirm," he responds. His voice is still soft, but his words are becoming clearer. "I can move both my legs but my left hurts. It's stuck in something. Richards?"

The only answer I can give to that is a headshake."Stay as still as you can. I've got you...I just need a moment." I glance at my watch again, tilting the luminous face to cut the glare—sixteen forty-three. Time is lying to me. It feels like an hour has passed. The other units will be here in a few minutes, once they have cleared the area. I dip into my pocket and pull the first aid kit out to stanch the bleeding from my leg. I am desperate for water, but I can't see any.

I take out a pressure dressing and a bandage. Snipping at the dressing with shitty blunt-nose first aid scissors, I make a hole and carefully ease it over the inch of metal protruding from my thigh. Then I wrap the bandage around my leg and either side of the shrapnel. The pain is excruciating. It will have to do. I am cold and sweaty, and hope I don't pass out.

I peer up and out of the gap in the vehicle armor right behind where Elliot is still buckled in. The harness holds him at a strange angle with gravity pulling him downward and to the right. He's squirming, trying to get free.

I can't reach to unclip his rifle from the sling without exposing myself. I tug the pistol from his holster, eject and check the magazine then ensure the weapon is safe before passing it to him. He grips it tightly, knuckles white.

I reach down for my own pistol, struggling to extract it without touching the chunk of metal in my leg. It takes me a moment, shock making it hard to coordinate. I drop the magazine out, check then reinsert it. It takes me a few attempts to cock the pistol. I set the safety again.

When did I last clean my weapons? What if they jam? I force myself to take a breath. You cleaned them two days ago, after you went to the range with Mitch. They've never jammed and they aren't going to, Sabine. My hand tingles with a compulsion to check my pistol again. Don't. You just checked it, it's fine. I know what to do. At the range I'd hit a target ninety-nine times out of hundred. But here, I can't see anything to aim at.

My nose is running. I sniff, swiping my wrist over my face. "Can you call out?"

Elliot shakes his head. "Radio's busted."

I glance at it, and yes, it's been hit by a bullet or shrapnel. It's now a useless scrap of plastic and electronic pieces. My senses zero in on everything around me. Steam hissing from the engine. The smell of diesel is both sharp and earthy. The indicator seems to be stuck in a signaling position.

Click. Click. Click.

I won't think of spilled fuel and sparks from bullets hitting metal. I cannot. Distant shouting rises above all the other sounds. Foreign voices. Fuck, fuck, fuck, FUCK!

At intervals, a random cluster of bullets hits the Humvee. They must be shooting full-auto. Why are they wasting ammo? Shut up, Sabine. I try to condense myself even further into the space beside Elliott. "Do you have another radio, Corporal?" My heart is beating so hard I feel it knocking against my ribs and my breaths are now coming in ragged gasps. Stop panicking. Every attempt to control my breathing is met with resistance. I said stop panicking, Sabine.

Elliot shakes his head. I reach out and grab his wrist to check his pulse. Very fast and still strong, hopefully there is no major bleeding. I check him as best I can while trying to keep lines of cover on myself. I am ducking down underneath the dashboard and trying to jam myself out of sight of the hole above me. I can't see anything except sky, so there is no point in returning fire from where I am, and I'm sure as shit not going to pop my head out of the hole to get a visual.

"Don't move, sweetheart." Proper address protocol be damned. Human first, doctor second, army third. "I need you to be as still as possible. You might have spinal damage," I command. "Tell me where you have pain."

"Back. Left side near my ribs," he gasps. "Left leg. I think I blacked out." He looks like a young boy, so afraid. I suddenly feel very old. He is still wearing his helmet but his shades have been knocked off.

I lean forward to check his pupils and am stunned by the color of his eyes. Clear gray encloses understandably-dilated pupils. I exhale, surprised. They look odd, no…beautiful, set in his blood-flecked face. I lean closer to him and lift my right hand so I can ask him to track my finger.

A sharp punch on my right side forces the air from my lungs and I'm thrown back onto the floor, gasping. My legs jolt spastically.

Is that…did they?

Have I just been shot?

Yes. I've been shot.

My legs squirm in a strange, irregular rhythm and all I can think about is how being shot feels a lot different to what I'd expected. I think about being shot a lot, which is probably natural when your job deals with the aftermath of such things. I'd always imagined it as a sharp tearing or cutting sensation.

This feels like a burning sort of pressure, like someone hit me with a flaming brick. It's very uncomfortable but not totally unbearable. Yet. It's not unbearable *yet*, Sabine. Thank you, flight-or-fight. For some strange reason, the trembling in my hands has stopped and a strange sense of calm has settled over me.

Elliot tries to twist toward me. "Captain Fleischer!"

I cannot make my limbs work to signal that he shouldn't be trying to move. "I'm hit, but…I think I'm…okay," I blurt.

My words are more to stop him from moving than anything else. I'm sprawled on the floor, propped up against the edge of the dash. It's digging into my lower back and pushing my vest up. Hajji must have moved along the ridge to get in front of us. It's lucky the bullet didn't catch Elliot in the face, instead of just me in the torso. My spine is tight with fear, waiting for the next round to come through the broken windshield.

I shuffle to my left to get away from the opening and try not to be seen moving. Cautiously, I crane my neck to try and see the wound. There's a spread of blood over the side of my jacket along my ribs. The bullet seems to have come through at a shallow angle under my right armpit. I'm certain my right lung is compromised. Fucking hell, right through the damned gap in the vest. There's sharp pain in my back, I'm guessing from an exit wound. I can move my legs so it must not have hit my spine but it probably hit the rear armor plate of my vest after it exited. Maybe it bounced back. Can bullets do that?

I try to relax and concentrate on breathing regularly. Each breath is short and painful. Combined with increasing shock, this could fuck me over. I stare at my watch and check my heart rate. Racing. One hundred and thirty-six. Tachycardic. Not surprising.

I unfasten the right side of my vest and reach over cautiously with my left hand to check for an exit wound. Be careful, Sabine. The movement brings a sharp tear in my ribs, forcing an exhalation through my lips. Everything slides sideways for a moment and I'm aware of the moment just before I lose consciousness.

I come to with no idea of how long I was out. When my vision clears into blurry focus, I'm staring at dirty fabric, my forehead resting against the passenger seat. Elliot is swatting awkwardly at me but can't reach me. I groan, still tasting blood but it could be from where I bit my tongue in the initial accident. Or it could be from my lung. Probably my lung. I push myself back up to lean against the dash.

"I returned fire," he mutters. "Seems to have shut 'em up for now."

I try to process what he's said. Has hajji gone? My head swims as I reach around and continue to make a gentle exploration with my fingertips, my teeth clamped hard together. I pant short breaths through my nose. There's a fist-sized hole in my back, just underneath my scapula. There's my exit wound. Christ, it hurts. I fumble in my pants pocket for another bandage.

I bring the package to my lips and tear the wrapper with my teeth, spitting out bits of plastic. "Squads have to be…coming. They'll clear then…evac us out." Every word is labored around my panting as I struggle to draw a full breath. I feel fluid in my chest and suspect I've got a hemothorax. Try not to panic. Right…

"Copy." His voice fades into the sound of more bullets making contact with the vehicle.

I pass the rolled bandage around behind myself, trying to push it into the wound as best I can. I let my right hand drop to press against the wound under my armpit. When the bandage in the exit wound feels like it's in place, I lean back using the surface behind me to keep up the pressure.

The pain makes me gasp and fluid bubbles in my throat. A sudden choking sensation fills my chest and a cough forces its way out of my lungs. Clusters of stars dance in front of my eyes. I shriek. There's the real pain. Nausea washes over me and I feel myself sliding sideways again, my head drooping.

I'm starting to feel woozy. Do not vomit. You will pass out and aspirate on your puke. Do not vomit. The pain has increased, tearing through my back and I can feel more fluid gurgling in my chest. It's blood, you can admit it to yourself, Sabs. It's blood.

The average-sized female has a blood volume of about four liters. What is fifteen percent of four liters? Am I average sized? Think. I can't. Each breath exits with a wheeze and I can feel warm blood in my mouth and on my lips. I want to cough to clear my lungs but I'm too fearful after what just happened.

The bullets contacting against the metal set up a regular beat, lulling me into a trance. I try to think of something to keep myself conscious. Where is the squad? My eyes close, just for a moment. I'm just going to rest them. They are so dry. Just for a moment. I startle as I realize what I'm doing and force my eyes open. Start a list, Sabs. What can you think of to keep yourself awake?

Surgical procedures. Swimming at the beach. Movie plots. Cooking. The periodic table. I remember the conversation I had with Rebecca last week. My thoughts slide easily into sex. Sex with Rebecca. The taste of her lotion and the way her fingers tangled in my hair. Her hips bucking up to meet my tongue as it slid inside her. Her guttural groan and the way she…

I grunt, defeated. It seems vulgar to think of such things at this point. I dispel the thoughts. I refuse to think of my family or Mitch or that I never said goodbye to anyone before leaving this morning. I will not think about how I want to tell Rebecca I love her but haven't done it yet. Thinking about it would let fear we won't be extracted creep in.

I suddenly remember the conversation I had with Bec about telling people what they mean to you, in case something happens. If I wasn't in such an awful situation here then I would be laughing at the ridiculous irony. My head droops again and I have a strange feeling of standing and staring at my body as though it were a practice cadaver from med school.

I see my insides laid bare. I look at the mess made of my bone, lung and muscle as the projectile traveled through my body. What's that muscle called again? Think, Sabine. Latissimus dorsi? I can't remember. Open your textbook to page forty-three, then peel your skin back and have a good look. What?

Something touches my leg. "Doctor! Eyes open and on me!"

Did you just give a superior an order, Corporal? I shake my head. I don't want to open my eyes. I want to nap. Just a short one before I have to go back into surgery. I haven't had lunch yet and I've lost two patients today. Wait. What? No. I mumble something I don't even understand.

"Why did you become a doctor?" Elliot asks suddenly. A loud grunt makes me open my eyes. He's bracing himself against the dash, still unsuccessfully trying to jerk his left leg free.

I hate the doctor question. Everyone expects you to say it's because you like helping people. I do, but that's not my reason. "I like cutting into people," I say like a smartass, giving him a little smile, which he returns. I can hear the distant grumble of a diesel engine. Relief floods through me and I let my head bump back against the dashboard. "We're…s-saved," I say lamely. I'm wheezing like an asthmatic. The pain is so raw, I want to weep.

A cluster of bullets spray the metal, reminding me that we are anything but. The sound reminds me of hailstones hitting a car during a thunderstorm. Elliot lets out a little exclamation, jerking sideways against the belt holding him in place. "Fuck!" he cries out. "I've been hit." He groans and drops his pistol onto the floor near my leg. I can't reach to pass it back to him.

"Where?" I ask him frantically. Speaking brings a fresh round of pain under my ribs. "I can't move." I'm pinned by their gunfire and my gunshot wound.

Fear amplifies and fills my belly. I have to put a mental clamp down on my bladder. Thank you, body. As if I don't have enough to worry about without adding potentially pissing myself to the mix. I move my right arm to keep pressure on the entry wound with the inside of my bicep.

Elliot finally responds. "Ughhh." He shudders. "I'm not sure. I think the vest caught some, my hip maybe." He makes a small movement with his left hand as he tries to find where the wound is.

"Put pressure…on it," I tell him, as if he had no knowledge of basic first aid. He runs his tongue over his lips, turning his head to stare directly at me. Those gray eyes are wide with fear.

If they shoot at us again, I'm going to have to return fire but I can't use the rifle one-handed. Pistol it is. I inhale, contemplating twisting somehow to get a shot out of the hole in the roof. How stupid, as if you could even move that much without passing out, Sabine. I close my eyes and swallow another mouthful of blood, trying to imagine the angles I will need to shoot from my current position. Do not even think of recoil.

I have no idea how I'm going to shoot with a bullet wound on the right side of my torso. I can't move that arm. It's going to have to be southpaw. I shift the Beretta to my left hand. I can't do it. The shots will go everywhere and all my target practice averages will be skewed. Stop it, Sabine. I can't do it. I'm not a soldier. I'm not. I'm a doctor.

Why aren't they here? I sneak another look at my watch—sixteen forty-six. Has it really only been seven minutes? For the first time since we were hit, I begin to cry. Not sobbing, just hot tears sliding down my cheeks. I am terrified and the pain is verging on unbearable.

I've moved somehow and can feel hot blood running down to my waist. I lean back again, trying to keep some pressure on the exit wound. I'm nauseated and when I swallow more blood, I gag on it. I can't move my head in time and vomit bloody mess onto my lap.

The retching brings another level of pain. My legs begin to quiver uncontrollably. I take a few seconds to get myself under control, bending my head to wipe my cheeks on my shoulder. It's so hard to breathe and everything hurts. Concentrate Sabine.

We are trapped.

Elliot stretches for me and grabs at my calf, all he can reach. He wraps a large hand around my leg and holds it tightly as the rattling boom of a fifty cal gun cuts through the air.

CHAPTER TWENTY-SEVEN

The fifty goes quiet, replaced by familiar rifle fire. I count off seconds in my head, until the sounds from the firefight are finished. Two hundred fifty-one. When I hear engines pulling around and muffled yells confirming the area is clear, I begin my count again. Seventy-two. Head silhouettes appear in the bright light of the gaping hole. Saviors.

Someone stomps around on the metal above me before the driver's side door is opened, pulled off the hinges and tossed aside. Two people-shaped things appear, reaching down into the cabin. They're people-shaped, because they are people, Sabine. *Our* people. I watch listlessly as they start work on Elliot. He is still holding on to my leg.

A man drops through the hole made by the explosion, bringing a large bag with him. Why he didn't come through the rear doors? It's a little crowded up front with three of us inside the space. The newcomer sets his bag down and unzips it. He holds a hand out to me. "Can you hear me, Captain?" His voice is deep and masculine, matching his square jaw and Paul Newman blues. "I'm Private First Class Learmont."

Sorry, PFC Learmont but you will always be Paul Newman to me. I ignore his hand and nod apathetically. Apparently satisfied by my response, Learmont moves to check Richards, crouching and picking his way carefully over the interior so he doesn't slip in blood. Why is he even bothering? It's obvious the man is no longer alive. "No…need," I mumble. "I've confirmed. Sixteen forty-one."

Learmont grabs the dangling left wrist anyway, his Adam's apple bobbing convulsively. He gags, dry heaving a few times. I don't blame him, because the sight is not only gruesome but the stench is awful. Not to mention the flies which have so rapidly found a feast. He nods, clears his throat and tries to appear casual as he moves back to me. The look on his face gives him away. He is anything but casual.

Learmont kneels in front of me, wedging his bulk against the vehicle frame. He helps me sit up, graciously ignoring the expletives I spit at him when pain takes me. Learmont waits until I'm under control, then pulls my vest off, cuts away the fabric of my jacket and holds a pressure dressing against my back. His gaze moves back to Richards's remains and a stab of empathy shoots through me. A train wreck. We cannot keep our eyes from going back to the horror.

Learmont reaches for my wrist and fumbles for a good spot. "I'm just here to make sure you're stable then we'll transport you to the hospital. Can you tell me your injuries, Captain?"

"Shrapnel in…my leg, artery seems intact. Shot, entry under my armpit I…think. Exit just above my scapula. It's…hemorrhaging again," I pause. "A lot. My lung has to be…com-compromised, my chest is tight and…I'm having t-trouble breathing. Hemothorax. Blood in my pleural ca… in my chest."

Learmont makes notes on a small pad.

"Heart rate?" I ask, perhaps a little rudely. I glance over to watch how they are handling Elliot. Adequately.

"One hundred forty-eight."

I turn back to him. "Are you…sure?"

"Yes ma'am," he says assuredly.

"I was…one thirty…six at sixteen forty-four," I tell him. He scribbles in the notebook again. I rub my lips together. Causes of increased heart rate: anxiety, shock, blood loss, fear. All of the above.

Elliot is wearing a collar and the team is dressing his gunshot wound. I want to say something reassuring to him, but I can't think of anything. When they free his leg and move him, he lets go of my leg and in its absence, I'm aware of how warm his hand was. I wiggle my toes.

"We just have to figure out the best way to get you out of here, Captain." Learmont checks the bandage on my right leg and leaves it alone. He lifts my arm from the entry wound and replaces it with a pressure dressing.

I am defiant. "I can m-m-move, I just need…some help." I don't want to wait for them to cut the side of the vehicle open and I do not want to be pulled out the back past the remains of the man with the sweet brown eyes. To push my point, I begin to wiggle my ass, trying to move toward the bright shaft of sunlight in the roof. I see stars again and let out a short scream.

"Captain, I need you to stop moving." A gloved hand on my uninjured left shoulder halts my attempt at momentum.

I look up at him, trying to catch my breath. "Please. I just want…to go home. We're…almost there." I'm a few seconds away from begging. I need to see Bec. I have to.

"I understand, ma'am, but I have to be sure you'll make it."

Good point. I give a loose-wristed wave. Learmont moves with quiet efficiency, checking my vitals again. I find myself running through the process in my head. At least I am mentally sound. He cuts away my sleeve and pulls an IV kit from his bag. Fluids, excellent. It doesn't take him long to prep a site. I avert my eyes to stop myself from instructing him.

He inserts the cannula first go, which surprises me. I take a look. Not bad, as my veins must be crap. He tapes it in place with trembling hands before he connects the bag. As he holds it above his head, I smell the masculine scent of his deodorant.

"Didn't think I'd get it, did you?" Learmont grins, nose wrinkling slightly.

"No." At least I am honest.

He chuckles. "Neither did I."

"It's hard…when you don't…do it often," I concede. He digs in his kit to offer me an analgesic inhaler but I shake my head. "No. No thank you."

Learmont wiggles it in front of my face. "Are you sure?"

I am emphatic. "Positive." I need to be lucid. I need to talk to Rebecca when I get back. I need to tell her I love her. I need to tell her that I can't be without her.

He lifts both eyebrows but doesn't ask again. He has reached the limits of his first aid. All that's left for him to do is to take me to surgical. I struggle for another breath. "Give me…a marker."

Learmont rummages in his bag and pulls out a thick black marker. He holds it out, unsure. I grab it and lean hard onto my left shoulder. "Count my ribs on the right. In the…space between number five and six. Make a mark." I'm mumbling.

Apparently, I make enough sense for him. One-handed, he pulls the tattered fabric of my jacket and tee out of the way, then runs his fingers over my bare skin. It makes me shiver and I feel the cold wetness of the ink against my ribcage.

"If I go blue and pass out…cut there and use the scissors to make it bigger, use a finger to move my lung then…then insert a tube to drain it."

His eyes are wide. "I don't think I can."

"Then hurry…the fuck up and take me b-back to surgical."

Learmont twists around and calls for one of his teammates. I don't catch the name. The rear doors are flung open, banging hard against the metal. Sunlight streams through into the cavern. I scrunch my eyes closed and hear a second squad member make his way through the space. "Jesus. Oh fucking hell." The voice is unsteady. "Oh God."

"Thomas. Pick up your bundle," says Learmont, not unkindly. "Come on, we've got to move him and get the doc out. It's gotta be through the back, man. He's gotta be bagged before we can get him out. Go grab Benson. Let's get the gunner in a bag and take him home."

He speaks with a forced calmness but I catch the edge of emotion in his voice. Boots sound on metal again as the man I know to be Thomas climbs back out of the ruined carrier. I keep my eyes closed, trying not to imagine them pulling Richards from where he is jammed in the turret. I don't want to watch them struggling with ruptured intestines, slippery with blood and shit, and I can't bear to see their faces as they cope with their revulsion. The sounds and smells are enough.

Their retching and angry sobbing bombard my ears. With my eyes closed, I wonder why I'm finding this so difficult. I deal with death and gore on a daily basis. It's my life. I reassemble men and women. Most of the time I succeed. Sometimes I fail. Despite my job I have never witnessed the cause of their trauma. This is real. I'm struggling. Learmont's voice is right near my ear. "Captain? We're going to move you now."

I open my eyes, blinking as they adapt to the brightness again. "Mhmm. Roger."

"We'll keep you on your back, I'm afraid it's going to be a little uncomfortable, but it'll put pressure on the exit wound."

"Keep my…head up," I demand. If they lay me flat for too long gravity will work against me and I will choke as the blood in my lungs moves along my trachea. I don't think I could cope. The pain is enough. I'm embarrassed at being covered in puke and other bodily fluids. Bodily fluids that aren't all mine. I can't breathe enough to make an apology. The men support me as they pull me forward and gently roll me onto the stretcher. It's excruciating. Despite myself I let out a loud scream.

"Very sorry, Doctor," says a faceless man to my left.

I lift my hand a fraction to acknowledge him, too tired to summon the energy to placate him. It's not his fault. I am jostled through into the open air. The stretcher settles in the dirt and I bite down on my lip to keep from crying out again. I settle for a sort of gurgle in the back of my throat.

Dizzy. It's taking all my concentration to not pass out again. I don't want to be intubated in the field. I want Bobby to do it. I roll my eyes to myself, as though I could force myself to stay conscious. You're conscious because your nervous system wants you to be, Sabine.

They leave me on the rocky ground with Learmont watching over me. I watch the squads. One team preps Elliot to be transported, the other strips the wrecked vehicle. The troops pull everything serviceable from it, including weapons, ammo and the medkit bags. When I'm lifted and carried again, a flash of color catches my eye. I move my eyes to look at it without turning my head. The sun is beginning to set and a shaft of light is streaming through a break in the clouds. It reflects off a pool of my blood that has seeped through the fabric stretcher into the dirt. It is mesmerizing.

The deep redness of the setting sun seems to amplify the color of my blood, contrasting with the dull brown-yellow of the dirt. It's beautiful, in a horribly morbid way, and I crane my neck so I can look at it until I am loaded and driven away.

CHAPTER TWENTY-EIGHT

The rapid rough drive shakes me and I have to shove my fist in my mouth to stop from screaming. My head spins and I come to as I'm being rushed through the hallways I walk every day. The ceiling has a strange diamond pattern. I become obsessed with looking at it as we move through. There's a strange dreamlike tinge to everything.

Drawing each breath is a struggle, like a four-hundred-pound weight is sitting on my chest. This is a strange experience, being on the other side going in as a casualty, not waiting for one. Everyone knows it's me. I can see the horrified faces of people lining the halls and I roll my eyes, trying to catch the gaze of someone. Anyone. "Why haven't you as-as-ssessed me?" The question is directed at no one.

"It's already been done, Sabine." The voice is familiar but I can't pin it down. All I know is it's not Bec.

"What?" How did I not notice?

"Everything's okay, we've got you now."

"Where's Elliot?" I mumble but nobody answers. I try to take a deep breath so I can speak louder, but before I can, they carry me through the doors into theater. What delicious irony. It is operating room number one. My favorite. My head has fallen so my face rests cheek down. I don't bother to move it. I'm on a ship, rocking in the ocean. There is noise around me but I can't isolate conversations, nor can I pinpoint specific things people are doing.

I am held eye-level with waists. Someone hasn't double knotted their gown. Sarah squats so she is level with my face. "Sabine." She gently pushes sweat-dampened bangs off my forehead with her elbow. "Mitch and Amy, and Colonel Keane are just scrubbing now." She moves away and is replaced by Bobby.

"Sabine, Sabine," he admonishes me. By the way his eyes are creasing I can tell he is smirking under his mask. "Did you miss me that much?" Arrogant bastard.

I flash him a tight-lipped smile. They lift me up onto the table, rolling me to my side so the stretcher can be removed. My smile fades as pain radiates through my body. I cannot help but scream and again, I feel myself slipping into unconsciousness. It takes all my willpower to keep my eyes open. I need to see Rebecca. I need to see Mitch. Where is Amy? I try to look backward to the scrub sinks, but I can't move my head enough to see anything but walls.

A sharp pinch tells me Bobby is inserting another cannula. "Had anything to eat or drink recently?"

"Food, uhh…twelve sixteen," I rasp. "Water, two hours ago but I vomited. Twice."

Bobby chuckles. "Good. Makes my job a whole lot easier. You still rocking that A-positive blood?"

My legs are quivering. Everything tilts and I close my eyes against the nausea. "Last time…I…ch-checked." I groan, tasting blood again. My uniform and boots are cut off, the shears cold against my skin.

Bobby clips a pulse oximeter to my left forefinger. It's too tight. "I know it's rude to ask a lady but what's your current weight?"

Before I can answer, Mitch speaks from a few feet to my right. "One hundred and twenty-four. All muscle, baby." I force my eyes open in time to see him lean over me. I am so desperate for him to touch me but he is gloved and sterile, and I'm not prepped. His eyes are moist above his mask. "What's this about, darlin'?"

"I just…w-w-wanted to…make an entrance." I gasp. It's so cold in here.

"Well, you sure did. You attention-seekin' bitch."

He moves away and Amy steps in, crouching down beside me. "I might get an eyeful of your junk, love. I hope you waxed recently." She winks, then she is gone.

The cacophony in the OR grows as I'm prepped. Now that I'm lying down, the blood is starting to move up my trachea, bringing a new wave of panic. Can't they tell it's choking me? There's blood in my mouth and I have no choice but to swallow it. Where is Rebecca? I cannot see, or hear her. Didn't Sarah say she was scrubbing? My legs shake uncontrollably. I am so cold. I hear the theater doors swing open again.

I smell her unmistakable scent, mixed with a fearful undertone. It's the sharp smell of sweat from someone who is afraid. I turn my eyes and catch sight of her but she isn't looking at me. A vein bulges near her temple as she towels her hands and pushes them into gloves. Still, she won't look at me and I grunt, trying to clear my throat. I try so hard to speak but instead I choke on blood.

Mitch's voice wavers. "Sabine. Stop it. Hurry up, Bobby." Something cold runs through my hand.

I dream, but not of any solution to my current dilemma. My dreams are an assortment of shapes, sounds and people I know. They do not wear their own faces, yet I know who they are. I climb a ladder into a tree house and when I make it to the top rung I am somehow standing in The Louvre. Before me is the Mona Lisa.

I wait with excitement for her to stop looking so self-satisfied and to tell me what I should do. She doesn't. The man next to me is wearing a well-cut suit. He whines about how da Vinci's masterpiece is bigger than he thought it would be. I'm part of an anime movie, which is confusing because my breasts are suddenly a lot larger than they should be. I do not defeat the shadowy villain. Bec and I are at the beach. She looks fucking amazing in a bikini. A snake eats my shoes. Thank you for being so fucking unhelpful, subconscious.

* * *

There is sudden rawness in my throat. Something is jamming my tongue down and pressing against my cheeks. It's claustrophobic. Immediately, anxiety grabs me. I can't quite get my eyes open and when I try to take a breath, something stops me midinhalation. It's an awful sensation, like pressure building in my chest.

I am intubated and on a ventilator. My anxiety turns to full-blown panic. It seems my brain doesn't register that oxygen has been introduced into my lungs and I try to take another breath but cannot. The pressure then decreases as the ventilator valve lets air draw back. Oh God. I can't vocalize anything with the tube in my throat.

I force my eyes fully open. Despite knowing I shouldn't, I scrabble clumsily at my mouth with my left hand, trying to grab at the tube. It's futile. My hand is so heavy that I cannot get a grip on the plastic. The feeling of being on the ventilator is terrifying. Is my lung fucked? Why am I awake? After another mechanical push and pull of air in my lungs, I double my efforts to get the vent tube. I shouldn't be touching it, but I don't care. I want it out.

There is another building of pressure in my chest. I realize I'm not alone. Voices are rising over the sounds of frantic movement around me. I manage to get my fingers on the plastic tube, but my hand is snatched away and held firmly against the bed. My right hand is not being held, but I can't move it to try again to tug at the thing in my mouth. There's a slow hiss and the pressure eases from my lungs again.

"Sabine, it's Rebecca…Keane." Her voice is quiet and calm.

I move my head to find her. Tears leak from the edge of my eyes to run down the side of my cheek. Please, pull it out. Please,

please, please. My eyes are now locked with hers as I squirm against her restraint of my wrist, digging my nails in to whatever they touch. Forced inhalation. Panic. Forced exhalation. Panic. I can feel a finger stroking my hand, but she keeps it pinned down.

"Everything's fine. Relax, relax. We're just checking functions. You're fine. I know you're scared but we're going to sedate you now. Sabine, I need you to stop trying to breathe over the vent."

I can't help it. Each breath is stopped by the ventilator forcing my lungs to expand. Then my attempt to inhale cuts over the exhalation valve opening and releasing the air in my lungs. It's like I'm choking all over again. I claw ineffectually at her hand as a shadow creeps into my peripheral vision and I feel myself sliding back under again.

* * *

I wake gradually and notice I'm in a small room by myself. Lucky me. They must have moved a bed into the empty office beside the recovery unit. Or am I in Germany already? I lift a heavy left hand to feel if I am still tubed. There is nothing but an oxygen mask there. Good, I can breathe on my own, but anxiety still twists my stomach into a hard ball. My throat is sore, like I have a nasty case of strep. Other than that there is a distinct lack of pain, which is novel given how intense it was before I was anesthetized. Hello narcotics.

Rebecca's soft, exhausted voice comes from my left. "Leave it alone, Sabine." No, I'm not in Germany. I turn my head to see her sit up and shuffle to the edge of the chair. I try to drag the mask down a little so it's not jammed so close to my eyes. Her hand closes around mine and she pulls it away. "I said leave it." She readjusts it. The oxygen smells stale and dries my nostrils.

Every time I try to talk, my tongue refuses to cooperate. I give up. She pulls a few strands of hair back from my forehead. "Do you need anything? Do you have any pain?"

I shake my head. My mouth is so dry. I try to mime drinking, though I imagine the action makes me look more like a drunk at a bar.

"You're thirsty?"

I lift both eyebrows and try to make an affirmative sound. It sounds like a goose honking. Rebecca glances at her wrist, twisting her watch around from where it has slipped face down. "You've been off ventilation for three hours. You may have ice in twenty minutes."

I glare but she ignores me. Again, I try to force out some words, but there's no saliva so I cannot swallow to get them out. I want to know how long my surgeries took and what they found. I want to know all the details. Did Elliot come through? I'm propped up into a sitting position with all the monitors behind me, no doubt deliberately so I can't see them.

I squirm on the bed, taking a few experimental breaths. My right hand won't cooperate Shit. There is no pain, but the right side of my torso feels so stiff. I finally manage to lift my hand about an inch from the bed. Rebecca turns to face me, with both elbows resting on the mattress. I smell stale coffee on her breath. "Stop it. You have a chest tube in. Do I need to sedate you again?"

I shake my head. No. No more sedation. I manage to push out a hoarse and breathy, "Whaaat."

Rebecca tilts her head at me, her disheveled hair flopping around. She looks exhausted, with dark shadows under her red-rimmed eyes. "I'd always heard doctors make the worst patients but I never believed it. Until now." She reaches for my hand, holding it between both of hers and bringing it to her lips. She has what looks like fingernail scratches over the back of her hands. I think they are mine, from my earlier attempt to get free of her grasp and pull my ventilator tube out. Not exactly the way I wanted to mark her skin again.

A gentle knock on the closed door behind her interrupts us. Rebecca drops my hand abruptly. The door opens and Mitch wanders into the room, pausing a moment. To one who doesn't know him as well as I do, his face would give nothing away but to me it is as clear as anything. He knows something is going on. My friend bows his head. "Colonel Keane, ma'am."

"Boyd."

Mitch closes the gap between us, leaning over to fetch my chart from the end of the bed. My eyes widen in anticipation, but he keeps it away from my view. I watch him writing and stare expectantly at him. Mitch shakes his head and drops the chart back into the holder. "How would you rate your pain, Sabine?"

I lift a middle finger. There. One out of ten.

His mouth lifts into a smile. "Any difficulties breathing?"

I lift my shoulders in a small shrug. It's labored and uncomfortable but not impossible.

"I think perhaps you need to rest a little longer. I'll send someone in with somethin' to help you sleep."

No, you asshole. I'm thirsty. Tell me about my surgeries. I turn my head toward Rebecca as though I could somehow influence her to overrule him. She shakes her head at me and reaches for my hand, covering the action by placing two fingers on my wrist.

* * *

I wake again and find Mitch wedged into the tiny chair beside my bed. When I move, he startles and sits up, swiping a forefinger in the corner of his eyes. "It's alive." He reaches for the glass of water beside my bed, bending the straw down to offer it to me. I suck greedily, but before I can take more than a few sips he pulls it from my mouth.

"Prick," I rasp.

"You know I don't enjoy watchin' people puke," Mitch responds, setting the glass back down. "How you feelin'?" he asks softly, wiping the corner of my mouth with his thumb.

"Tired. I...don't think I can work tonight." I laugh inwardly. At least I can still amuse myself. My voice is gravelly and it's taking a great deal of effort to talk. "Time?"

He laughs. "You always were lazy." He reaches out to caress my cheek, his hand sliding up to push my hair back off my forehead. "You're thirty-one hours post-op." Thanks for the epic knock out, guys. Mitch grabs my hand in both of his. "Sabs, let's not do the thing where I tell you how terrified I was. Then I tell you how glad I am you made it and finish off by demandin' you never do it again, yeah?" His lips are clamped tightly together. He's trying not to cry.

"Agreed," I whisper.

"Good."

"Tell me," I demand.

He demurs slightly, but still he runs me through the damage and the surgery. Punctured and collapsed right lung, broken rib, hemothorax. Minor lacerations and contusions. Everything repaired and hunky-dory. My leg wound is straightforward but they think there may be some nerve damage which explains the radiating pain. We will have to wait but it should be fine with some therapy.

I want to talk about being aware of the intubation, but the thought of it makes my bowels feel like they are turning liquid. I can't count of the number of times I have told a patient not to try and breathe over a ventilator. Now I know how fucking stupid it is. I couldn't help it, no matter how hard I wanted not to, I just had to try and draw a breath. I won't say it to anyone ever again. I run my tongue over my lower lip. "How's the driver?" The sound of my voice is grating.

"No complications. Leg fracture, tib-fib. Coupla lacerations and bruised ribs from the vest catchin' the bullets. Bullet wound was minor, mostly a fleshy. He's on his way to Landstuhl right now."

Good news, he will be fine. I lift my finger to point at the water. "Please."

Mitch lifts it to my lips and lets me have another small mouthful. I clear my throat. "Mitch, I need to talk to you about something." It cannot wait. I need to get it out.

"You need to tell me you're leavin' everythin' you own to me for saving your ass?" He sounds hopeful.

The corner of my mouth twitches into a smile, but I won't be sidetracked. "No. It's about Keane."

He looks surprised. "What about her? Did someone tell you what a fuckin' dictator she was with your surgery? Seriously, she was out of control. Frantic, demandin', totally over the top." He sniffs, mouth twisted. "She apologized when we were done, but I gotta tell you, it was a pretty hard job, Sabs, and she made it harder."

I raise my eyebrows. "No. I didn't know. Sorry." I look at the door and he catches my meaning immediately. Mitch rises from his chair and pushes the door closed while I try to catch my breath again. Speaking has made my chest tight and my ribs painful. He settles back in the chair, looking at me with expectant suspicion.

"She came to my house while I was on leave. We slept together." I get it all out, but it takes a few pauses so I can breathe. There. Straight to the point.

Mitch looks incredulous, his mouth hanging open until he speaks. "Christ Sabine. It's one thing to dream about it, but to do it? The fuck were you thinkin'?"

My voice is barely audible. "We were thinking…about our mutual attraction."

He shakes his head. "How? What happened? She asked and you told? Fuckin' hell, she's your superior! I mean, I know you're both commissioned, but Jesus, you're in the same unit! And not to mention…" He indicates between the two of us. I know exactly what he means.

My head snaps up. "Mitch, it was mutual. We both know it's been coming. You joked, but it wasn't a joke." I wheeze and drop my head back to the pillow to try and catch my breath. It takes a little while and he is silent the whole time. I try again. "I don't know what to do. I can't risk discharge. You know what that would mean for my father. We were off base and there has never been anything…unprofessional between us. No favoritism or anything since." I am trembling from the effort of my monologue and tears are starting to slide down my cheeks. "I just don't know what to do. I can't leave right now and I can't spend the next four years pretending like we never…" I have to stop.

Mitch's face softens. Others' crying upsets him. "Don't cry, darlin', please. It's okay." He pulls a package of tissues from his pocket and wipes the edge of my eyes. "Did y'all speak about it?"

"Sort of, yes. No." I grunt softly, trying to clear my throat and I feel a twinge in my back. I grimace.

"Pain?" Mitch asks, shifting to the edge of the seat.

"Yeah. And I feel a little nauseous."

Mitch gets up hastily. "I'll organize a PCA, and send a nurse in with another emesis basin. We'll talk more about this later." He looks down at me, with a single eyebrow raised and a hopeful expression. "Tell me one thing. Was it any good?"

I open my eyes wide. "Understatement of the century."

He smirks. "I thought as much."

CHAPTER TWENTY-NINE

Whenever I wake, someone is in the room with me and I'm beginning to feel as though they have some sort of roster going to make sure I'm never alone. Or perhaps it's to stop me from climbing down the bed and grabbing my own charts. Everything is fuzzy-edged which I attribute to my drugs. I'd wager opiates are featuring quite highly.

I tease Bobby. "Short straw again? They must be desperate if they left an anesthesiologist in charge."

He's watching a precious football replay on his laptop. From what I can hear, the Bears are having a decent start to their 2009 season. Bobby shrugs nonchalantly. "It's fine, gives me some downtime. You're a poor conversationalist, Fleischer." He pauses what he's watching and looks up at my monitors.

"All okay?" I still cannot twist around to look at the screens. I need to talk to someone about this.

He nods. "Yep. Perfect."

"How's my oh-two sat?"

"Saturated. Any pain?"

"Only you. In my ass."

Bobby laughs and sets down his laptop on my side table. He shoves his stethoscope in his ears and lifts the edge of my gown away from the drains in my torso. The metal is cold against my skin, setting off a deep shudder as it touches me. It seems their Watch Sabine Club includes an oath to keep me out of the loop. I grunt, knowing it will give him an amplified blast of sound through the earpieces.

"Hey!"

"You deserve it. You're all awful."

"I know." Bobby settles back down in the chair and taps a laptop key to resume his game. My eyes slide closed as I listen to the commentary.

I doze off and wake again to see Amy in the chair, reading but I can't keep my eyes open long enough to talk to her.

Mitch arrives later with my laptop and a red Jell-O cup for me.

I push it aside. "I'm not hungry."

"Fair enough." He peels back the foil and eats Jell-O while I power up my laptop. Mitch speaks around mouthfuls. "Next time I'll bring banana pudding if you're just going to give it to me. You're three days post. You should be eating."

"I have been eating. You could bring me coffee. I'll eat that. Drink rather." My right arm is worryingly clumsy. It's probably from the wound in my back and armpit, not nerve damage. That's got to be it. My hand wasn't damaged. It moves. I'm not going to lose range of motion or the sensation and dexterity I need to operate. Stop worrying.

When everything has booted up, numerous emails from my family appear on my screen. Evidently my RED form was processed and everyone knows what's happened. I know they were notified, but I haven't thought to ask for details. I'll need to call them soon to reassure them that I am fine, relatively speaking.

"Office said your mama has called every day, all aggravated wantin' to speak to you," Mitch tells me when I turn the laptop around to point out all the emails.

I exhale. "Oh?" I am now beginning to feel some discomfort, tight and aching like I'm being held in a vise.

He nods. "Mhmm. Keane notified, but I spoke to your mama the first day and she knows what's happenin'. Been givin' updates and I told her you'd call soon as you could."

I struggle to sit upright and he leans over to push the pillow up behind me. "Thank you, Mitch. For everything."

He waves me off. "Couldn't have you dyin'. The family probably wouldn't like me so much if that happened. I need those parcels." Mitch's smile is too bright. He's using humor to deflect how upset he is.

My own smile is weak. "I guess not, though someone would have to take my place as the army golden child. Maybe my father would forgive you." I wave behind myself. "Is the PCA up there?"

He reaches up and passes me the button, hooking the cord over the bar beside me to keep it out of the way. I thumb it hard, listening for the beep then I drop it to rest on the bed beside me. "What do you rate it?" Mitch asks.

"About a six," I mumble. Bad, but not the worst.

"Having any side effects from the narcotics?" Mitch drops the empty Jell-O cup in the trash and stretches toward the end of the bed for my chart.

There's no point lying. "Dry mouth. I'm still a little queasy." I shift the tube in my nose, trying to stop the left prong from poking my nostril.

"About to puke queasy or just a distant sort of feeling?"

We've moved back to Doctor and Patient. I don't like it. "Distant. I'm not going to puke on you. No dizziness. Do you want to know if I'm constipated?"

Mitch flings the chart cover open. "You shouldn't be. We're giving you something for that." He grins.

"When can I read it?" I close the laptop and shove the table away. The meds are starting to work. I feel lighter.

"When you're no longer under the influence of drugs." He reaches into a pocket and pulls out a chocolate bar. My lips are clamped so tightly together, I must resemble a puppet. It has no effect. Mitch smiles sweetly at me, then unwraps the candy bar and takes a bite. He leans back in the chair with his feet resting on the frame under the mattress.

Mitch looks relaxed, as though he is settled on the couch watching a game with a beer by his side. I know he is acting with this feigned casualness to annoy me. "So, what are you going to do about this Keane thing, darlin'?"

I roll over onto my left hip so I can look at him, letting my stiff right arm rest against my side. All the IV tubes are caught in the blanket and I snatch at them with my good left hand. The pulse oximeter has shifted from its correct position on my forefinger. I waste time fixing it and trying to think of a response. After almost a minute of stalling I manage to come up with, "I don't know." It's not an evasion. I really do not know.

He blows a raspberry at me. "I don't believe you."

"Have you thought any more about your application for Forward Surgical?" I don't want him to be any closer to the action than we are here. I couldn't bear anything to happen to him, and now I know we're not immune to the dangers it would seem like tempting fate.

"Stop avoidin' the subject, Sabine."

"I'm not. I just don't know. There's no good answer." I gesture helplessly. "I want to be with her and she wants the same, but we can't." I feel like my fingertips are in a bowl of cotton wool.

"Keane's career army, right? Hell, she'll make colonel in another five years." What he doesn't say hangs between us. Why would she give that up? Mitch exhales, long and loud. "I suppose you just gotta wait until your obligation is up, and deal with distance while you're workin' some cushy civvie job back home."

I gnaw on the inside of my cheek. There's nothing I can say, it's all been said.

Mitch leans forward and takes my hand. "I'm sure it'll work out, if it's what you want. You sure? You love her?"

"I am and yes, I do."

"Well, then just let it play out as it wants to. There's always a way. But you need to talk to her about it." He looks like he's just managed to cure cancer and end world hunger all in one moment.

"We've *been* talking—there's no good solution," I whisper.

I catch sight of Rebecca in the doorway just before she knocks on the frame. Mitch drops his feet from where they are hooked up on my bed and stands to greet her politely. "Ma'am."

She smiles. "May I come in?"

I nod, head wobbling. Oh, morphine, you silly thing, you. "Of course, Colonel."

Keane moves into the room and stops at the end of the bed. Her mouth is open slightly and I catch the confusion in her expression.

"I'll leave ya'll to it." Mitch picks up the wrapper from the chocolate he so rudely ate in front of me. "Colonel."

"Mitchell."

Mitch gives me a pointed look as he closes the door. Yeah I know, buddy. Rebecca grabs my chart and looks through it, flipping a few pages back and forth. I assume she's comparing something. I frown. The way it's going, everyone in this damned hospital will have seen it and put their notations on it, before I even get to look. She moves to the head of the bed and drops the chart on the bedside table, just out of my reach. Rebecca drags the stethoscope from around her neck. "How are you feeling?"

"Annoyed."

Her mouth twitches as she readies the stethoscope. "Why is that, Sabine?" She moves my gown to the side. Hello.

"Because nobody will tell me anything!" I exclaim croakily, looking up at her.

"You don't need to know. You need to concentrate on recuperating." She places the diaphragm on the left side of my chest and I flinch at the cold metal on my skin. The edge of her palm brushes my breast. My stomach tightens and I'm certain she would hear the stutter in my heartbeat.

"I don't feel any fluid." I am petulant to cover my embarrassment.

Rebecca lifts a finger. "Be quiet please." She moves the stethoscope around, forehead furrowed. "Breathe in."

I comply.

"And again."

I comply again.

"Can you sit up for me?"

"I'll need some help, please."

She helps me move forward away from the pillow, keeping a hand on my shoulder to support me. "How'd you sleep?" She slides the stethoscope in through the opening at the back of my gown.

"Okay."

I keep quiet while she listens, aware of her thumb massaging the tense muscle of my neck. "Any pain around the dressings or chest tube?" Rebecca pulls me gently back to the pillow.

I jiggle my shoulders. "A little, and some stiffness and weirdness." Very scientific, Sabine.

Rebecca moves back to the chart and begins to write. "Stiffness and weirdness you said? Is there a rating scale for those?" She shows her dimples.

"Don't tease."

Rebecca chuckles and finishes up, pushing the chart away. "I think the chest tube can come out this afternoon. We'll move you to Germany in the next day or two, then we can start thinking about recovery. It'll be months—you'll go back to the States." She sits in the chair and crosses her legs.

"Wonderful." Months of recovery, therapy and then evaluation prior to redeployment. Being discharged on medical grounds would be the perfect solution to everything but I'm under no illusions. I'll recover enough to return to full duty, either sent back here or even to Landstuhl. Maybe I'll get lucky and be assigned to a hospital stateside. There's nothing about my injuries that would affect my surgical ability, and the general weakness will go away. I clear my throat and reach for the PCA again. Just a little more. I thumb it, listening for the beep indicating analgesic has been dispensed. Nothing. Fuck. I press it again just to be sure. Nope.

Rebecca looks at me and then up to the control module. She stands and thumbs through data on the screen and I hear electronic tones as she makes an adjustment. "Try now, Sabine."

"Thank you." I press the button again and the machine beeps loudly. "Why haven't you moved me on to Landstuhl yet?"

"Because I want you here where I can make sure you're all right. I need you near me until I know…until I know you're really safe."

I smile. "You're going to get in trouble."

"Yes, I know and I don't care." Rebecca settles back down in the chair beside my bed. "I thought I might come with you."

I drop the PCA button. "What do you mean? Come where? Germany?"

"Home. I've spoken to HR and handed in my letter of resignation."

"*Really*?" I'm incredulous. "Why now?"

"Because." She runs her tongue over her lips. Her eyes glisten with tears, which she wipes away quickly. "I want to come home with you and help you recover. I want us to be settled when it's time for you to leave the army and come back home for good. We can deal with you finishing your contract, deployments and the distance later."

My heart pounds as I try to take in what she is saying. "Is that what you want?" I'm starting to float.

She reaches out to hold my forearm. "It is. I told you that you'd changed my perspective but if I can be honest, I wasn't totally certain before. I wanted it and I wanted you, but I was scared to make such a drastic change to my life."

"I get it," I say softly.

"Sabine, I cannot even begin to tell you the terror I felt when I heard your name on the incoming call. That fear is a million times worse than fearing a life change."

I shift my arm so I can take her hand. Our fingers interlace. Her hand feels soft, like a marshmallow. I wonder if it tastes like a marshmallow. I swallow a laugh. Morphine. Such a serious conversation and I'm almost high.

Bec lifts her eyes up to the ceiling as though she's trying to stop tears from falling. It doesn't work and she leaves them to roll down her cheeks. "I felt so…helpless. I was paralyzed by fear, Sabine. There aren't words to describe it. I knew right then it was because I love you. I love you so much and I want to be with you, and this can work." She wipes at her eyes with her free hand. "It seems so simple now, why didn't I see it?"

I choke a little and she sits up, panicked. "No, no," I wheeze. "I'm fine. I'm just...I don't know. Relieved? Happy?" I wrinkle my forehead, trying to push past the fogginess. "Full of opiates and unable to find a word? I love you. I love you too," I blurt.

She laughs, adjusting my gown back on my shoulder.

"I'll be deployed again after I've finished my medical leave." I stare down my right side. "Assuming this arm works properly. It feels like it will, but...it's so weak."

"You know this injury isn't one that will affect your surgical career," Bec assures me.

"What will happen? You'll be back in the States and I could still be away on deployments or working in Germany until I'm out." We'll be apart but there will be no more stress and worry about slipping up or being caught. No threat of being disciplined or worse. I lift my chin and look into her eyes. "Are you sure you can wait for me back home?" She knows exactly what I'm really asking her.

"You know I will." The laugh lines at the edge of her eyes crease. "I've already waited most of my adult life for you, Sabine. I'm not letting a few more deployments or some distance come between us now that I know you're really mine."

CHAPTER THIRTY

In the four days since the ambush I've spent my time in a dreamless bliss, cushioned by opiates, or being made to do shit like get up and take weak and wobbling steps around the room. I should be making better progress than this.

I'm not sure what time it is when I wake, drenched in sweat and thrashing from a nightmare about disjointed bodies coming to life. I can't breathe to cry out and bile burns the back of my throat. An alarm is blaring from the monitors behind me. I know the sound. It's my heart rate. Too fast.

I jam my eyes closed, each ragged inhalation sending pain through my torso as I try to draw a full breath. The image of a body being pulled apart by faceless men is seared on my mind, like poorly developed film. Sudden light floods the room, giving everything a red tinge behind my closed eyes. It looks like blood. I force my eyes open, squinting in the artificial brightness.

"Shhh. Relax. You're okay, Sabs. You're safe. It's just a dream." Amy presses an oxygen mask to my face. I try to pull it away, but she pushes it even harder against my nose.

I grab at it again, gasping. "Take it off! Take it off. I'm gonna puke." My words are muffled against the plastic, echoing in my ears.

Amy pulls the mask away and snatches an emesis basin from the bedside table just in time. Each heave sends stabbing pain through my ribs. My body is trembling violently. I begin to cry. "I had a bad dream, Ames."

She pushes damp clumps of hair off my face, frowning. "Oh Sabine."

Kathy pops her head in the door. "Everything okay?"

Amy reaches one-handed for my chart. "Peachy, thanks Kath. Can you get me alprazolam point five milligram please?" Xanax. She flips a page back and forth. "Actually, make that one milligram."

Amy sets my chart down and offers me water. I swish liquid around my mouth to clear the taste, then spit it into the basin. My fists are tangled in the blanket as though giving them something to hold might stop the tremors in my arms.

"We can up your antianxiety dose if you like," she says gently. My teeth are chattering so much I can't answer her. Amy runs her hand over my sweaty forehead. "Are you cold?"

"Mhmm."

Amy stands to check the monitors and reset the alarm. She looks exhausted. "All vitals within normal range, love. No fever." There's no physical reason to be cold, Sabine. This is psychological. A panic attack.

Amy makes a few notes on my chart while I'm trying to calm myself down. The trembling has settled, but my gut is still twisted with anxiety. Is this PTSD? Am I broken? Will I ever be the person I was before, or will my life now be spent running from nightmares?

Kathy shuffles back with the pill. The bitter coating sticks to the back of my throat before I wash it down. I give her a weak smile. "Thank you."

"No sweat. Call if you need anything else."

Amy nods absently, still scribbling. I lean back against the pillows while she finishes. She sets the chart on the table then drops the railing down and sits on the bed. "Do you wanna talk about it?"

I shake my head. I can't talk about it, not yet. "Will you hug me?" My voice is soft and so pathetic.

"Of course, honey. Come on, shuffle over this side." She pulls the railing back up and waits for me to move over. I settle on my left side, pillow propped against the bed rail.

Amy kicks off her boots and pads around to the other side of the bed. She helps me shift all my wires and tubes, readjusts my blanket then carefully climbs up into the bed. "Are you comfortable, little spoon?" She holds me gently, the warmth of her body permeating the woolen blanket.

I hold her slender forearm. "Mhmm."

"I'm fucking shattered, been working extra to cover your sorry ass. I might fall asleep. Hope Keane doesn't come in and catch us," Amy whispers.

I turn my head, twisting to look back at her. "What?"

"I don't want any trouble now," she singsongs.

I take a shaky breath. "I don't...she won't..."

"Shhh, it's okay. I've had an inkling for a while now, Sabs. The way she was with your surgery confirmed it. That, my friend, is lurve."

"You won't tell?"

Amy laughs in my ear. "Of course not, sweetie. I'm so happy for you. Now try and go back to sleep."

I shift slightly. "If you snore, I will. It'll be just like always."

She gives my waist a gentle squeeze. "Deal."

"Ames?"

"Yep?"

I close my eyes. "I'm gonna miss you."

"Me too, Sabs. Me too."

* * *

Not even Rebecca's influence can hold me at Invicta any longer, and seven days post-op I'm sent to Landstuhl. My goodbyes are too quick and too public for my liking, and I leave

Afghanistan with things unresolved. Someone has given an order to keep me sedated and I spend a hazy, disjointed week in Germany before I'm flown home to the States and taken to the Army Medical Center in D.C.

Mom and Dad are staying in a hotel nearby, and are with me every moment of allowed visitation hours. They only leave when I have a dressing changed, am made to do my two-hourly shuffling lap of the floor or get sent to therapy—both physical and psychological. My mother is now better at not asking how I am every few minutes.

She still fusses though, bringing books and supplies for me and my roommate, Leigh, whose family lives in California and can't visit. Leigh was patrolling with another soldier who stepped on an IED and was killed instantly. The explosion blew off Leigh's left leg below her knee. She wants a prosthetic so she can return to active duty. My father is very impressed.

When my parents leave, Leigh and I barely speak, too spent from our physical and mental exertions. Our main conversation consists of a sleep-hoarse, "Are you okay?" when one of us wakes the other with a nightmare. It's oddly comforting to have someone who gets what I'm feeling.

I'm pretty sure she's sick of the parade of medicos, my colleagues, who come by during the day just to see how I'm going. They make jokes about my laziness being in bed, and how they are going to make me a sling so I can stand up and operate. I laugh dutifully and then when they leave I try not to cry.

Time moves in a nonlinear way and I can't pin down the passing of days properly. Jana visits when she can, but she's trying to cram in as much work as possible so she can stay with me when I get out of the hospital. Daddy and I talk and play endless interrupted games of chess. I win maybe one game in five and even then suspect he has thrown it. Mom joins us for canasta and my win rate improves marginally.

Mitch calls me the second week and I hear the smile in his voice. "Keane called a meetin' today, told us all she was leavin'. You wouldn't happen to know what that's about, would you?"

"I might."

"Good for you. See I told ya'll it'd work out."

"We're not through it yet, Mitch." I roll over, turning my back to my roommate, and lower my voice. "She's not here, plus I still have to finish my service obligations." They have assured me I'll make a full recovery and return to active duty as good as ever. In body at least.

He snorts. "A minor detail. You'll get through it and if you deploy again, I'll be helpin' you."

"What do you mean?"

"I'm leavin' my FST app till you discharge for good. Someone needs to keep an eye on you when Keane's gone."

I blow a raspberry through the phone. "Yeah, right. More like you need my help." My heart lifts. I'm not going to be alone.

He laughs. "You know, she came to see me and thanked me for my discretion. In the tradition of clichéd best friend threats, I told her she'd answer to me if she broke your poor heart. Very respectfully, of course."

Of course he did, I can imagine it. Mitch sniffs. "Anyways, I bought a card special for this call and I think it's almost outta credit. Email me. We'll set up a video call."

"I will. Love you, Mitch."

"Love your guts too, darlin', and I've seen some of them."

* * *

The television drones on in the background while my mother completes Sudoku puzzles, counting out loud. My father left a short while ago, probably to go outside for some fresh air. I'm jealous. It's stale and claustrophobic in here and I'm reaching my tolerance for being hospitalized, not that my threshold was high to begin with.

Leigh was discharged yesterday and I'm yet to get a replacement roommate. I'm half-dozing, half-listening to a soap opera when the phone rings. I lean over awkwardly and grab the handset. "Hello?"

The line crackles. "Sabine? It's Rebecca."

I glance at my mother. She doesn't appear to be listening, at least not actively. "Hey."

"Were you sleeping?"

"No, just watching TV and trying not to go insane with boredom."

She laughs. "Well, be glad. It's a madhouse here."

"Mmm."

"How are you feeling?"

"Just a sec, I'll get my chart."

"Sabi—"

I cover the phone with my hand. "Mom, can you pass me my chart please?"

My mother looks around. "What chart?"

"It's there. See at the end of the bed? The folder thing."

"Should you be looking at it, sweetie?"

"I'd just feel better knowing exactly what's going on, Mom." I give her my best smile, the same one I used to seal the deal on getting my first pony. Mom fishes my chart from the holder and passes it up to me.

"Thanks." I wedge the phone between my ear and shoulder and flip the chart open, scanning the notes. "Okay."

Rebecca sounds exasperated. "Sabine. I asked how you were feeling. Not what your status is."

"Oh. Well, I'm feeling like I'm in the hospital recovering from an explosion and a gunshot wound."

"You're such a smartass. And your mom's there."

"Yes, and I know." I glance up at my mother and move the phone away from my ear. I need something to get her out of the room. "Mom, could you please find a nurse or a doctor and check if I'm allowed something to eat?"

"Of course, honey. Anything in particular?" She gathers her purse.

"Maybe a sandwich? The canteen should be open. Something with mustard, please."

I wait until she is gone and lift the phone again. "Sorry about that. I just…I need some privacy."

"You're terrible. She's going to be trying to find someone for half an hour."

My mom will be fine. There's something important I need to say. "I miss you, Bec."

There's a long pause. "I miss you too. It's dark without you here." She clears her throat. "Okay. Let's start with pain score. Don't lie."

* * *

After I hang up from Rebecca's latest call, Mom looks over at me. "Who keeps calling you? I know it's not Mitch, that boy hates the telephone."

Oh shit. Butterflies knock against my ribs. I clear my throat. "Colonel Keane."

Mom pauses. "Your boss? She notified us of the incident. How nice of her to check in on you, Sabs."

From the corner of my eye, I see my father shift. He knows a superior officer calling nearly every day is unusual. I lick my lips. You're going to have to tell them sooner or later, Sabine. "It's not just that, Mom."

She sets her magazine down on my rolling table. "What do you mean?"

The beep monitoring my pulse increases tempo. "We, um, we…well. We're involved."

"Involved," Mom repeats.

My father is silent. I daren't look at him but I feel as though I need to keep talking, to explain. "It happened off base, I was home and it's all away from work." My nose stings as tears pool in my eyes. They spill and slide unencumbered down my cheeks to drip from my chin. My voice cracks. "I love her." Daddy rises from his chair and leaves the room without speaking. I cry even harder.

Mom moves to sit on the bed and hold me. "You know how he is about rules, honey," she soothes. "He'll be all right, just let him work it out."

I'd suspected he would be upset about it, deeming it a disrespectful circumvention of command chains and protocol or some shit. Beyond all that, I'd hoped he could see what it means to me. What *she* means to me.

Dad returns an hour later and he doesn't seem angry, more contemplative than anything. Mom gathers her purse and leaves the room, muttering about finding decent coffee. My father sits in the chair next to me, his elbows on his knees with hands clasped together. He leans toward me. "Tell me all about it, Sabine. Not the facts, but how you feel."

I pick at the threads of the hospital blanket. "It just happened, Daddy, I swear. Nothing inappropriate, or predatory or disrespectful." I'm ten years old again, trying to explain how I managed to break the kitchen window.

"Is that why Victoria—"

"No! This was after and had nothing to do with it."

He listens to me explain what happened and more importantly, how I feel about Bec. Dad leans back in the chair. "Well, she's leaving the service and I hear they'll be legislating to change DADT anyway, Sabine. Maybe it won't be so hard after all."

"Maybe…"

He squeezes my hand. "I've always known you never intended to stay in the army and you only joined up for me and your opa." He pauses, Adam's apple bobbing. "I'm sorry if I ever made you feel like the only way you'd make me proud was to be in the military. It's not true. I've been proud of you your whole life."

I swallow gummy saliva. "It doesn't mean I don't enjoy the work." It's the truth, I do love the work. I just don't love being in the army.

He reaches up to wipe tears from my cheeks. "I understand, honey. I love you."

"I love you too, Daddy."

He gives me a sly smile. "And just think, you're even going to get a medal."

"I think I'd prefer something less painful than a Purple Heart."

When they leave for the night, I lie in bed and think. How I would cope with parents who weren't so supportive? My mother lives for her family and she will support me as she has done my entire life. Despite my father's misgivings about what's happened, he loves me and wants me to be happy.

It's nearly ten and I'm in a groggy, semi-asleep limbo when the phone rings. I roll over slowly and pick it up. "Mmm 'lo?"

"Sabine?"

I would know this voice anywhere. I exhale. "Vic."

She sounds on the verge of tears. "I heard what happened. Jana called me. Are you okay? Jesus, I can't even…" She bursts into full-blown crying. "Sabs, I'm really sorry. About everything."

I'm not sure what to say. Perhaps I should give a passive-aggressive speech but all the anger and resentment is gone. I listen to her cry and the only words which come to mind are, "I'm sorry too." There are no tears. I've cried for what I lost and it no longer matters.

"Are you okay?" she asks again, voice quavering.

"I will be." It's not exactly answering her question, but I know it's better for her to hear that, rather than how I am feeling right now.

"What happened?"

"Just a job perk, Vic."

"One you won't tell me about, right?"

I laugh, setting off a sharp twinge of pain in my ribs. "Right."

"Just like old times." I hear her inhale on a cigarette. "We weren't always awful to one another, were we?"

"No. Things were great. Until they weren't."

She laughs. The sound seems so foreign to me now. "I suppose that's a good way of putting it."

Despite everything that happened between us, I still care about her. I run my tongue over dry lips. "Are you happy?"

"I am. You?"

My answer is instant. "Yes."

"I suppose it all worked out in the end then, yeah?"

I smile, thinking of just how well it worked out for me. "Yeah." I push myself up on the pillow behind me. "How are the boys?"

"They're good. Brutus caught a mouse. I nearly died." She laughs again.

I grin, trying to imagine it. It would probably be the first thing the cat has ever caught. "Hug them for me? And kiss that furry little head of his."

"I will."

"Vic...thanks for calling."

CHAPTER THIRTY-ONE

I'm discharged from the hospital the next day, which is too soon according to Rebecca. "At least I know there's doctors everywhere in case something happens," she tells me down a bad telephone line. Her voice is tight with stress. "What if—"

"It's been almost four weeks, Bec. If something was going to happen, it would have happened." I stare out at my mailbox. "It's fine. I love you."

My parents make sure I'm settled and comfortable before they go home and Jana plays her Partner of the Firm card to work from home so she can stay with me for a few weeks. She purchases a pair of walkie-talkies because call bells are apparently *so last decade* and sleeps down the hall in the spare room. I sleep with my door open and could just call out but she thinks I'll like the walkies.

The first morning she's in my house I'm awake before dawn and decide to give her a call. I thumb the button on my walkie. "Mother Bird, this is Nest. Do you copy? Over." Nothing. "Repeat. Mother Bird, this is Nest. Do you copy? Over."

I hear her hitting the bedside table before a groggy voice tells me to, "Get fucked."

"Mother Bird, you didn't identify yourself and you forgot to say over. Over." The sound of the handheld hitting the wall echoes through the house. I laugh so hard that I have a coughing fit. Jana comes racing into my room with her hair in disarray and her eyes panicked. That worked just as well as the walkies to get her in here.

She works on her laptop, leaving papers strewn at the foot of my bed while I watch television, read and email everyone I can think of. Every day, a clerk comes by to pick something up or drop off thick files for her. She helps me shower until I get sick of her fussing and send her out of the bathroom.

Jana takes me for my therapy—physical and psychological—then tells me about the cute soldiers she's seen while I'm in my sessions. She comes in when I wake up crying out and sweating from a nightmare, reassuring me as she curls up by my side until I fall asleep again.

When it takes a Xanax and thirty minutes of breathing exercises to leave the house, she's gentle and patient as she tries to help me calm down. We stroll very slowly around the block, me hobbling with a stick, limping badly and growing more and more frustrated with myself. Jana soothes me every time I get snappy and teary, or startle whenever there's a sudden noise. She cooks and tidies. We talk and laugh. The whole thing feels like we are teenagers again. I love having her with me.

But I still don't have Rebecca. She is due back home the fifteenth of November and even though it's less than two weeks away, I haven't heard anything firm from her yet. I want to know exactly when she will be on my doorstep.

Jana makes a note on a legal pad and glances at the television. "Women's soccer again?"

I thumb the remote. "Hush. You should be working and I need something to make me feel better while I convalesce."

Jana closes her laptop and climbs into bed beside me. "What's the score?"

"I don't know. It's an old game and I don't watch it for the sport, Jannie."

She swats at me, settling carefully against my shoulder. "Why don't we stretch while you're watching?"

I groan. My sister has turned into a physical therapy dictator. Even when I'm trying to relax in bed, Jana makes me do exercises to strengthen my leg and keep my right arm from seizing up. I get stiff if I don't move regularly. I can't be stiff. I need full range of motion but her constant insistence seems to trigger a sibling annoyance response in me. "Fine," I sigh.

The muscles in my back complain as Jana pulls my arm forward. I'm still obsessed with wiggling my fingers slowly, making sure each one moves on command. She mouths numbers and when she gets to twenty, she releases me and starts up with her new favorite topic of conversation. "I fucking knew something was going on with you. Tell me again. What exactly did she say? Was it like a slow sultry burn? Or just straight up this is how it is, now take me on the kitchen table?"

"She said words, Jana." I bite my lip to stop my smile. Withholding information makes her crazy.

My sister's expression would wither flowers. "Sabine. This is like a classic love story. Against all odds and shit. What does she look like?"

"Like a person. A very attractive person."

"Haven't you got a photo?"

"Nah…"

"If you weren't so damaged, I would fucking hit you."

Jana goes to get my lunch, leaving me to worry. It's nice to have her so excited about Bec and me but there is still a long way to go. I've had fear dreams of her leaving me or being forced to stay in the army. Her reassurances do not reassure me.

"So any idea of when?" Jana asks the moment she's back in the room.

"Soon." I shrug. "We've hardly spoken in the past few days. She's busy with her last days of deployment and I'm stuck in a fucking rut, unable to move in any direction. I seem to be recovering so slowly. Thought I'd be right by now." I still need pain meds and I'm terrified that I'm going to be addicted to them. And I can't sleep without nightmares. The thought of going outside, let alone back to work terrifies me.

Jana sets a sandwich and a banana on my bedside table. "Be patient. You're not indestructible."

"I know," I snap at her. My sister's face is blank as she sets my pill onto the table. I grab her hand and squeeze it. "I'm sorry, Jannie. I'm being such a shit."

"Yeah, you are." She grins cheerfully. "You need to stop holding yourself to such stupid high standards, Sabs. You got exploded and shot, and you…" The grin fades, her jaw going slack.

I raise an eyebrow. "You okay?"

Jana nods, slowly. "Yeah…I guess I'd never actually really thought about it until right now." She shakes her head. "I, uh, I'm going to put dinner in the slow cooker. Eat your lunch, you cantankerous bitch." She kisses my forehead and leaves the room. My sister isn't like me. She loves therapy and I'd put money on the fact that she's making an appointment right now to work through her feelings about The Incident.

I grab my laptop. My mailbox has five new messages. Mitch, Amy, Amy, Rebecca, Bobby. Rebecca's was sent five hours ago.

Sabine,

I miss you. I'm not sure what else to say, I feel like there's no words to describe the emptiness of not having you here. I miss you. I said that already. Sorry I haven't called, things are crazy at the moment with unit changeovers.

I won't talk about work, it's crass. How are you?

Still no firm transport date. How fucking surprising. Amy says she has a jacket of yours.

I'll bring it home with me.

I'll call when I can. I miss you so much, and love you even more.

Rebecca.

I close the laptop, drop it on the end of the bed and roll over, ignoring the rest of my lunch. The note about my uniform reminds me that I'll need to order a replacement and boots for when I'm cleared to go back to duty. My clothes were cut from me back at Invicta and would have been burned as medical waste, the ashes scattered across the dirt. Right now, I wonder if part of me was scattered along with them.

* * *

A couple of days after Bec's email, Jana and I take an early morning walk around the streets. We share giggling judgments about people who still haven't taken their Halloween decorations down and she turns around to check the ass of every guy who jogs past. After breakfast and another round of seemingly endless stretching, I climb back into bed. Jana pulls the duvet up over my waist and gives me my book. I smile up at her, offering a facetious, "Thank you, nurse."

"Hush, you." Jana adjusts the cover over my legs as I flip my book open.

I'm woken by the doorbell ringing, interrupting a weird dream about raking leaves with a fork. I need to stop falling asleep randomly. Stupid drugs. Stupid recovering body. Jana taps a laptop key. "It'll just be Shawn with some work."

"What time is it?" I ask her, wiping my mouth with the side of my finger. Sleeping drooler strikes again. I push myself up into a sitting position. The book falls off the bed with a loud thud.

"Almost noon." Jana bends down to get my book and sets it on the bedside table. "Any pain?"

"A little," I admit. A little back pain and a twinge from my broken rib, which still complains if I breathe too deeply. "I… let's just go half a pill, okay?"

She is already halfway out the door. "Okay, boss. I'll be back."

I make my way to the bathroom and close the door. It's a habit. Even though my sister has watched me pee repeatedly, I still want a little bit of privacy. I half-fall, half-sit onto the toilet. It takes me some time to get organized and I haven't heard her come back by the time I've managed to stand and tug everything back up. I'm tying the string in my sweats when I hear her call out, "Sabs? Everything okay in there?"

I flush and move to wash my hands, leaning against the sink. "Yes," I respond. "I've been peeing for thirty-five years, Jana." I push the door open. "I'm sure I can—"

She is not alone.

"Manage," I finish.

Standing next to my sister and wearing a very smug expression is Rebecca. I let out a cross between a squeak and a sob.

"I brought you a gift," my sister says drily. "Are you going to thank me?"

"Thank you, Jana," I respond automatically. Rebecca and I make eye contact. She never said she was coming back now, but she's here.

"Nonreturnable, I'm afraid." My sister looks sideways at Rebecca, who is standing just inside the doorway. Jana comes forward to get her things while I lean against the bathroom door.

Bec's out and she is here. I can't stop looking at her. She cut her hair, just a little, and she has my favorite expression on her face, the one of amused delight. It makes her left cheek lift and shows off that dimple. She's here. I want to cry.

Jana stops in front of me, widens her eyes and whispers, "Holy shit." She quickly unplugs the laptop, balancing it on her palm. "I'll be downstairs in the den. Holler if you need me."

"I won't," I say instantly.

She stops next to Rebecca and places her free hand on Bec's arm. "I've been replaced. Devastated."

Rebecca smiles and turns to watch her leave. I notice she is carrying a small tub of yogurt and a spoon, as well as my medication. She steps forward and gestures to the doorway. "Your sister looks just like you."

"She's shorter."

Rebecca comes closer. "I've been given a detailed rundown of your pain pill routine and I think she might trust me enough to give you this dose." Bec holds up the yogurt. "Do I have to feed you this beforehand?" Her eyes are shining with tears.

I wipe my eyes. "Yes. Yes you do."

"That's what I thought."

I state the obvious. "You're here."

"I'm here. Thought I'd surprise you." She takes the final step toward me. "Say please."

My eyes search hers. "Please."

She grabs my hip gently and gives me the sweetest kiss, then enfolds me in a hug and helps me back to the bed.

CHAPTER THIRTY-TWO

We agreed to take it slowly and that she should sleep in the spare room but after I have a thrashing nightmare the second night, she climbs into my bed. Bec wraps herself carefully around me and when I wake again, she holds me tighter. We cry together and talk about The Incident for the first time. Now, we call it *our* room.

After another few days she cancels the lease on her shoebox apartment and begins to move in to my bigger house. I should have known taking it slowly would never work—I need her like I need oxygen. She sleeps in my bed but we're not sleeping together, even though my physical therapist and surgeons assure me it's okay to be intimate.

My want of her is as desperate as ever but in the back of my mind there are images of muscles tearing loose and something inside breaking. I know it's irrational, yet I can't shake it. The Wizard tells me fear of intimacy is common with PTSD sufferers. It's unfair and I hate that there's another thing that's been turned on its head. Rebecca's been sweetly patient with me as I've pulled away from kisses which were becoming heated, or stilled when I've become overwhelmed at the thought of making love to her.

Now, she's in bed doing a job application on her laptop while I lie beside her and read the same sentence of my book over and over. I can't concentrate, because I'm suddenly thinking about how cute she looks with her glasses sliding down her nose.

I'm thinking about random things like the precise way she cuts vegetables for dinner and sets the table with my knife and fork the other way around. The hitch in her voice whenever she asks if I want to talk about anything. The taste of her. How she looks in jeans. The crease in her cheek just before she gives me a smile and turns it into a dimple. The way I remember her feeling inside me.

It's going to be okay. She won't let me be hurt.

Rebecca seems caught off guard when I suddenly set my book down, shift her laptop to my bedside table and climb over to straddle her. I kiss her hard and she responds with a soft groan. "You're sure?" she asks.

I answer her by pulling first her glasses then her tank top off. "I'm sure. I want you, honey. I *need* you so badly."

Her hands are under my tee and tugging it over my head before I can say anything else. She pulls me down and kisses me, tender and gentle but I feel her desperation as we rediscover each other. We help each other out of our clothing with fingers clumsy from pent-up desire and when my foot catches in my pajama bottoms, we laugh together as I try to kick them off.

Bec places a hand on my leg to stop me from moving. "Let me help." She slides down the bed, her lips softly trailing down my stomach before she frees me. I watch her pause, as if she doesn't know what to do or where to go next. She hooks her fingers in my panties and tugs them down, tossing the scant fabric aside before she slides her own off.

I let my eyes roam to take all of her in. Her landmarks, those delicious dips and curves. I reach a hand out to her. "Come back."

She settles on my left side, away from my healing injures, half on and half off me. Bec brushes too-long hair from my eyes. "I've missed you, Sabine."

"I'm sorry," I whisper.

"That's not what I meant." Her voice catches. "Don't apologize. Ever." She leans over, her hand on my neck and our lips meet again. This time it's my tongue that gets in first and when hers meets it, my stomach twists and I know we are back in the place we belong. We fit together the same way we did so many months ago, as if no time has passed. I'm overwhelmed by the sensation of having her so close again, but it doesn't matter because my body remembers hers and how to be with her.

Bec makes love to me with her hands and her lips, reclaiming my every inch and when I move, she pins me down. "Wait. Let me…" She spreads me and I feel the wet heat of her tongue against my throbbing clit. "You taste exactly the way I remember," she says throatily.

The thought of her tongue inside me makes my body clench and brings a fresh flood of arousal, but now isn't the time. I have a more pressing want. "No," I murmur, reaching to try and pull her back up.

She climbs carefully over my torso and settles beside me again. "No?"

I hold her face and pull her in for a kiss, tasting myself on her lips. "I want you up here. Here with me." I guide her hand downward, moaning softly as she cups me and dips her finger inside my wet folds. She has hooked her leg over mine, locking us together as if she actually thinks I would want to be anywhere but here with her. She plays me expertly, pushing me toward my release.

Bec bucks underneath me when I reach and gently circle her with a finger. She's so wet that I slide right into her, my thumb slipping over her clit. Bec bites my neck but it doesn't stifle her cries. She stops vocalizing long enough to murmur, "I love you, I love you," into my neck.

I tense and cry out hoarsely, fingers moving reflexively against her and Bec joins me moments later, adding the sounds of her climax to mine. We lie tangled together, damp with sweat and trembling, and I wonder why I had been concerned at all. There's no longer time to worry about the unknowns, not after everything that's happened.

Rebecca runs her hand over my stomach and breasts, her touch light yet so decisive. I shiver involuntarily as her fingers pause near the patches of healed skin over my ribs. She lifts herself up on her elbows. "Are you okay?"

I crane my neck to watch her. "Yes. Perfect."

Her lips brush over the ragged pink skin of my scars.

* * *

I drop the pile of mail onto the kitchen counter, curious about the disappearance of my girlfriend. When I went outside to quickly check the mailbox she was in the kitchen. Then I got caught talking for half an hour to our neighbor about my deployment and our Thanksgiving plans. Now Rebecca is nowhere to be seen. "Bec?"

"Yep, I'm in here," she calls from upstairs.

I lean against our bedroom doorframe enjoying the sight of her in an old pair of cut-offs and a tank top, both splattered with paint drops. The floor and furniture in the room are covered with drop cloths. She's painting the walls I prepared so many months ago. How much things have changed. It seems like another lifetime.

Her tone is cautious. "I hope you don't mind, I found all this in the spare room closet while I was putting some out-of-season clothes away." She reaches for me as I step inside the room.

"It looks great." I take her hand, running my finger over her palm. When I bend forward to kiss her she responds eagerly, careful not to let the paint roller touch me. I rub the tip of my nose softly against hers. "You know, I think I finally figured it out."

Her forehead wrinkles. "What exactly have you figured out?"

I take a deep breath. "I figured out what you taste like."

It takes her a moment to connect the dots from that night. Our first night. “And what’s that?” Her voice is quiet, her head tilted as she studies me.

“Home.”

The word catches in my throat. I try again.

“You taste like home.”

Bella Books, Inc.
Women. Books. Even Better Together.
P.O. Box 10543
Tallahassee, FL 32302
Phone: (800) 729-4992
www.BellaBooks.com

More Bella Books Titles
from E. J. Noyes

Alone
Ask Me Again
Go Around
Gold
If I Don't Ask
If the Shoe Fits
Integrity
Pas de deux
Reaping the Benefits
Schuss
Turbulence